continued on next page . . .

Falcon and the Sword

"Medieval romance at its best. Beard paints a lively and colorful portrait of the thirteenth century with vivid descriptions, sharp narrative and an engrossing, original plot. She is at the top of her form." —*Romantic Times*

"A sensitive, thought-provoking story with an original plot, fascinating characters, and a vibrant setting. Another bestseller for Ms. Beard." —*Rendezvous*

A Dance in Heather

"Lively [and] endearing." —*Publishers Weekly*

"A nice interweaving of medieval British history, pageantry, and love." —*Library Journal*

"Every scene is beautifully rendered . . . a nonstop read." —*Romantic Times*

"Vivid and compelling, the fifteenth century springs to vibrant life . . . From roistering festivals in ancient castles to teeming life in medieval London, she paints an astonishingly vivid picture of the times; and a bold lord, his fair lady and their love . . . a memorable read." —Edith Layton, author of *The Crimson Crown*

"A glorious love story in every sense—alive and vibrant, enthralling, and intriguing . . . I couldn't put it down until the last page." —*Rendezvous*

Very Truly Yours

Julie Beard

JOVE BOOKS, NEW YORK

This is a work of fiction. Names, characters, places and incidents are either the product of the author's imagination or are used fictitiously, and any resemblance to actual persons, living or dead, business establishments, events or locales is entirely coincidental.

VERY TRULY YOURS

A Jove Book / published by arrangement with
the author

PRINTING HISTORY
Jove edition / April 2001

The Penguin Putnam Inc. World Wide Web site address is
http://www.penguinputnam.com

ISBN: 0-515-13039-7

A JOVE BOOK®
Jove Books are published by The Berkley Publishing Group,
a division of Penguin Putnam Inc.,
375 Hudson Street, New York, New York 10014.
JOVE and the "J" design
are trademarks belonging to Penguin Putnam Inc.

PRINTED IN THE UNITED STATES OF AMERICA

10 9 8 7 6 5 4 3 2 1

*To my darling daughter, Madeline Jing,
and to the generous people of China for sharing
a national treasure*

Prologue

In the shadows of his lodgings near Whitehall, over-looking St. James's Park, Jack Fairchild slowly raised his head. Behind his closed eyelids, light blinded him. It was the searing, painful light of inevitability, of a realization that came too late. He tried to swallow, but couldn't. His head slumped. It was over.

Life as he'd known it would never be the same. Like a desperate man clinging to the familiar as it slips away, he reached out and combed the sleek, dark red mahogany Chippendale table where he'd dined privately with so many beautiful women. The satiny feel of the expensive wood on his fingertips, and the soft squeak of skin on polish, soothed him. He sighed and his eyes fluttered open.

He consciously tried to memorize every lovely detail—the green striped silk wallpaper; the warm glow of dozens of candles in the tinkling crystal chandelier overhead; the smell of fresh flowers on the sideboard; the rich, almost gaudy red Oriental dinner set imported by the East India Company, always plentifully dressed with fashionable delicacies—Russian caviar, Portuguese hams, Laplander reindeer tongues, lobster patties. Of course, he'd taken it all for granted. What a fool he'd been!

Never again would he be admitted to the all-important and prestigious Almack's, he thought as he listened to the rumble of carriage wheels over the damp cobblestones below. Indeed, if he did not act soon, he would instead be listening to the uneasy breathing of those who spent restless nights in debtor's prison, desperately hoping for a reprieve that would never come, for Jack was thoroughly in dun territory. Overnight John Calhoun Fairchild, heir apparent to Baron Tutley, had become impoverished.

The late-summer breeze fluttered around his perspiring temples, chilling his overheated skin, and knocked the dread letter to the floor. He did not retrieve it. He knew it by heart. He'd read it over and over again since its arrival this morning.

My Dear Mr. Fairchild,

   Imagine my surprise learning upon my return from the East Indies that you are now the sole proprietor of the Fairchild Tea Company, having inherited said company from your late father who, I understand, died a year ago at his own hand. A gunshot wound to the head, wasn't it? I had hoped to collect money owed to me from him, but now find you responsible. I expect three thousand pounds by the end of the month, or I will take action, sir. You wouldn't be the first gentleman to land in debtor's

*prison, so do not expect leniency from me. I shall
visit soon and expect the payment in full.*

It was signed Lord Abbington. He was a shareholder
in the import company that had put Jack's father out of
business. Abbington knew very well that the Fairchild Tea
Company was insolvent. Jack had spent the last year paying the rest of his father's creditors. Until the moment
he'd been unfortunate enough to inherit the failing business, Jack had had no interest in it. He'd never wanted to
follow in his merchant-father's footsteps. It had been expected that he would inherit his maternal grandfather's
title. Therefore, he'd studied law to suit his own fancy,
with no intention of earning a living from it. After all,
work was beneath a member of the Upper Ten Thousand.

He couldn't resist giving charity, though, and had spent
untold hours in the Chancery courts, using his skills as a
lawyer on behalf of indigent men who were one step away
from debtor's prison, or there already. He'd worked tire-
lessly to keep honest, poor men out of the very place he
would soon be headed, an irony that was too bitter to
swallow tonight.

Two years ago, however, the heir apparent of the Tutley
barony had become the heir *un*apparent, as it were, when
his grandfather had turned on Jack and his mother, cutting
off all contact and financial support. A year later, Jack's
mother and father had died from a combination of too
much drink and too much crushing debt. His father had
killed himself; his mother simply lost her will to live. His
lovely, poor mother had lived like a betrayed waif in a
netherworld of her father's making simply because she
had not known what price she would pay for marrying a
man she did not love.

Despite his parents' scandalous deaths, Jack had clung to his former social status as a member of the *haut ton* for the last year through sheer charm. But he possessed an inconvenient sense of honor that had compelled him to use all of the remaining funds in his trust to pay off his father's debts, and the illusion of fashionability he'd struggled to maintain could not ultimately survive this coup de grace to his finances. When this letter had come, announcing the very real possibility that he might be imprisoned for his father's debt, Jack's house of cards had crumbled. He didn't even have enough money to try to gamble his way out of this one. Last night, he'd lost his last hand at White's.

That left him with only one way out.

He reached for the duelling pistol his father had used to blow a hole in his head. With sweat streaming down his brow, he picked up the weapon, hating it, but needing more than anything in the world to end his sorrow this way. His hand was trembling, and he could hardly still it long enough to finish the task. He had just raised the pistol in the air when the door flew open behind him.

"No, Mr. Fairchild, you cannot do it!" cried out his secretary. The portly Mr. Clayton Harding ran to his side and gripped Jack's wrist, jerking his employer's hand toward the ceiling. "I won't let you! The situation isn't that dire!"

"Let go, Harding," Jack said with sangfroid, regarding him with as much perturbation as he would a pesky fly.

"No, sir, I won't let you take your own life!"

"Take my own life?" Jack blurted out a disbelieving laugh. "I had no such intention, I assure you. Now let go of my arm before it goes numb. Really, Harding, you have the most dramatic sense of perception. If I wanted to kill myself I'd lie down in front a carriage in Hyde Park and save my creditors the price of a bullet."

Still frowning, Harding loosened his grip and chuckled uncertainly. "You mean you weren't going to kill yourself? I saw that the pistol was missing and assumed the worst. I did not see you in your room and feared you—"

"Lud, no! It is not even loaded. I was simply going to throw this blasted gun in the fire." Jack glared at the pistol in his hand. "If I can't melt the metal, I'll at least burn the handle until it's useless. I loathe the damned thing for all the trouble it's caused me."

Harding looked suspiciously at the fireplace. It did indeed roar with more life than was warranted on a warm summer evening. Then he looked at Jack, who merely arched a brow and gave him a crooked half-smile.

"Very well, Mr. Fairchild. I see your point. I wondered why it was so hot in here."

"Yes, I'm sweating like a bloody pig. Now remove your hand so I can finish this nasty business. I can't keep the pistol that killed my father, nor can I sell it to some poor unsuspecting chap who doesn't know what a curse it bears. If not for this weapon, Henry Fairchild would be around to take care of his own debts. I blame him, and this weapon, for the burdens I now carry, so let me find some peace at last."

When Harding let go, Jack threw the wooden and metal contraption in the fire, then dusted his hands, which trembled with the significance of the act. "At last I have some revenge against the fates that have contrived such an impossible future for me."

He leaned his tall, languid body against the hearth and gazed fondly around his drawing room. "I shall miss this place very much, Harding. It's been a good life here in London."

Harding went very still, raising his nose in the air as if sniffing disaster. "You speak in the past tense, sir. I never like to hear you speaking of London in the past tense."

"The plans are already made, I fear. I've corresponded with Mr. Pedigrew, an old family friend in Middledale who has retired. I've arranged to purchase his law offices. He's going to let me use them on credit for a year."

"Middledale." Harding grimaced. "Why, that's in the Cotswolds."

"Yes, it's rather picturesque there, I fancy."

"Picturesque! You might as well move to the Scottish moors! Do you know how far Middledale is from London?"

"Yes, and I don't care. If I never come to Town again I will be glad of it."

"You may not care, sir, but I most certainly do. You test the limits of my loyalty if you expect me to resign my life of pleasure here for the exasperation of country life."

"I don't expect you to come with me if you do not wish it, Harding," Jack said, pushing off the hearth and going to the window, looking down at the moonlit street with a wistful sigh. "But if I don't want to starve, or end up in debtor's prison, there is only one thing left for me to do— work for a living."

"As a solicitor?" Harding asked, growing pale even by moonlight standards. "But then you'll be a man *in trade.* That will finish you off in the polite world. You'll be thrown out of the best clubs in Town."

"What choice do I have? If I stay here I'm sure to land in debtor's prison. If I lose myself in the country, I'll have at least a month, and maybe more, before Abbington can find me. I know the odds of paying off my debt are against me, but would you rather I simply loll around and wait for an arrest warrant?"

"Earning money would be so much more palatable if you were a barrister," Harding bemoaned, wringing his hands. "Then you would not be cast out from good society. But no! You were too intent on charity cases to spend the required time eating with the benchers until you could be called to the bar. Now all you are is a lawyer, a solicitor who must hire barristers to plead your cases in court."

Jack turned from the window and with a neat twist of his wrist straightened his starched, white cravat. "You make me sound like a blasted ragpicker, Harding. How can you possibly blame me for this predicament? I fully expected to be a wealthy baron, not a barrister. I did not know you'd take my plight so personally."

Harding's eyes simmered in a pool of regret. "I have stood by you, Mr. Fairchild, because I knew your potential. You have greatness in you. I might have been secretary to a government minister, you know. But I chose you, sir."

Jack swallowed hard, feeling the weight not only of his own future, but of Harding's as well. "Thank you, old boy. I know you've been loyal. I do not plan to let you down."

Hearing his own declaration, waves of cold and heat washed over him at once. He had to survive. And he would. His fortune lay in Middledale, he was sure of it.

One

few days later, when Middledale was less than a mile away, Harding tried once more to dissuade his employer from country life. However, this time his arguments were punctuated by his own grunts and groans whenever the swaying carriage hit a bump in the road and jarred his gout-swollen feet.

"It's not too late, sir," Harding said. "We can spend the night and turn back on the morrow." He pressed a kerchief to his florid brow and watched his elegant employer for signs of weakness.

Jack merely turned the page of the book of poems he was reading.

"If all you need is money, Mr. Fairchild, you could—ouch!—go to a money lender." After hitting a pothole, the carriage pitched left, then right. Harding heaved to and fro, while Jack casually shifted his weight.

"Go to a money lender?" Jack replied without looking up. "And watch a three-thousand-pound debt multiply ten-fold before I could pay it back? No, thank you."

"Then plead with your grandfather."

"He would never lend me, much less give me, a single groat." Jack's jaw muscles ticked at the insult. Then he looked up, pinning Harding with his infamously beautiful eyes. "He loathes me because I am my father's son. And since that is a fact I will never change, I do not expect him to reverse course at this point in time. He can't deny me his title in due time, but he can damned well keep his fortune from me and so he shall."

"Then plead with your friends."

Jack grinned sardonically, finally giving up and closing his book. "You know very well my friends are all women. Their husbands wouldn't take kindly to giving charity to their wives' lover."

The secretary sighed forlornly at the truth. Jack Fairchild had wasted his talents and grace and good looks on impoverished men and the wives of powerful men, instead of cultivating the elite of the beau monde. For a sharp-witted man, he was impossibly oblivious to his own deficits and attributes, or how he might have used both for his own gains.

He did not, for example, fully appreciate or take advantage of his own beauty, as Harding surely would have had he been so blessed. Jack Fairchild cut the kind of riveting figure that even men could not help but notice. Given Jack's natural grace, his dashing mane of onyx hair, and his high, ruddy, lean-cut cheeks, his conquest of women was taken for granted. Expected even. And the extent to which this behavior did not inspire jealousy was owing to the fact that everyone, including the husbands of his lovers, sensed that Jack just couldn't help himself. A beautiful man had to have women, didn't he?

This unspoken contract required gentlemanly discretion, naturally. While he might ruin a woman's ability to love her husband by having an affair with her, Jack would never be so inconsiderate or selfish to even think of stealing her permanently. So he was always forgiven. After a fashion.

The one time Jack had been called out by a jealous husband, he'd quickly proven his skill with the pistol, lodging a bullet in the man's arm. Of course, the scandal had forced him to spend a year abroad, but his impudence had been forgiven by Society in due time, and ultimately only served to enhance his reputation as a rake.

Did Jack feel remorse for his indiscretions? Not as far as Harding could tell. He'd told his secretary on more than one occasion that he was doing womankind a favor. He had seen his own mother's misery in a loveless marriage. And Jack knew that the majority of women were similarly locked into unhappy political arrangements, as the rich were wont to be. He considered one night of passion the least a woman might expect from life.

"And what about the women?" Harding now asked with resignation. "Will you spend your time doting on them in Middledale, too, distracting you from the business at hand?"

"No, I'm a changed man. I've done with the fairer sex. I must work now. I will not let anything keep me from my efforts to restore my fortunes." Jack looked out the window. "Ah, here we are! We've arrived." He cast Harding a sardonic grin. "And just in time to spare me an interview with the Inquisition."

Jack and his reluctant secretary arrived in the perfectly charming town of Middledale on a perfectly radiant summer day. The village was tucked in and around the bends and curves of a great hillside, so that one couldn't see the entire length of the main street at a glance. One had to go exploring, shifting this way and that, rounding a milliner's shop in order to see the farrier, and rounding that to see the cobbler's shop, walking in the shadows of quaint stone buildings, enduring the curious stares of the locals.

Jack ordered the carriage to stop at one end of town, determined to walk the length of it to his new offices.

"Here we are!" he announced as he climbed down the carriage step. "What a lovely village, eh, Harding?"

"Charmed, I'm sure, sir," Harding grumbled. His legs, already burdened by his weight and a nasty case of gout, hit the hard cobblestone street with a wobble from days of disuse during the arduous coach ride from London.

"This is a cozy nest of humanity!" Jack enthused, his face alive with interest, his eyes taking in everything—the prettily weathered hand-painted signs over stores and taverns, the rainbow of fruit and flower stalls along the way, the simple-looking folk who did business here, the genteel ladies strolling down the thoroughfare with wide-brimmed bonnets and fringed parasols. "And the air is so fresh."

"Fresh?" Harding moaned. "Foul smelling if you ask me."

Jack let out a peal of joyful laughter, clapping him on the back. "Oh, Harding, you amuse me. You chafe at the smell of flowers on the breeze, loamy earth from the fields nearby, the smell of sunshine in your nose, and the pleasant aroma of horses? Good God, man, I suppose you miss the choking pall of fumes that hangs over London like a dreary shroud."

"Yes, sir, I do, rather," he said, holding a kerchief to

his nose. "At least the stench of burning coal is familiar."

The empty coach drove on to their destination at the end of the thoroughfare, leaving Jack to stride and Harding to hobble after him through the scenic village.

Jack had fond, though distant, memories of Middledale from childhood. His mother used to take him here on shopping excursions from Tutley Castle and would buy him candied treats. She'd once bought him a pair of shoes here. They'd hurt like hell, but he'd been so proud of them. They'd smelled richly of leather, just as the shop did now when they passed by its open door.

Jack pulled a coin out of his pocket and tossed it to Harding. The secretary caught it between his perspiring palms just in time. "What's this, sir?"

"Buy yourself a new pair of shoes when we get settled, Harding. I owe you a favor or two. Besides, we need to at least look prosperous if we're to attract prosperous clients."

"You shouldn't be tossing money about, Mr. Fairchild," he said, but tucked the coin in his pocket nevertheless. "You've little to spare."

"My life is going to take a turn for the better, Harding. I have one last, small nest egg I've kept for such dire circumstances that not even you know about. Enough to allow me to keep my carriage, though I won't have more than a housekeeper. And I have a month to spend it. So for the next few weeks, we will live as we always have, at least until Lord Abbington catches up with me."

He winked conspiratorially at his secretary, then stopped abruptly when he rounded another corner and could see the length of the town for the first time. He was pleased to note it was larger than he'd remembered. Carriages passed with surprising frequency, the horses step-

ping highly. It had rained recently, and the men had to
skirt rain puddles that swallowed up patches of red pavement, now and then tipping their hats to ladies and nodding to men who seemed marvelously unaware of them.
Ah, sweet anonymity, he thought.

"I just might make a fine country gentleman, Harding.
At last I'll be free of the lure of London's scheming ladies. I'll be a philosophical country squire, a man to be
respected. Perhaps even a gentleman farmer with a sheep
or two and boots to muck about with in the pastures."

At that very moment Harding nearly stepped in horse
dung recently dropped by a passing four-in-hand. He skit-
tered sideways, his nose crinkling at the lambasting smell.
"Pastures, eh? Muck about in them if you please, sir. I'm
not setting foot outside your firm's premises."

Jack scowled at him good-naturedly. "Harding, you're
acting like a bloody dandy. Get hold of yourself, man.
You once told me we needed a visit in the country."

"Yes, sir." The portly fellow wiped a kerchief over his
reddened brow. "But I meant only a visit. And I didn't
realize it would be so . . . so clean here. The air is so fresh
it hurts my lungs. And this village is so . . . so puny."

"Only compared to London. Small is good, Harding.
This is the sort of town where people get to know one
another, who look after each other. Trust me. This will
be a new start for us. Why, look at the women here."

He discreetly motioned to two ladies promenading their
way down the other side of the street, chatting like mag-
pies beneath their pastel-colored parasols. "Look how
plain they are. Not a spot of rouge on their cheeks. I won't
be in the least tempted, by Jove. I'll be free at last. Free
from the wiles of women. Free from the desire to take

them in my arms and entangle myself in sordid emotions. Free from—"

Splash! A spray of muddy rainwater spewed from beneath a carriage wheel into Jack's face, drenching him in an instant. The cold water spiked his cheeks, shutting him up immediately as not even Harding could do.

"Bloody hell," Jack muttered, looking down at his soiled coat in utter dismay as the water trickled down the back of his neck.

"Here you are, sir," Harding said matter-of-factly, handing him a kerchief, remarkably without so much as a twitch of a smile. "So much for country life."

Jack wiped his face. He was just about to laugh when he heard the squeak of a carriage coming to a halt. He looked up and to his astonishment saw the offending vehicle stop in the middle of the street, four gorgeous white horses clomping their hooves impatiently on the cobblestones, snorting in protest. Liveried footmen in white powdered wigs hung on the back of the barouche. They jumped down to open the door, but fell back when a woman with an enormous hat peeked out the window and waved them off. She stared at Jack with amethyst eyes, her face looking every bit like a perfect cameo.

Jack was speechless. Stunned. As much by her consideration as by her startling beauty. People in London would never stop a carriage to see whom they'd run over, much less splashed. He took a step forward, then froze.

"Good God, I've seen her before," he whispered to Harding.

"Not surprising, I daresay. Turn and run while you can, sir," his plump companion replied.

"Who the devil is she?"

"I believe she goes by the name of Trouble."

"Do you recognize her?"

"No, but all women are trouble where you're involved."

"Are you very well, sir?" she called out, her voice gentle and yet traveling the distance with confidence.

"I like her already," Jack murmured.

"It doesn't take much, sir," Harding replied sotto voce.

"Are you hurt?" she called again.

"If I said yes, would you linger to tend my wounds?" he called in reply.

"Oh, God!" Harding muttered, dropping his forehead in his hand. "Here we go again."

"I daresay not," she shot back, her eyes sparkling. "But your companion seems ill. Perhaps he needs a ride."

Jack strolled forward, an unseen strand reeling him in like a hooked fish. "My companion is in perfect health, if you don't count his gout."

"Oh, please, sir," his mortified secretary beseeched.

The closer Jack drew, the better he was able to see the confection poised for the tasting. Her fresh, pale beauty beamed from beneath her cornucopia of black curls. Her lips were poutingly full, yet intriguingly wide. And most captivating of all, she seemed unaware of her own astonishing appearance. Her gaze cut the distance without interference from batting lashes or a fluttering fan or any other familiar female weapons. She simply regarded him steadily, lips slightly parted, thoughts churning in the priceless gems that were her eyes. She was clearly a woman with her own mission, though a hint of resignation in her countenance hinted it was not a happy one. She was the most evocative combination of worldliness and innocence he'd ever seen.

"I do appreciate your concern," he said when he drew close enough to speak in normal tones, then glanced down at his soiled garments with exaggerated dismay. "Though I am a bit wet."

"I am so very sorry," she said, sounding not in the least remorseful. Laughter bubbled from her before she managed to control it, pressing the fingers of her gloved hand to her lips. She frowned at the spots of mud on his cravat. "Did my carriage do that, sir? How dreadful. Please accept my apologies."

"If you insist, I will."

He grinned and strolled closer, realizing he really hadn't seen anything of Middledale until now. She was utterly fetching in a low-cut gown that constrained ample breasts. Her skin was as fresh as Devonshire cream, brushed lightly with the color of raspberries. When he caught her gaze and held it by sheer force of will, she reluctantly offered her hand, and he reached out for it with tingling anticipation. He was known in London for his clever ability to charm an introduction from a lady without ever warranting a direct cut. He bowed low, barely holding her fingertips, barely brushing his lips to her hand, and yet the contact sizzled.

"All is forgiven, I assure you, ma'am." He could not discern a ring beneath her kid glove. He righted himself, not letting her fingertips go until she started to frown in reproach. "Or is it miss?"

She cocked one delicately arched brow, but still did not look away. Slowly, her ravishing eyes focused on his nose, and he realized she wasn't going to let him force an introduction from her after all. She seemed to be fighting a smile as she gazed at his nose. Jack looked down at the tip and saw, to his chagrin, a dollop of mud. He sucked in his cheeks and gave her a simmering glare.

"Upon my word, Miss Whoever You Are, you should have told me."

Her laugh was as gay and bright as a cascade of silver bells. "Miss Whoever You Are! You mean you don't remember me?"

He frowned and wiped the mud from his nose, trying to recall the facile replies he always held in store for such occasions.

"Your beauty, my dear, would be impossible to for—"

"You don't!" she crowed triumphantly. "Then I have the advantage. Oh, this is famous!"

He smiled openly at her refreshing lack of false modesty and raised the quizzing glass dangling from his waistcoat, stealing only a quick glance at her full breasts before aiming it at her face. "Clearly, you have the advantage in every way that counts."

Her eyes narrowed on him consideringly. "What brings you here so far from London?"

He shrugged, stalling. Where the devil had they met? And precisely how much did she know about him? "I am making Middledale my home."

Her smile fell momentarily, and she frowned. Then, recovering her composure, she tilted her head coyly. "More is the pity for the ladies of London. Well, you must have much to contend with. I will steal no more of your precious time. I am glad, sir, that you suffered no injuries save for your pride."

Her eyes teased him, and he wanted to teach her a lesson with a long, slow kiss. By his estimation she needed one badly.

"Good day, sir."

"Good day." He still did not know whether she was a

miss or a ma'am. As bold as she was, doubtless a ma'am. For only married women would flirt so audaciously without fearing the repercussions.

With that, she withdrew, leaving him uncharacteristically speechless. The coachman cracked his whip and the carriage lurched forward. Jack watched with a frown on his forehead and a grin on his lips.

As the carriage rounded a bend in the road and disappeared, he turned to his secretary. "By Jove, Harding, I've been bested."

"Indeed, sir. In every way that counts."

Liza resisted the urge to look back to see his reaction. Instead, she pressed against the plush velvet seat and breathed hard until the pain searing beneath her breast subsided. It had taken every ounce of her inner strength to be so blithe when her heart was tearing in two. And yet, her body had taken on a life of its own and she'd felt the tempest a man like him could produce merely by his presence.

She squeezed her eyes shut, willing the image of Jack Fairchild from her mind. She could not feel. Heavens, no! Not now. Not when it was too late. Feelings were the last thing she needed now. God's teeth, why would a man like him come to tempt her just when she had resolved herself to an unfeeling marriage? Of course, he hadn't come for her at all. He didn't even remember her.

This was God's way of punishing her for being too much like Desiree. For wanting what a true lady should never have. Lord, it was all too ironic. She laughed incredulously. Her fair-haired younger sister sat beside her in wide-eyed wonder.

"Liza!" Celia hissed. "Are you well? You were flirting with him!"

Liza bit her lower lip and slanted her a jaded look. "What of it?"

"It was marvelous! Though you're not supposed to, you know. Mother would never approve. You're nearly engaged."

"Oh, fiddle. What does it matter? I'm going to marry the viscount. He doesn't care as long as he gets my money."

Celia pressed her hand. "I wish you wouldn't. You don't love him. Even I can tell that much."

Liza turned away.

"Who was that man? Did you really know him? You were splendid, sister dear. You had him all tied up in ribbons."

Liza smiled as tears inexplicably filled her eyes. "He is the only man in London I ever wanted. And I scarcely even knew him."

"Really? You met him in your Season?"

"Seasons," Liza amended dryly. She reached out and tucked a wayward curl back into her sister's pale green bonnet. Celia's eyes were a sweet, soft, cornflower blue. Her blond hair was a gleaming tumble of loose and charming curls. She was delicate and fresh, much sweeter than Liza could ever be, Liza thought with great affection. Then again, perhaps she, too, had been that innocent eight years ago. Liza had spent three Seasons in London, and two exiled in the country, before she'd succumbed to her merchant-father's benevolent plots to marry her off to a nobleman.

"What's his name?" Celia persisted.

"Jack Fairchild. He was a rake of the first stare. Though

he's older now, age seems to have merely lent him more sophisticated grace. It's not fair. We had but one dance together, but it changed my life." Her raven-colored brows furrowed neatly. "Whatever could he be about, moving to the country?"

"A rake?" Celia said, her blue eyes widening further. "Perhaps he's been reformed. Did he steal your heart?"

Liza shrugged. "We danced only once." But once was enough to know she'd find heaven in his arms if given half a chance. It was then that she'd had a profound re-alization. She didn't want to marry. Her mother would never allow her to marry a rake. And if she couldn't have the sort of man she really wanted then she wouldn't have any at all. With a singular determination that astonished even herself, she'd steadfastly refused to succumb to So-ciety's expectations that she marry for something less than bliss—companionship, land, or a title. The fact that one dance with Jack Fairchild had been powerful enough to inspire this conclusion did not bode well for her now. He'd unexpectedly thrust himself back into her life at the most inconvenient time. A time when she had, finally, agreed to marry. But not for any of the aforementioned reasons.

"He was out of the question for me and so I did not pursue him," she said nonchalantly.

"What a pity," Celia moaned.

"I doubt he would have been interested in any event. He only seemed captivated by married women."

"Oh, how scandalous!"

Liza turned her head, grinning at her sister's gasping exclamation. "Do you think so? I found it terribly roman-tic."

"Oh, Liza, think how much excitement he'll bring to Middledale!"

"That's what I am afraid of."

His reappearance in her life would be a test of her resolve. A test she would fail at the peril of her entire family. She could neither fail them, nor inform them. For not even her parents knew why she had at last agreed to marry. Nor could they ever know.

Two

Jack sighed as the carriage turned the corner and took half his being with it. There was something very unusual about that young woman. What was it? Who was she? And why did he care at a moment like this?

"Damn it to hell," he muttered as they continued on toward their destination.

"Yes, sir," Harding said, "rotten luck about the mud puddle."

"Not that, Harding. Did you see her?"

"Hard to miss with that hat."

Jack looked down at his secretary with exasperation. "And I didn't even notice her bloody hat. Didn't you recognize her beauty?"

"Oh, yes. That. I did, rather."

"It didn't set your blood to a boil?"

"A roiling boil, sir."

"That's good then, I'm not the only one."

"No, but you're the only one she wants. I saw it even from afar."

"But how do I know her? Think, think," he chanted, tapping the palm of his hand on his forehead. "Aha! I remember. Her name is Liza. Liza what? Liza . . . Liza . . . ah, yes. Liza the Untouchable." Jack shook his head and laughed. "That's what the young swains called her because she wouldn't set her cap at anyone, no matter how noble or landed or rich."

"Why not?"

Jack shrugged. "I have no idea. All I remember is one enchanting little dance with her. How bloody awful for me to have forgotten."

"Age is setting in, sir."

Jack scowled down his Roman nose at his impertinent secretary. "Watch what you say. I could fire you, you know."

"Would you, please? Then I could return to London."

"There is something about her I can't quite identify. She's terribly reckless for a beautiful young woman in such an expensive carriage. She is challenging the world to interfere with her plans, whatever they are. She may not know it, but she is."

"Oh, Lord, sir, how can you deduce such a fantastic notion from one conversation?"

"Easily, Harding, I know how to read women. She needs me."

"She can't possibly need you, sir, she's too young. And if she's untouchable that means she's unmarried and a woman doesn't even know what she needs until she's married and then it's too late. So you needn't concern yourself in the least."

They continued their stroll, arguing as they often did

about the virtue of helping the fairer sex. Helping, of course, being a delicate word for something far more gratifying. Suddenly they arrived at their destination. Number 2 Hanley Street. His carriage was standing in the street.

Jack looked up at the quaint law establishment, taking the key from under a moss-covered brick in the front as old Mr. Pedigrew had instructed and opened the weathered red door. He was immediately greeted with a stuffy plume of dust motes. They danced about in the sunlight like a jostling crowd at a fashionable ball.

Jack coughed and blinked, stepping his way into the old-fashioned room. Dark green velvet French draw draperies suffocated the two windows facing the street. Rows of musty law tomes, snug in mahogany cases, reeked of mold. The walls were handsomely decorated with floral moldings and pastoral paintings. The furniture was scattered about in a cozy fashion. On one Sheraton sofa lay a sleeping young man who looked suspiciously like the supposedly industrious articled clerk Jack had been promised. He wore crumpled clothes that smelled even from a distance as if they'd been lived in unabated for weeks.

"Ahem." Jack cleared his throat as Harding looked around in dismay. "Are we keeping you from your slumber, my good man?"

The lanky, unkempt man woke lazily and yawned without embarrassment. "What's that you say?"

"I said," Jack repeated emphatically, "are we keeping you from your sleep? I'm John Calhoun Fairchild. This is my new establishment. And I assume you are my articled clerk."

"Right," the young man said with a long stretch. "My name is Giles Honeycut. You can call me Giles."

"Why, thank you, Mr. Honeycut," Jack said dryly.

"You may call me Mr. Fairchild. This is my secretary, Clayton Harding."

"Mr. Harding to you. Come, come, young man," Harding tutted, "is this how you always look when you come to your place of employment?"

Giles rubbed his loose, tawny locks of uncombed hair and grinned. "Most of the time, I daresay."

"In that case," Jack said, "your services will no longer be needed. Thank you, Mr. Honeycut. You may go now."

Jack turned and headed toward the back offices.

"I said you could address me as Giles," the young man called after him, not in the least alarmed. He rose and tugged up his breeches. "Excuse me, sir. Oh, Mr. Fairchild!"

Jack stopped and turned with a cool smile. "Yes, Mr. Honeycut?"

"I'll go if you want me to, but I must warn you that you won't do well without me."

Jack's features lit with amusement. "Quite confident in your abilities, are you, Mr. Honeycut?"

"Giles! Please call me Giles. I am rather confident, you might say, sir. I grew up here, you see, and I know where all the business is. I know, for example, that the butcher wants to look into changing his deed. Old Widow Farnsworth wants to change her will to cut out her ramshackle son. And Farmer Plowright is planning to sue his landlord."

"I see." Jack crossed an arm over his chest, rested his other elbow on it, and stroked his clean-shaven, sculpted cheeks. "Are you trying to bribe me into keeping you, Mr. Honeycut? I suppose if you are, then we should be on more intimate terms. Giles, are you trying to blackmail me?"

The clerk's earnest-looking features wilted. "Oh, no, sir! I wouldn't think of such a thing. I'm simply trying to make you understand my value as an employee."

"I see. Well, certainly your assets are evident. But to own the truth, Giles, I could have found out about these clients myself, as I intend to do."

"Yes, sir, but again I have the advantage there."

"How?" Harding barked impatiently.

"You see, the butcher is my cousin once removed, old Widow Farnsworth is my aunt, and Farmer Plowright is my mother's mother's cousin's uncle. He remembers me every Christmas."

When Giles ended this litany with an innocent smile, Jack exchanged a significant look with his secretary. "Well, Harding, I think we're cornered."

"Yes, sir," the secretary replied, biting the words through clenched teeth. He was very protective of his employer and didn't like even the hint of a swindle, especially not in their own camp. "But I'll not work with a sight such as this. Go home and clean up, young man. You're an embarrassment to your profession."

Giles shrugged nonchalantly and started for the door. "Mind if I stop by the tavern for a pint or two on my way back?"

"Yes, as a matter of fact, I do," Jack replied. "When you return, if you're not half-sprung, we'll discuss the terms of your employment. I'll continue your compensation at the same rate as Mr. Pedigrew. If you have any aunts or cousins who engage my services, there will be a nice raise in it for you."

"My relatives will most certainly engage your services, but I can assure you they won't pay their bills."

"They won't pay their bills?" Harding asked, scratching

his bald spot. "Then what good are they to Mr. Fairchild?"

"A man's got to keep busy, doesn't he? It wouldn't do for Mr. Fairchild to sit around with nothing to do. Why, I hear in London that barristers hang about the courts trying to look busy hoping a solicitor will think they're in demand and hire them on to argue a case. Now, in your situation, sir, Mr. Cranshaw is the man you want to impress," Giles continued, oblivious to the secretary's gaping mouth and reddening cheeks. "He's the client you're looking for."

Jack's chiseled lips twitched with a mirthless grin. "A relative of yours?"

"No. How I wish!"

Jack let out a soundless laugh and thrust his hands on his hips. "I believe I've been roasted by my own clerk, Harding."

The balding secretary nodded in agreement as he began to sort the mound of papers scattered on the front desk. It was either that or strangle the young clerk.

"Mark my word, Mr. Fairchild," Giles said, "Mr. Cranshaw is the man you want."

"I vaguely remember my grandfather mentioning the family. Is this the Cranshaw who has made such a fortune in the wool trade?"

"Among other things. You'll thank me plenty when you arrange a meeting."

"And how will I do that?"

"Through your cousin, Mr. Paley."

Jack crossed his arms again, this time with a smile of admiration. "You do have intelligence about everyone in this town, don't you?"

"Your cousin is Mr. Cranshaw's glover," Giles continued, ambling his way toward the door. "Mr. Cranshaw keeps his wife and girls in the finest gloves. Mr. Paley has invited you to dinner tonight."

Harding looked up with proprietary interest. "I handle all of Mr. Fairchild's appointments, young man. Mind you tend to your own bailiwick."

"The invitation is there on the desk," Giles explained. "See for yourself. But if I were you, Mr. Fairchild, I'd arrange to have Mr. Paley give you a letter of introduction to Mr. Cranshaw."

"Just how wealthy is Mr. Cranshaw?"

Giles winked. "He has more money than God, sir. And he's a right proper gentleman with two daughters who are pure as the driven snow."

"Are they married?" Jack asked, careful not to sound too interested.

Giles shook his head. "No, but one's near engaged, I hear. The old man has mills and sheep all over the country. He lives on top of the hill."

Giles opened the door to the glorious morning and pointed to a stately, gleaming mansion that stood like a golden sentinel on a hill overlooking the town. Jack followed him and looked closely. At the sight of the enormous house, his pulse quickened. Birds were singing, and for once they sounded like harbingers of great fortune. Jack returned to Harding's side with a smile.

"Yes, Harding, this was a very good move indeed. Leave the door open, Giles, we need fresh air in here. Country-fresh air!"

"Very well, then, I'll be on my way." Giles took off without further ado, clearly a man of his own leisurely destiny.

Jack frowned after him, then realized he couldn't expect country folk to hold to the same manners or fast pace

that he'd grown accustomed to in London. Life was
slower here. Work would get done in its own time. And
if all of Giles's relatives couldn't pay their bills, at least
this Mr. Cranshaw would, and handsomely.

Still, Jack glanced down disapprovingly at the clerk's
cluttered desk and noticed a stack of mail nearly a foot
high.

"What in bloody hell does Giles Honeycut do around
here? Giles!" he called out and jogged to the door, shouting after him. "Giles! What is this mail doing here?"

The clerk, who had his hand on the tavern door, returned without so much as a sheepish grin. He sauntered
back to Jack's side. "What's that, sir?"

"Surely Mr. Pedigrew isn't still receiving letters here.
What is all that mail doing on your desk?"

They went inside to survey the clutter of sealed letters.

"This is where the post comes," Giles explained. "A
fellow named Jenkins from Waverly brings it in for the
Royal Mail. Jenkins is a postboy of sorts. A drunken sot,
really. You see, Middledale is too far off the beaten path
for the Royal Mail coach. So Henry ferries letters to and
from Waverly, earning what money he can in tips from
grateful customers. Your job, sir, is to collect the postal
fees for each letter that comes in and make sure Henry
transports them to the Royal Mail guard. Now and then
Henry runs off with the money and drinks himself into a
stupor. Then you have to settle up with the guard out of
your own pocket."

"Over my expired corpse," Harding said, dropping the
stack of mail back on the desk with a thump. "Mr. Fairchild will not cover anyone's incompetence in such a
fashion."

Giles shrugged. "It doesn't happen often, sir, and Henry

is worth his considerable weight in gold. It was worth the trouble to Mr. Pedigrew to make sure the mail came here, what with all his dispatches to London. Waverly is quite a ways away, and you'd have to make the trip yourself every time you wanted to post a letter. Jenkins makes just enough to quench his thirst and feed his nag."

Harding glowered at the clerk.

"His rickety old beast of burden is on her last legs, sir."

Jack deftly placed his hand on Giles's angular shoulder. "If Jenkins brings the mail here, that must mean everyone in town will be stopping by regularly."

"Everyone but Mr. Cranshaw. He can afford to send his servants to Waverly. Likes his privacy."

Jack grinned cunningly. "That means I'll get to know everyone in town quickly. All the better for business. Thank you, Giles."

Giles made a quick exit, and while Harding grumbled in his wake, Jack wandered back through the adjoining rooms, one of which was his personal office. To his great relief, it was both spacious and charming. Windows facing out the back of the building shed light on rows of empty bookcases, and there was a handsome mahogany desk and several delightful Chippendale chairs suitable for even the richest clients. He'd just begun inspecting his desk when the door to the front office opened with a bang.

"Right. Now, 'ere it is, mate, the latest mail," came a slightly slurred voice. "This bundle is fresh from Waverly, just off the Royal Mail coach. I collect from you, sir, and you collect in turn from those who receive the letters. And see this one 'ere? I'm returnin' it. And I expect my due, mind you!"

Jack went to the adjoining doors and quickly learned that the postboy, as Giles had quaintly and archaically called him, was a big, stocky bear of a man with three days' growth of beard covering his beefy cheeks. When he stepped fully into the office, he brought with him the distinct aromas of leather and liquor.

"You owe me one shilling and sixpence for this letter," he hiccuped, running a hand under his crusty nose.

Harding looked at the letter and frowned. "Why, this missive came from Middledale and it was supposed to travel to Fielding. Let the guard collect there when he finds the person to whom it was written."

Jenkins scratched his stubble of a beard with a square paw and focused his rummy eyes on Harding. "Look 'ere, mate, let's get off to a good start, shall we? This letter couldn't be delivered because it 'as no name."

Harding's eyes narrowed on the missive. "That's because someone dropped it in a puddle." He snatched the letter and pointed at the weeping address. "There was a name and an address written here above the town of Fielding, but everything but the word Fielding has been blurred. It's no wonder it couldn't be delivered. I daresay it was dropped in the rain."

"Right! And therefore I'm returning it."

Jack had been watching from the doorway and decided that now was a propitious time to intercede.

"Good afternoon," he said amiably and introduced himself, treating Jenkins like a proper gentleman. The combination of respect and charm from Jack partially thawed the man's foul mood.

"Look 'ere, Mr. Fairchild," he said, "I 'ave to be strict about collectin'. If I didn't, no one would pay me. It's my job, you see. As you well know, anyone can post a letter for free. It's the person who does the receivin' who 'as to pay the postage. Sending letters is an expensive business, fourpence for the first fifteen miles alone. Why, a letter goin' seven hundred miles costs seventeen pence. And if there's two sheets of paper the cost doubles. If word gets around that the Royal Mail doesn't mean business about collectin' at the end of the run, then people will go about sending letters willy-nilly with no thought to who 'as to pay. The Royal Mail guard says this letter went all the way to Fielding, but the receiver could not be found. Since there is no name on the return address, and nothing but the word Middledale, I 'ave to collect from you."

"With all due respect, Mr. Jenkins, how do I know that this letter ever made it as far as Waverly, let alone Fielding? Now just suppose, for argument's sake, you accidentally dropped it in the rain on your way to Waverly and decided to make the new lawyer in town pay his dues, as it were, before he grows wise to your scheme."

"Oh, sir!" Jenkins said, his fat, chapped lips turning down in horror. "I would never, ever take such advantage of a gentleman. Trust me, sir, if this ever 'appens again, I'll spend me own gin money payin' for it. It's simply, ye see, Millicent needs to be reshod. Practically lame, she is, poor old girl."

His eyes filled with tears and he motioned to the open door, where a tired old mount stood with drooping eyes and protruding ribs.

"Your nag?" Jack surmised.

Jenkins nodded solemnly.

"I understand, good man," Jack said, entwining his fingers behind his back and nodding sympathetically. Jack looked consideringly at Harding. He put an arm around his secretary, pulled him aside, and said quietly, "Now, Harding, I know what you're thinking. We can't afford it, but poor Jenkins can't be expected to take such a loss.

He says the Royal Mail did its best to deliver the letter."

"He very likely passed out in a puddle twenty paces down the road and can't remember what the devil happened to that missive," Harding whispered. "If Jenkins figures you're an easy mark, he'll bring back half the post without making any effort to reach the Royal Mail coach. Isn't it bad enough that Giles says Jenkins has been known to drink away the postal fees before they ever reach the mail coach?"

Jack glanced up at the anxious Jenkins, then murmured, "Jenkins has an honest face. Let us give him the benefit of the doubt." He reached into his pocket and raised his voice. "Very well, Mr. Jenkins. I'll pay for this letter, even though there is no hope of recovering the costs. But I hope I don't see the likes of this again for some time to come."

"No, sir." Henry exhaled a liquorish breath and smiled broadly.

"But you'll never find out who sent that letter," Harding grumbled. "You'll never recover your money."

"Then let my generosity be a kind offering to my new town. Eh, Mr. Jenkins? This looks like a good place to make my home."

"Indeed, sir." Jenkins looked so grateful Jack thought he might burst into tears. "You're a good man, Mr. Fairchild. And I'll make sure everyone 'ears about it."

Jack grinned contentedly and caught his secretary's eye, giving him an I-told-you-so look. When Henry left, he said, "I could do far worse, Harding. Perhaps word of my good deed will travel faster than word of my reputation as a rake."

"One can only hope, sir," Harding replied stoically.

Three

After exchanging other letters with Harding, Jenkins staggered out the door and went directly to the tavern down the street. Jack quickly forgot about the missive as he explored his new establishment. He surveyed the cozy quarters upstairs, where he and Harding would live. Then he returned downstairs and retrieved his trunks from the carriage. He had just settled himself behind his desk to review his stack of debts when Giles returned. The articled clerk had changed into outdated but clean clothes. He looked and, more importantly, smelled like a new man. He even appeared to be more alert.

"If it's jolly good with you, sir," he said, poking his head into Jack's office, "I'll gather the briefs old Mr. Pedigrew left for you before he retired."

"Excellent," Jack replied, fingering the letter. The water-stained paper waffled at his touch. "Look here, Giles, can you interpret this handwriting?"

"What's that, sir?"

"Do you recognize the handwriting?" He handed over the letter. "Was it written by someone here in Middledale?"

Giles flipped over the weather-worn missive with a quick shrug. "Sorry, sir. I don't recognize it. But this was written by a member of the fairer sex, to be sure."

Jack cocked his head. "How do you know?"

"I've seen enough mail come through this office that I've developed an eye for it. A woman's way with the quill is more delicate." He squinted at the smeared address. "Fielding, it says here. And Middledale is the only mention of its origination. Well, if it was written by someone here in the village, I don't recognize the handwriting."

Jack stroked his chin. "That's odd, wouldn't you say?"

"I suppose someone here could have written it and tried to hide his or her penmanship. A very private letter perhaps."

Jack leaned forward. "Fascinating. Who do you suppose might be inclined to such privacy?"

"I don't know, sir. But it wouldn't take much effort to find out. Just break the seal and read the signature."

Jack leaned back and shook his head, his sensibilities recoiling at the prospect. "I couldn't, I'm sure."

"Mr. Harding said you paid out of pocket for it." He dropped the letter on the desk in front of his employer. "If you find the sender, you can get your money back."

"But in the process I would have breached her privacy. And she would know it. If it's a she."

"If I were the sender, sir, I'd be grateful to have my letter back. You don't have to read it. Just glance at the signature."

"But if, as you say, the handwriting has been disguised,

would the sender have signed her name? And if she'd bothered to disguise her identity, it's very likely because she doesn't want anyone to know the letter's contents."

"You'll never know, sir, until you break the seal and read it for yourself."

Jack hesitated. "I shall consider your argument."

And consider it he did. Jack could scarcely concentrate on the briefs Giles brought him. There was something absolutely mesmerizing about the letter. Of course, he'd always been attracted to the forbidden and elusive, at least where women were concerned. This poor missive looked so forlorn, the parchment discolored and mud-splattered, wrinkled and bent. Who could guess what sort of critical intelligence it might contain? Perhaps it informed someone of an inherited fortune. Or perhaps it had been intended for a mother whose daughter was nearing her last breath. Or maybe it had been sent by a scorned lover who was begging forgiveness and threatening to kill herself. The possibilities were endless. And what would happen if any of these sorts of messages did not reach their intended destination? What a peculiar responsibility now sat on his shoulders simply because he had taken it upon himself to pay for it.

Jack's fingers seemed to crawl of their own accord across his desk until the letter was safe in his hands. He held it to his nose. Was there still the faintest whiff of perfume, or was he imagining it because Giles had told him the writing had come from a woman's hand?

"Oh, this is absurd." He slid his thumb under the top fold and broke the wafer seal. The paper, which folded in on itself and had thereby served as its own envelope, sprang open, revealing an intricate scrawl, much of which had also bled after getting wet. His gaze combed to the bottom of the page, and when he saw that it was signed only with the initials "L. C.," he sighed in frustration. He'd have to rely on content to figure out who'd written it.

"Dearest Mrs. Halloway," he read softly to himself with a slight sense of guilt. "I hope this letter finds you well. I am writing to inform you of my decision on whether to marry Lord B. I can confide in you alone, for you are the only one who knows the real reason why I am even considering marriage to his lordship."

"Hmmm," Jack said, shifting uncomfortably in his chair. So this missive was very much intended for privacy. He shouldn't read any further. But how could he return the letter if he didn't know who'd sent it? He silently read on:

I have finally come to a fateful conclusion. My inclinations on the subject were decided two days ago when the viscount and I were walking in the garden with Aunt Patty. I tripped over a rock the gardener had misplaced, and his lordship merely laughed. And then while Aunt Patty and I did our needlework in the shade of the old oak, he strolled through the rose garden. When I looked up a few minutes later he was fornicating with the new chambermaid, quite literally. Poor girl. Of course, I had to come up with an excuse to let her go, for it was clear that this had been a prearranged rendezvous. It is one thing for a servant to be prevailed upon against her will, but this clearly was not the case. The truly shocking thing about it was that the viscount had timed it for this occasion, when he knew I would be in the garden to watch. And he did so in such a location that

*he knew I was the only one who would see it. Bless-
edly, I could only see them from the waist up, for
the roses impeded my view. What I saw filled me
with disgust. They were like two rutting dogs. Forgive my frankness, my dear Mrs. Halloway, but I
think it necessary that you fully understand the
depths of his lordship's depravity, since you alone
have advised me in this matter. Thank heaven Aunt
Patty didn't see it. She was oblivious as usual. Before it was all over, his lordship looked up at me
and grinned. I knew what he was about. He was
trying to show me the power of his position. He
wanted to make sure I understood precisely what
sort of marriage he was offering me, and now I most
certainly do. I smiled back at him, unwilling to give
him the satisfaction of my distress, though you can
well imagine how I felt. In light of this incident, I
must marry him, for I know he would be willing to
go to any lengths to ensure he gets his hands on my
dowry; for he has no scruples. I have accepted his
offer and Father is proceeding with negotiations for
a marriage settlement. I can only hope my decision
will benefit Desiree. I know you will understand and
agree with my conclusion. Please write when you
can and let me know how you are. Give my love to
your cousin.*

Yours,
L. C.

Jack stared in numb disbelief at the beautiful, deeply
slanted script. He felt as if his head had just been twisted
backward and everything was topsy-turvy. This letter

made no sense. It reeked of such apparent grace and maturity that the contrast to the crude events described could hardly be fathomed.

"Why, she can't marry such a jackanapes!" he muttered to himself, then wiped a hand over his weary features. Good God, how many more women would impale themselves on duty, or status, or any number of other misguided notions of what constituted a good reason for marriage? What on earth could possibly make marriage to this cretin nobleman necessary? Jack ached for this girl. And though he did not even know her, he knew what misery was in store for her.

Jack's parents' marriage had been a match made in hell. His father had been the son of a wealthy merchant. Jack's mother had been a blue blood, the daughter of a baron whose finances had temporarily taken a tumble nearly thirty years ago. Lord Tutley had needed an influx of money to restore his personal fortune, as his barony barely provided for itself. So he'd convinced his daughter to marry an untitled but rich man whom she did not love. The handsome settlement from Henry Fairchild had solved Tutley's financial problems and had in fact led to investments that eventually made him very rich.

Jack's father, of course, had been motivated by the opportunity of marrying into the aristocracy, of having a noble son, since Baron Tutley had no other children or grandchildren to inherit the title. There was no thought whatsoever given to affection, much less love, and none had existed in their pragmatic union. No one in the *Ton* expected love in marriage, but Jack's mother had been unique. Her father had indulged his only child with great affection, and then had foolishly expected her to enter a loveless marriage. The rest of her life was an open wound that would not heal. Jack well remembered the emptiness of Fairchild House, the clock ticking endlessly and deafeningly in the sitting room as his mother frowned over her needlework, waiting for her husband to come home from the clubs.

Later, when all pretense of an affectionate marriage had disintegrated, Jack remembered the formal dinners at a table so long that his parents never had to risk eye contact. Jack, who negotiated a peace in the middle of the table, could hear himself chew in the painful silence. The only other sound was that of his father's knife cutting too deep into bloody meat and scraping the fine china with a ticklish squeak. It was a raging, deadening silence born of indifference that had grown from ignorance and disappointed expectations. The discomfort in their home had been so great that as Jack grew older the very notion of marriage gave him the same deadening, sickening feeling he'd had whenever he contemplated his parents' marriage. It wasn't a logical thing, for he knew happy marriages did exist; rather his reaction was instinctive, so deep-rooted it never occurred to him to try to cure the problem.

Jack had simply sworn as a child never to marry for convenience, and since he wasn't intimately acquainted with love matches, the thought of marrying for companionship never presented itself as an option in his mind. Truth was, the very notion of any kind of marriage at all made him physically ill.

And so as he clutched this letter in his hands, picturing what was in store for this poor young lady, perspiration beaded on his upper lip and he grew light-headed. He pinched the bridge of his nose, grimacing as he fought for a steadying breath of air. This poor lady. This poor, dear girl. She couldn't do this. She simply couldn't.

Giles popped in. "Mr. Fairchild, you'll need to find out—"

"Giles," Jack jumped in, wiping his upper lip, pinning his clerk with a serious frown, "who do you know in this town who bears the initials L. C.?"

Giles shrugged. "Why, a few people come to mind."

"Yes, yes! Who?" Jack gripped the edge of his desk.

"There's the rat catcher's son, Liam Carew. And a yeomen's wife named Lu—"

"Someone who might be considering marriage to a viscount," Jack cut in impatiently.

"Oh. That would have to be Miss Liza Cranshaw."

Jack sat up slowly. "Liza?" The image of the woman in the carriage careened in his mind. "Not her. Oh, Lord, surely not her."

"She is the daughter of Mr. Bartholomew Cranshaw."

"Cranshaw?" The significance of the name finally penetrated like a swallow of bad gin. Jack cleared his burning throat. "You mean—?"

"The man you need to hire you as his solicitor. The richest man in town. The only rich man in town, in fact."

"Bartholomew Cranshaw? Of course." Jack let out a bark of mirthless laughter. "Liza Cranshaw is his daughter. Naturally. How could it have been otherwise?"

He leaned back in his chair and pressed his hands to his face as he felt himself sinking into a quagmire he could ill afford. The once untouchable Liza Cranshaw had finally decided to marry, and she'd made the worst choice imaginable. If Jack could possibly convince her to forestall her marriage to this contemptible viscount, her father would undoubtedly be furious with him for interfering in such an ostensibly good match. Then there would be no way to win Mr. Cranshaw's favor and earn the living Jack so desperately needed.

And yet if Jack let Liza Cranshaw go through with this dreadful plan, he'd never forgive himself. Somehow saving someone else from misery seemed especially important given his tenuous situation. The chances of saving his own arse at this point were painfully slim. But there was a real chance he could spare Liza Cranshaw a life of misery. And if he were clever enough, perhaps he could do it without sabotaging his new life here in Middledale.

He lowered his hands and eyed Giles, who stared at him as if he were mad.

"Is there something amiss, Mr. Fairchild?"

"Yes, Giles, a great deal." He smiled so charmingly that Giles was utterly baffled. "I need to give this letter back to Miss Cranshaw."

"Oh, it's her letter, then? I suppose she didn't want her father to know she was sending it, or she would have had one of his servants take it to Waverly. I'll run it up to Cranshaw Park for you, sir."

Jack tucked the letter in his waistcoat before the clerk could grab it. "No, that won't be necessary. I'll just go visit my cousin and get my letter of introduction to Mr. Cranshaw and take it to Cranshaw Park myself."

"Very good, sir."

Jack leaned forward and said confidentially, "Giles, do you know which viscount Miss Cranshaw is entertaining as a possible match?"

"Oh, yes, sir. Viscount Barrington."

"*Barrington,*" Jack rasped. "Oh, good God." That explained everything. Barrington was a complete ass, a so-called nobleman who didn't have a noble bone in his body. He was so bereft of good judgment and good character that Jack felt like washing his hands every time they played cards together at the clubs in Town. How on earth had that scoundrel convinced such a beautiful and rich heiress to accept his suit?

"That settles it, Giles. I must intervene."

"What, sir?"

"Never mind. Look, young man, do not mention this letter to anyone. Do you understand? Especially not to the viscount's servants."

Giles nodded slowly. "Of course. You can trust me, sir."

"Good. For I'm about to cause a great deal of trouble. Don't tell Mr. Harding, will you?"

"What are you going to do, sir? I've heard all about your scandals in London."

Jack gave him a resigned look. "Have you? Word travels fast."

"Are you going to start a scandalous affair?"

Jack could tell by Giles's keen look of mischief that he had a great deal of potential. Jack rose and straightened his waistcoat, donning his mental armor. "I doubt very much that an affair will be effective. But I'm going to do battle, my boy, and if I succeed, I will prevent a young lady from making the worst mistake of her life."

Four

That afternoon Liza declined to walk with her sister through the grounds, which was a way they often passed their idle time before dinner. Instead, she decided to write a letter to Mrs. Halloway. Thoughts burned and tumbled in her mind, and she was eager to express herself to the only confidante she could trust. Though Liza had received no reply to her last missive to Mary Halloway, who was a widow and a longtime family friend, there was so much she wanted to say, and most of it had to do with Jack Fairchild.

Liza settled herself in the luxurious and stately library at her favorite escritoire. The writing desk overlooked the windows exposed to the south lawn. It was a bright day, and the sun beamed warmly through the mullioned, bubble-pocked glass.

As Liza trimmed her quill with a small knife, shaving the ink-stained tip against her thumb, she wondered what she should say about Mr. Fairchild. She tried to picture

him in her mind's eye. It was easy to do. Her breasts
tingled as her memory filled with images of his faintly
tanned flesh, of a snugly fitting brown coat and tight doe-
skin trousers on muscular legs. His white teeth flashed at
her in an unhesitating smile, and his eyes crinkled with
charming kindness. And yet he had not been kind to her.

One dance with Jack Fairchild had changed her life.
One kiss from him had stirred her from youthful ignorance, teasing her with a passion and a seductiveness she
knew she could never have. It had been so long since that
night that she'd forgotten just how exquisitely beautiful
he was. She was now almost numb to the tumultuous feelings he had sparked in her, and the changes in her that
had resulted. Yes, he had destroyed her innocence with a
single dance, which was testament to his personal power,
but she no longer mourned that lost innocence, and the
changes in her were now integral to who she was. But
while she no longer felt the careening loss she'd felt that
fateful night eight years ago, she could not fathom or control the anger, the confusion, and the excitement he elic-
ited in her now.

What was it about Jack Fairchild that stirred her so,
then and now? She pictured in her mind his poetic features—brooding yet charmingly ironic eyes, expressive
eyebrows, a graceful and strong nose, bold and sensuous
lips, a square jaw, high cheeks, wild and handsome hair.
A pleasing list, but it was more than looks that conspired
to upend her life.

When he wasn't smiling, his powerful eyes seemed to
be waiting for something, looking for proof that the world
was indeed a better place than he had known it to be. He
was holding out for something better, determinedly, even
though she suspected that cynicism was a permanent mist

in his constitution, clouding his natural love of life. It was
that hint of cynicism that lured her, that made her want
to prove to him something that she did not even believe
herself—that the world was good and fair to those who
were good and fair in turn.

He was a prophet of love and doom and she his dis-
ciple. She wanted to signify his existence, to soothe the
rawness she saw chafing just beneath the surface of his
skin. Even more, she wanted him to want her. For if
someone so difficult to please, so determinedly single,
wanted her, then she would be as powerful as she wanted
and needed to be. Much more than she knew herself to
be.

She dipped her sharpened, featherless peacock quill in
a pot of black ink and began to scratch her thoughts on
the page.

> *Dear Mrs. Halloway,*
> *There has been a most interesting development in*
> *Middledale since last I wrote. I have become reac-*
> *quainted after a fashion with a most distinguished*
> *and notorious gentleman from London. He—*

The door creaked open behind her. "Greetings, my
dear," came the bored-sounding voice of Lord Barrington.

Liza's hand jerked, and her floundering quill scrawled
ink across the page. Every muscle in her body tensed, and
she whipped open the left-hand drawer of the escritoire.
She slid the letter inside and was about to close it when
the viscount reached for the note.

"What is this, my darling? Something you don't want
me to see?"

A wave of the viscount's cloying clove-scented sweet

waters wafted over her shoulder as his shadow fell on the desk. When Liza saw his fingers touch the paper, twin bolts of fury and fear ripped through her, and she slammed the drawer as hard as she could.

"Ow! Damn!" he cursed, pulling his jammed fingers free and shaking the pain from them. "What the devil is wrong with you, Liza?"

She looked up, taking care to smile sweetly. "I am ever so sorry, my lord. I didn't hear you coming up behind me. I shut the drawer unaware that you were reaching for my personal correspondence."

He pressed a bloodied knuckle to his lips and pinned her with his cold gray eyes. "How in hell could you not have heard me? I spoke as clear as a bell."

Liza shrugged and stood, placing herself directly in front of the drawer. "I suppose I wasn't expecting you. I would not imagine that you would ignore all rules of propriety and visit me without a chaperone. Then again, you call me by my Christian name without asking my permission. So I suppose I should not wonder."

He crossed his arms and tapped one of his fine black boots on the Aubusson-covered floor as he considered his response. He made no pretense of charm or affection. He rarely smiled for anyone except her father, and that would doubtless cease once he acquired Liza's considerable dowry.

"Your parents don't care if we spend a few moments alone as long as they acquire a titled son-in-law. That's all your merchant father cares about. I've come to tell you that we will announce our engagement in three weeks at a party here at Cranshaw Park. I trust that meets with your approval."

He ran his hand through the limp blond locks that

would never stay in place and strolled to the French doors, looking out at the lawn. Robert Barrington had always seemed to Liza like a twenty-seven-year-old schoolboy dressed in his father's finest and thoroughly out of his own league. Though he always wore richly cut clothing made from exotic textiles and brandished exquisite jewel-encrusted snuffboxes that would be the envy of the demi-monde, Lord Barrington lacked a certain grace. His hands were square, his eyes were cold, his lips were unpleasantly thin, and his hair was the wrong texture. He wasn't un-attractive. He simply possessed none of the elusive qual-ities that could hold together such disparate factors in an agreeable pose. He had none of the savoir faire that made his addiction to gambling seem like a charming eccen-tricity. He was only happy in the gaming halls, and had gambled his way to ruination. Marrying a rich merchant's daughter would be his only salvation, and to his credit he had conjured enough warmth and charm to convince Liza's father that he was truly interested in the family business. But she knew better.

The only time Liza ever saw Barrington smile genuinely was when he was shuffling cards. In any other environment his gray eyes darted about, impatient with everything, set-tling on nothing for very long.

"In a few weeks," he continued, thrusting his hands in his pockets, "after we announce our intended nuptials, we can make our union official in the way that counts the most."

She blinked several times, then caught his dreadful drift, though she didn't let on.

"What do you mean?"

His mouth widened to show a gap-toothed grin. "Oh, come, my dear, don't tell me you're that naive. It's not

uncommon for two people who are engaged to warm the
bed before the ceremony."

The image of making love to Lord Barrington made her
queasy, and she gripped the table for support. She swallowed hard. "No, I have not heard that," she lied.

"It's true." He sauntered forward and trailed a finger
down her neck to the V of her plush bosom. It made her
skin crawl.

"Don't, my lord."

"Oh, Liza, do not be such a prude." His fingers fanned
out over her breast and he squeezed.

She grabbed his wrist and flung it away. "I have no
intention of doing anything before it is absolutely necessary, and then only as often as necessary."

He reached under her hair with one hand and swooped
for a sensual kiss. His tongue churned in her mouth like
a chimney sweep with a feather duster. When he pulled
her closer, she thought she'd suffocate. Not knowing what
else to do, she bit his grotesque tongue, just hard enough
to elicit a yelp. He jumped back.

"Hell! What the devil?"

She wiped the back of her hand across the saliva he'd
left on her mouth and blinked innocently. "Did I do something wrong? Isn't that how it's done?"

He stared at her venomously, touched his tongue, and
when his fingers showed no blood, he sullenly took out a
jade snuffbox. He loaded the tobacco in the crook of his
thumb and snorted it loudly. He sniffed again as the per-
fumed mixture penetrated the membranes of his nose.

"I see that you are very inexperienced, my dear," he
said, smiling mirthlessly. "You should have asked Desiree
to teach you a thing or two."

"Don't ever speak to me of her again," Liza hissed,

smacking him hard on the cheek. When he merely laughed, she turned and hugged her upper arms, hating herself for letting him bring so much gracelessness out in her. He would take her down to his level one way or the other. It was simply a matter of time.

He smiled sweetly. "Poor Liza. Just a silly virgin. Don't worry, darling, I'll teach you everything I know."

He left then without saying good-bye, thankfully having forgotten the letter. She nevertheless tore open the drawer and ripped the half-written missive to shreds. She could not embroil the unwitting Mr. Fairchild in her miserable life. It was too late for comfort. All there was left to do was dream of what might have been and prepare for the horrible prospect of consummating her marriage to the despicable Viscount Barrington.

That evening, Jack accepted the Paleys' invitation to dinner. They lived in what was once known as Deerfield Rectory a few miles out of town. The house was typical of the stone dwellings in the Cotswolds, a quaint and sturdy home surrounded by green fields and wildflowers. It was the sort of place where one could almost smell the sunset and hear the woods sigh at night as the trees settled into slumber.

As Jack approached in his carriage, he breathed deeply the calming country air and prepared himself for the bittersweet visit he knew awaited him. For his cousin had the one thing Jack would never have, what he never even considered having—a happy marriage. Seeing Arthur Paley's contentment always made Jack feel hollow, half-lived, and though he enjoyed these infrequent visits, before they were through he was always anxious for a breath of London's foul air and some sort of affirmation that his cynical outlook on life was justified.

Jack was warmly greeted by his cousin, Arthur, a decent-looking and lanky man of unexceptional ambition, and his entire brood of twelve children. The boys all looked ruddy and obedient, and the girls were fair and sweet. Standing in a row, they looked like a living staircase, ascending from high to low. What a picture they made! Just like a painting, Jack thought, wistfully coveting the life of a country squire. He greeted them all with charming deference, and watched with a stifled smile as each bowed or curtsied to their esteemed distant relation. Jack saved an embrace and a warm greeting for their mother, Theodosia, the softly plump and loving matron of the flock.

While the girls helped her prepare the meal, and the boys finished their chores, Jack and Arthur strolled the land, talking about old times. The tension that had gripped Jack in London began to dissipate amidst the quaint setting, even without so much as a sip of brandy. The men, though very different in disposition and fortunes, had always been close. The older they grew, the more they appreciated one another. By the time they returned to the house for dinner, Jack was relaxed and laughing and quick to praise everything about Arthur's life in the country.

During dinner he groaned in approval of Theodosia's cooking, and looked more closely than he ever had at each of her good-natured children, who were seated along benches on either side of the long, rough-hewn dinner table. The youngest child was a wee blond moppet in a little white cap who sat next to Jack. She looked up at him throughout the meal with such blatant adoration that he thought for the first time in his life that children might not be such a terrible curse after all. The only curse would come with marriage to the mother they would require.

"So, Jack, tell us what you plan to do in Middledale," Theo said at the end of their pleasant meal after they had all eaten the last of her delicious mutton stew. "Will you be here long?"

Jack wiped his mouth on a napkin and exhaled a sigh of satisfaction as he pushed aside his empty plate. "I plan to make a home for myself, and I hope it is as cozy and full of good food and fine temperament as yours."

Theo blushed at the compliment. Her husband also beamed at the praise. Arthur Paley had always looked up to Jack, even though Arthur was older by a year. Arthur's mother had been the daughter of Lord Tutley's half-sister. Though distantly related, Arthur was nevertheless second in line to the title. Assuming his claim would never be exercised, Arthur had lived his life happily and humbly as a glover and gentleman farmer, never seeming to covet all that Jack stood to inherit.

There was another distinction between the men. Arthur's mother had been happily married, as was Arthur himself. It was in part a function of never having been burdened with the expectation of producing an heir for a great estate, which was an irony considering his large brood of children.

"Come, Jack, and join us by the fire with a sip of port," he said. "There is much to talk about."

At the signal from their father, the flock of well-mannered children scattered like mice at the sight of a cat. When some giggled, others reprimanded. And together they all cleared the table and helped the maid-of-all-work clean the dishes with remarkable cohesion and enthusiasm. Jack had never seen any half-pints so well behaved in London. Come to think of it, he never saw children in

London. They were always kept in nurseries while the adults entertained themselves.

"Come here, coz," Arthur said and drew a curtain that separated the kitchen from the hearth room. "I'm afraid we have much to talk about, and we won't have peace with the children about."

"Normally I would agree with you," Jack replied, taking a seat opposite Theo, who knitted next to the fire. "But your children are undeniably well behaved."

"A good thing, considering there are so many."

The fact that Arthur had had twelve children in spite of his modest means indicated that he either was more passionate in nature than his rather sallow cheeks indicated, or that he'd made a love match. It was the latter, Jack thought, and he grudgingly admired his cousin for it. Happiness aside, there were lines of worry imbedded on Arthur's forehead that hadn't been there five years ago.

Was it any wonder? The bills such a family produced must be enormous. Jack noticed that Theo's gown, though she'd undoubtedly donned her best for the occasion, was somewhat faded. And some of the children's clothing seemed too small for their growing bodies.

"So many mouths to feed," Arthur said, as if he had read Jack's turn of thoughts. He poured port and handed a glass to his guest, shaking his head.

Jack sipped the liquor, letting the potent fumes fill his nostrils, and nodded his approval. "You must indeed have debts to pay if you provide all your guests with port as fine as this."

Arthur smiled. "I'm glad you approve. I keep it in the cupboard. It's your grandfather's favorite. I always hope one day Lord Tutley will visit and I can offer him a good glass. I know it's unlikely. In the meantime, Theo and I have been visiting Tutley Castle faithfully. I want him to know I have honored the family reputation and my duties in spite of my humble circumstances."

There was a longing for recognition in his voice that tugged at Jack's heartstrings. He leaned back and sighed with bitter memories. "You shouldn't care a whit what Grandfather thinks of you or your family. How is the old bastard?"

"Old," Theo said with a smile.

"And a bastard," Jack prodded her.

"He is a good man in his own way," Arthur said, ever the family diplomat.

"You wouldn't have an unkind thing to say about Attila the Hun, Arthur."

His wide lips spread in a teasing smile beneath his bony cheeks. "And you wouldn't have a kind thing to say about Jesus of Nazareth."

Jack barked out a laugh. "Not true. I'm as pious as any man in London."

"Piously devoted to women, I should think." Arthur looked at him with furtive envy, but Jack smiled wryly.

"Not anymore."

"You truly mean to settle down, then?" Theo said with obvious surprise.

"I mean to make this my home and pay off my parents' debts."

"Will you take a wife?" Theo asked.

Jack shook his head. "Good Lord, no. Just hearing you mention the possibility makes my stomach pitch as if I were at sea on a small, leaky boat. Some people are made for matrimonial bliss. I do not harbor such hopes."

Arthur had been silently studying the peat smouldering in the fireplace. He suddenly cleared his throat, saying,

"His lordship doesn't have long to live, you know."

"I suppose I should be saddened by that news, but I'm not." Jack's face clouded over. "I haven't seen the old man in ten years. He didn't even come to Mother's funeral. His own daughter!"

Arthur shot him a sympathetic look. "I'm sorry. But I am not surprised."

"Neither am I. But still it outraged me."

"You two always were oil and water."

Jack snorted. "That's a decent way of putting it. What you mean to say is that the old man always hated me, and I hated him in turn."

Arthur and his wife exchanged worried glances. "Theo and I were discussing this a few days ago, when we received your surprising message that you were relocating to Middledale. Theo suggested your grandfather might like to see you."

"Not bloody likely," Jack replied.

"But will you see him? I'd like that, Jack. Do it for me."

Jack tipped back the last of his port. "Very well, Arthur. I'll do it for you. If for no other reason than to repay you for this excellent glass."

A warm silence followed this concession, during which time the clock chimed and the voices of the children, whispering and giggling as they tried to be quiet, filled the air.

"Jack," Arthur said, hesitating, and then continuing, "I've been thinking. If Great-Uncle Richard left his fortune to you after all, you would be able to clear your debts in one fell swoop. You are the eldest, in fact, the only remaining grandson. The title as well as the inheritance should be yours."

Jack sighed and shook his head. "Yes, and if pigs had wings they could fly. He'll leave me the title because he has no choice, but he wouldn't leave a farthing to me if the devil himself offered him another lifetime in exchange for it. Sadly, I could scarcely maintain the estate without his personal fortune. And considering I'm one step away from debtor's prison, I'll be an embarrassment to the title. I'm thinking of resigning it in your favor, Arthur."

Arthur turned pale. "Heavens, no! Jack, please don't. I don't want the responsibility. I haven't trained for it. You have. And once you have the title, they can't throw you in debtor's prison. Somehow you'll manage. Can you imagine me sitting in the House of Lords? A glover sitting next to dukes and ministers, commandeering a staff of servants?"

"Oh, dear!" Theo said in alarm.

"You will have the money to hire the best steward and secretaries in the land, Arthur. Haven't you thought of what power you will have with that fortune?"

Arthur bit his lower lip, and worry clouded his soft brown eyes. "I regret to say that I've been thinking a great deal about that money. I hope you don't think I want to steal your inheritance, Jack, but Mary, she's our eldest—"

"Of course I remember Mary," Jack interjected, though he realized with a guilty twinge he might not remember the names of the rest of the children.

"Mary is not well. She needs to see a physician in London. And Theo hasn't had a new dress in years."

"Don't worry about me, dearest," Theo admonished gently.

"I am sorry to hear it," Jack said, avoiding her gaze. He was afraid she might see pity in his face. And his heart was full of it. It wasn't right that a man who had married the woman he loved, and who had tried to be a good father, should suffer for the want of money. Jack had seen that too often. Prisons were filled with fathers who'd lost loving families because they couldn't buy their way out of debt. "Is there anything I can do to help?"

"No, no, thank you. We need no charity. And we don't need much. It's just that, I had always expected Grandfather to . . . to remember me in some small way."

"He will," Jack said reassuringly. "His hatred of me will see to it. Surely you will inherit his fortune. He's said to be worth nearly three hundred thousand pounds."

"Three hundred thousand?" Theo gasped.

"And he wouldn't give a penny of it to my mother when she was dying and hounded by creditors. Simply because she'd stubbornly refused to separate from a husband who had squandered his own fortune."

"He's a bitter old man," Theo said. "Don't you become bitter, too, Jack. You must learn to forgive him. Forgiveness is the most precious gift one can bestow on another. It makes the giver large in spirit."

"You're too good for this world, Theo," Jack said, shaking his head. Forgiveness wasn't on his list of aspirations. "But enough of this morose talk. I don't want his money. It's all yours, Arthur. So don't have a worry. Now tell me about Mr. Cranshaw. Can you give me a letter of introduction?"

"Oh, yes!" Arthur said, his pale cheeks regaining their color. "I'll write a letter straight away."

"Splendid," Jack replied. As soon as it was written he would leave. However pleasant, the visit exhausted Jack. It took a great deal of effort to see evidence of marital happiness and still cling to the inexplicable certainty that such love was not meant for the likes of him.

Five

A t ten the next morning, when any other young
lady of her station would occupy herself with
letter writing or needlework, Liza went out into
the park to practice archery. No one in the household uttered so much as a word of disapproval. It was a com-
monplace occurrence that everyone blamed on her father.

Bartholomew Cranshaw adored his eldest child, and
though he'd never bemoaned the fact that she was a girl,
he had indulged her interest in this sport. Archery helped
to teach her control and discipline, and had also proved
to be a useful outlet for her temper—a temper that had
been under considerable strain in recent months. Although
Liza may have appeared to outsiders to be almost strident
in her impatience over her parents' foibles, she was utterly
devoted to them and was entirely convinced that neither
her mother nor her father could survive without her practical, almost cynical understanding of the world. The more
fiercely Liza clung to this belief, the more frequently she
visited the shooting range.

On this fine spring morning she nocked her arrow on the first attempt and settled the wooden shaft into place on the bow. Her sister stood behind her, twirling her pink parasol over her shoulder. Liza already felt a trickle of sweat between her breasts, but she wanted no shade. Let her face become hideously freckled for all she cared, she thought petulantly. It would only serve to dismay Lord Barrington.

Oh, what a miserable, loathsome toad he was, she thought as she drew back her bowstring, picturing his face at the center of her straw target. The muscles in her shoulders tensed beneath the short puff sleeves of her white muslin gown. She pulled until her arm muscles ached and then she let the arrow fly. *Thwomp!*

"Perfect!" her sister declared. "You hit the mark straight on."

Liza turned with a triumphant smile to Celia, but froze when she saw they were not alone. Seeing her dismay, her sister turned as well and gasped.

"Well done," said Jack Fairchild in his deep, mellifluous voice. He stood not far away in a leisurely pose, leaning lightly on his walking stick, looking every bit as dashing as he had the day before. His dark brown coat was buttoned snugly at his slender waist, and beneath that his blue silk waistcoat gleamed in the sun. He wore buff-colored trousers that revealed a shocking bulge that she should not even notice. His high white collar and starched cravat perfectly framed his square, manly jaw and his full, sensuous lips seemed to stand out in contrast to so much crisp white and lightly bronzed skin. His hair cast about his forehead like black waves crashing into shore, but the real tempest resided in his eyes. They were not so teasing as before, rather they leveled her with a kind of troubled compassion that seeped into her like water into an unseaworthy vessel. Looking at him, growing weak at the sight of so much masculine beauty, made her think her ship was sunk already.

"Mr. Fairchild," she greeted unevenly, and cleared her throat, tipping up her chin. "What a surprise."

"Miss Cranshaw," he said. When he smiled the sun became his co-conspirator, bouncing off his fine, white teeth and winking in his eyes. "I've come to beg your forgiveness."

When he took a step forward, she had the unreasonable notion that he was going to take her in his arms. She made a start and had to stop herself from creeping backward. Her sister caught the aborted motion and shot her a stunned look. Celia had never known her sister to shrink in anyone's presence.

"Liza?" she queried, fidgeting with the lace collar of her rose-colored crepe dress. Her alarmed blue eyes peeked out from under her wide-brimmed bonnet.

Liza gave a short, violent shake of her head, setting her black curls flying. *Don't ask,* the motion said. *Don't ask why he undoes me so.*

"Will you forgive me for forgetting our dance?" he continued, sauntering to her side. "Upon further reflection, I avow I remember you well."

When his eyes crinkled with a wistful smile, she blushed. What precisely did he remember? Only the dance? "I am sure, sir, the evening was quite forgettable."

"I pray not. And now that my memory has been jogged, may we start again?" He displayed a well-formed calf and sketched a deep bow, taking her hand. His warmth penetrated her Limerick glove. She'd offered only two fingers, but he'd managed to scoop four in his firm grip.

"Miss Cranshaw, I am pleased to make your acquaintance again."

He gazed at her steadily as he placed his lips on the back of her hand. She felt the intimacy of that kiss all the way up her arm to her woozy head, nearly bowling her over. She stiffened and waited for his theatrics to cease.

"May I introduce my sister, Mr. Fairchild?" she said when he rose. "This is Miss Celia Cranshaw."

"Greetings, Miss Celia. What a pleasure." Jack turned his focus to the young girl, and her eyes widened in surprise at the force of his charm. He kissed her hand as well, and she stifled a girlish giggle.

Liza rolled her eyes, then quickly pasted a smile on when Jack turned his focus back to her. "What brings you here to Cranshaw Park, Mr. Fairchild?"

"I became lost. I decided to walk to your house to give your father a letter of introduction, but I lost my way when I tried to cut through the woods."

"You're lucky you weren't shot by our land agent," she said dryly, resting her bow against a bench. "He doesn't take kindly to trespassers."

"Then I should count myself fortunate that I stumbled on you, since you are armed only with a bow and arrow and not a gun. And I came at such a splendid moment. I have never seen such a shot from a woman before. Very impressive, Miss Cranshaw."

His eyes warmed with genuine praise. It softened her like water on a dry sponge. She smiled and blushed in spite of her wariness. "Thank you. I've worked at it for some time."

"Is that why you are still without a husband? They fear your marksmanship?"

At the mention of marriage, her stomach took a tumble

and she frowned. How could she explain to this handsome, lovely gentleman that she had finally decided to marry a man like Barrington? She'd once been proud of her independence. She'd relished the way people talked about her, half-admiringly, half-disparagingly, as if she were a unique creature to choose spinsterhood when as a rich merchant's daughter she could have the pick of England's land-poor noblemen. But now her own choice of a husband had robbed her of all moral superiority. Everyone knew Lord Barrington was a wastrel desperately in need of a rich wife. Everyone, that is, but her good-natured parents.

"Why have *you* never married, sir?" she asked, trying to deflect his inquiries, turning bright red when she realized what a personal question it was.

"I hold the unfashionable belief that one should marry only for love." He tapped his cane into a sprig of grass and regarded her thoughtfully, as if waiting for rebuttal.

"Unfortunately," he added wryly, staring blatantly at her mouth, "I'm not capable of true love. Surely you've heard that about me before."

"Yes, I have." When his gaze wandered from her lips to her eyes, she smiled sadly. "What a pity, Mr. Fairchild. Don't you think?"

He blinked with a flash of sadness in his nut-brown eyes, then grinned ironically. "Not really. One rarely misses that which one instinctively knows one cannot have."

"Cannot have or will not have?"

He shrugged. "Is there a difference?"

"What pretty words from such an experienced young blood."

"Not so young anymore," he interjected. "I am near to thirty-five."

She was twenty-five. That made him positively ancient. And yet age had done nothing to diminish the vibrancy that thrummed in his lean, muscular figure.

"How many hearts have you broken with such gracious humility, sir?"

He held up his arms as if she were a bandit threatening his life with a pistol. "Have I struck a bruise, Miss Cranshaw? I fear my charm is not having its usual effect."

"No." She shook her head and the raven coils spilling from her cambric cap bounced at her temples. Her eyes narrowed with a warning. "No, sir, do not imagine one dance with you left any impression upon me at all."

He lowered his arms and frowned with understanding. "Is that it, then?"

"Is what what, then?" she asked, her eyes flaring. He thought he knew her. The audacity of the man! The air was suddenly stifling. She reached down and snatched up her bow and grabbed an arrow from her quiver. She nocked the arrow and drew it back, letting it fly cleanly. For a moment, she felt glorious release. But then the arrow struck wide of the mark, and that only added to her exasperation. She turned on him. "Why tempt women with your peculiar brand of charm, sir, if you have no intention of going the distance with them?"

He opened his mouth to speak, and she cut him off.

"Oh, I've heard of your charitable efforts to pleasure unhappily married women. How magnanimous of you."

"Liza!" Celia gasped. During the course of their scandalous conversation, the younger woman's complexion had turned from pink to red to white. But Liza ignored Celia's shock—and her presence.

"I think you're selfish," Liza rushed on like a lemming that could not stop its mortal plunge into the sea. "You teach women to want that which they can never have. You know very well any respectable girl will never find such pleasure in marriage."

"Yes, I do know that. That's why I've never married. And will *you* now marry, Miss Cranshaw, you who were once called the Untouchable? It appears that, like me, you had your own reservations about the state of matrimony."

She shut her eyes against a wave of nausea. Marriage to Lord Barrington. Heavens, what was she doing? And why had this man come back into her life at the worst possible moment to taunt her with what might have been? She had to get ahold of herself. In fact, this would be the perfect test. If she could convince one of Society's acknowledged rakes that she was set on a happy course, then she could convince anyone. Even Desiree.

She opened her eyes and pilloried him. "Yes, I will marry. I'm soon to announce my engagement to Viscount Barrington."

He didn't flinch or blink. That was a good sign, wasn't it? She breathed easier.

"Will you marry him happily?" Jack asked softly, regarding her with those penetrating, dark-lashed eyes.

The word *yes* stuck in her throat, and she swallowed hard. "You are despicably impertinent, sir. Why are you hectoring me in this way?"

"Forgive me again, Miss Cranshaw, that was not my intention."

She drew back her shoulders. "What was your intention?"

"I brought you something."

"What could it possibly be, considering you did not even remember me yesterday?"

He reached into his pocket, then skewered her with a speculative look that made her feel as if she'd forgotten to dress that morning. Now she knew what Eve must have felt like just before she'd found three fig leaves.

"What is it, Mr. Fairchild? Do you have something for me or not?"

"Not," he said, pulling an empty hand from his pocket. "Unless you count this for something."

He stepped forward, his shadow falling on her face. She leaned her head back to look up into his strong, determined features. He gripped her arms and pulled her close like a sack of goose down. She started to gasp, but he swallowed the sound with his mouth. The faintest growth of whiskers brushed her chin. His lips were hard silk. His breath was delicious. She frowned in astonishment at the pleasure. She'd forgotten, completely forgotten what it was like. Then she groaned and melted in his grip. She leaned into him and breathed in his musky scent and felt a gnawing hunger for more; oh, so much more. Madness. It was pure madness, but for one moment she was alive again. Alive, God, yes, alive!

He drew back suddenly, watching warily, as if he couldn't quite believe he'd done it either. A moment later she heard a thud. They turned in unison and found Celia in a crumpled heap on the ground.

"Oh, good Lord, she's fainted!" Liza cried out, rushing to her side. "Poor girl, I've finally shocked her into insensibility."

"Prop up her head," Jack instructed, coming around to the other side.

Suddenly there was another voice.

"Halloo! Liza, is that you?"

As Liza cradled her sister's head, her own shot up in dismay. She squinted in the sun to see the approaching figure. "Mother is coming!"

A genteel and slightly plump woman came up over the hill. Smiling, she paused to brush back a stray strand of graying hair and catch her breath. When she spotted her youngest daughter on the ground, her lovely face turned into a mask of horror.

"Oh, dear! What has happened?"

"Celia fainted, Mama."

"What should we do?" Mrs. Cranshaw said. She rushed to Liza's side and looked to her eldest for guidance. "Liza, what should we do?"

"We should take her back to the house, Mama. She became . . . overheated." Liza exchanged a furtive look with Jack. Her mother followed her gaze.

"Who are you?" Mrs. Cranshaw asked, completely mystified.

"This is Mr. Fairchild. He was kind enough to stop and help. Can you carry her, Mr. Fairchild?"

"Of course." Jack scooped the still-unconscious girl into his arms, which was the least he could do after having caused the girl's distress in the first place. Ironically, he became an instant hero in Mrs. Cranshaw's eyes for merely rectifying the very problem he had caused. Liza saw it all transpire in a sinking instant, and she knew then she would have been better off aiming that second arrow at Jack Fairchild's heart, for if she did not take great care, he would soon capture hers.

Six

ack strolled through the portrait gallery at Cranshaw Park while the ladies and their servants tended to Celia in her room. How the devil was he going to explain that audacious kiss to Miss Cranshaw? God, he was getting reckless in his dotage. But it had seemed the only decent thing to do. He'd planned to give her the letter, but when the moment arrived it had seemed a cruel thing to do, to let this noble-hearted young woman know that her dreadful secret was known. And yet somehow he had to communicate the urgent message that she deserved more than Lord Barrington. At the same time, he'd been struck with an overwhelming urge to kiss her. Hoping she would get the message without words, he'd indulged himself. He'd quite forgotten about Miss Celia. Yes, indeed, he was getting too old to be a rake. He was losing his damned touch.

He pondered this dreadful thought as footmen carried in tea accoutrements—a three-legged teapoy and tea caddy, as well as expensive china and crumpets—placing them amidst a cluster of furniture in the center of the long hall. It was a two-story room reminiscent of the Elizabethan galleries of old, except there were few windows here. Oak paneling lined the walls in stately elegance. Candles burned in ornate wall sconces, and a rich red Turkish carpet cushioned Jack's feet as he strolled from portrait to portrait.

He was struck by the impressive array of paintings, which seemed somehow out of place. After all, Bartholomew Cranshaw had come from the merchant class and had made his fortune himself. It wasn't as if he'd descended from a long line of aristocrats who'd suddenly found themselves kicked out of the nobility into the gentry. Perhaps Mrs. Cranshaw had been of noble birth, Jack mused. He had no doubt he would soon find out.

"There you are, you dear man," said a female voice from one end of the hall.

Jack turned and found Liza's mother bustling toward him. She wore a feminine, old-fashioned over-robe of peach taffeta with a gathered ruffle at the neck. A white capote decorated with peach ribbons secured her salt-and-pepper hair, which was pinned up elegantly. Her cheeks were slightly plump and flushed, and despite a constant air of fluster, she was, Jack realized, an aging beauty whose features would have perhaps surpassed Liza's in magnificence in days gone by. She was an interesting contrast of frump and flair. She held out her hands as she closed the distance, clearly intending to greet him like family.

"My dear Mr. Fairchild," she said warmly, gripping his fingers. "How can I possibly repay you for rescuing my daughter?"

"I am afraid I haven't quite accomplished that yet, Mrs. Cranshaw," Jack replied with a blithe smile, returning her sturdy grip. He liked her very much, even though she was apparently oblivious to Liza's peril, a fact which her next comment confirmed.

"On the contrary, sir, Celia is already recovered. She's sitting up in bed and speaking with her sister at this very moment."

Jack cocked a brow, but wisely refrained from comment. He could only imagine the conversation between the young women. *Upon my word, Celia, if I hear you mention a word about that kiss to Mama, I'll never speak to you again!*

"Mr. Fairchild, please forgive my incivility," she continued, releasing his hands. "Please tell me who you are and why you've come to Cranshaw Park. Then I can give you a proper welcome. I am Rosalind Cranshaw."

Before he could respond, Liza walked into the room. She was no longer the flushed, bold girl he'd encountered in the deer park. With her hair pinned in coils at the back of her head and dressed demurely in white, she looked as fresh as a spring daisy. Her simple dress seemed to accentuate her stunning amethyst-blue eyes and rose-colored lips.

"Here is my eldest daughter, Mr. Fairchild, Liza."

"We'd met many years ago in London, ma'am," Jack said, unable to tear his gaze from Liza.

"Mama," she greeted, dutifully kissing her mother's cheek. Then she turned to him with downcast eyes. "Thank you, Mr. Fairchild, for helping my sister. I don't know what came over her." She flashed him a needling, mischievous look.

"Then you know one another!" Rosalind said enthusiastically. "Liza, dear, you must tell me all about this charming gentleman."

He watched admiringly as Liza's face concealed a multitude of emotions that he was too experienced to miss. Her eyes dulled with sorrow, then glinted with anger, then warmed with the pleasurable anticipation of the torture he was sure she intended for him. It would be her retribution for the kiss. Her intriguing lips curled with a tart smile.

"I am quite sure, Mama, that Mr. Fairchild would not want me to recall the past, for that is something most people would just as soon forget. Especially someone like Mr. Fairchild."

"So true, Miss Cranshaw." Jack grinned and pulled out his letter from Arthur. "Fortunately, I have a letter of introduction that exaggerates all my current attributes and ignores all past follies. It's from Mr. Arthur Paley. You may know of my family. My grandfather lives but an hour's ride from here, at Tutley Castle."

"Is he in Lord Tutley's employ?" Rosalind Cranshaw asked politely, taking the letter.

"No, ma'am, Lord Tutley is my grandfather. Arthur is also a relation."

"Lord Tutley is your grandfather!" Mrs. Cranshaw nearly burst with joy. "That is simply famous!"

Jack wondered that she had not immediately made the connection when she'd first heard his name. He would have imagined she'd heard something about Lord Tutley's heir, as they were practically neighbors. But the Cranshaws spent little time in London and were doubtless among the folk who deemed the *haut ton* a bit hedonistic. They probably heard little gossip, which might explain their ignorance about Lord Barrington's character as well. And since Jack's grandfather considered merchants his social

inferiors, they'd had scarce chance to acquaint themselves
with the goings-on at Tutley Castle.

"Now that you mention it," Rosalind Cranshaw said
with satisfaction, "I do recall hearing that the baron's heir
was a London rake."

"Mother!" Liza cut in.

It took Rosalind Cranshaw a moment to realize her
blunder. Then she smiled sweetly. "I meant no insult, my
dear. It is simply a fact."

Jack smothered a smile as they gathered around the
teapoy, the women taking the sofa and Jack settling in an
austere Hepplewhite chair.

"So tell me, Mr. Fairchild," Mrs. Cranshaw said, her
face positively beaming with anticipation, "will you be
our neighbor one day? Not that I should wish anything
untoward to happen to Lord Tutley, of course."

Jack accepted the cup of tea she had just poured and
sipped as he considered his response. She was trying to
find out if he was going to inherit the title, and if he did
that would make him a prime match for Miss Celia,
though he was far too old for her.

"I will doubtless take up residence at Tutley Castle,
ma'am, when I inherit the title. But my grandfather is in
fair health and I do not expect that day to come for some
time. Meanwhile, I have come to Middledale to practice
law. It is a passion of mine, and one I hope to ply on
your husband's behalf, should he have need of services
now that Mr. Pedigrew is retired."

"I will speak to him," Rosalind Cranshaw said, blinking
her large sapphire eyes. Clearly she'd been taken aback
by the implication that he had to work for a living.

"I am not the sort of man to wait around for my relations to expire, Mrs. Cranshaw. My father was a success-

ful merchant and he believed hard work was good for his son, even though he knew I would one day take my place in the House of Lords." Jack felt a tinge of amusement at painting such a whitewashed—and patently untrue—portrait of his father, but he sensed Mrs. Cranshaw could prove a valuable ally if she could be influenced in his favor.

"My husband will like your thinking very much, young man," Rosalind Cranshaw declared, smiling at him approvingly. "I daresay he shall hire you forewith."

"Father hire Mr. Fairchild?" Liza regarded him more skeptically over the rim of her cup. "I can scarcely imagine the infamous Mr. Fairchild working as a provincial country solicitor."

"Infamous!" Rosalind said with a throaty chuckle. "Liza, my dear, I have never seen you so impertinent."

Jack grinned openly, but wisely said nothing.

"Yes, you have, Mother," Liza returned defiantly. "Many times."

"It's not true," Rosalind hastened to reassure Jack.

"Come, Mama, you will soon have Mr. Fairchild thinking I'm a biddable female." Liza put down her cup, leaned back in a shockingly casual pose, and twiddled her fingers, shaking her head in disbelief. "No, Mama. I simply cannot believe that a man of Mr. Fairchild's worldly experience would ever be happy with rusticating in the country. I should think it's in his best interests to return to London at once."

"Happiness has nothing to do with my decision to live here. I am simply living up to my responsibilities."

"As am I," she said pointedly, arching one brow.

He lifted his chin and smiled teasingly. "Do I detect

that you are unhappy with my decision to move here, Miss Cranshaw?"

"No, Mr. Fairchild, she feels nothing of the sort," Rosalind Cranshaw hastily denied.

But Liza did not deny him. She sat up and turned her head aside, regarding the tray of delectables as if the task of picking out the perfect crumpet to eat was much more to her liking than looking at the likes of him.

"No, Mr. Fairchild. I would have to care about you in some fashion to be disappointed. I wish you good fortune in what seems to me an impossible task."

"I am greatly heartened."

"It is not my concern if you have gambled away your fortune like the rest of London's bucks."

"Liza!" her mother said reprovingly. "Where are your manners? Am I to assume your first meeting in London was not a pleasant one?"

Jack noticed with satisfaction that Liza's ears turned red. When he could no longer bear her embarrassment, he diverted her mother with a confession he knew would have to come sooner or later.

"I did not gamble away my inheritance. I spent it paying off my father's gambling debts. Forgive me for being so blunt, but I'm quite sure you would have heard rumors soon enough."

Liza set aside her tea cake and turned to face him. "Upon my word, what an honorable thing to do."

"Indeed," agreed her mother. "Mr. Fairchild, all you need to do is find yourself a rich wife and all your troubles will be solved."

"I wish I could, ma'am. But I do not believe that that is a proper reason to marry. A marriage of convenience is a crime against nature, don't you agree, Miss Cranshaw?"

He stared hard at her, and her soft wonder turned to sadness. Always with her that bloody sadness, like a weed in a luscious bed of flowers. He wished he could pluck it from her heart.

"Well, Mr. Fairchild," Rosalind Cranshaw said brightly in the awkward silence that followed, redirecting the conversation with all the subtlety of an out-of-control high-perched phaeton, "let me show you the history of our family. I am afraid we're not of noble blood, but I do have my own proud and respectable lineage to boast."

Liza's teacup landed in its saucer with a thud, and a pained expression rippled across her brow. At first Jack thought she might be embarrassed, anticipating that her mother was about to add branches to a meager family tree. Jack was always amused when families turned fourteenth-century horse thief relations into ministers of state. But there was clearly more to it than that.

"What is it, my dear?" her mother gently prodded, touching her back lightly.

Liza willfully wiped the frown from her brow and blinked away her concern. She kissed her mother's cheek, her eyes twinkling with utter devotion. "It's nothing, Mama. Forgive me. I had a stab of pain that was surely indigestion."

"Come, my dear, let us show Mr. Fairchild our history." She rose, guiding him over to the first painting. "This is Mr. Cranshaw's father, a very distinguished justice of the peace in Devonshire."

Jack nodded and raised his brows. "Most impressive, ma'am."

"Surely not to one in your position, Mr. Fairchild," Liza

said as she reluctantly joined their parade down the gallery.

"As a solicitor I appreciate the importance of running local affairs efficiently and fairly," he replied. "It's one thing to have one's case tried before the King's Bench at Westminster Hall, but often the best hope for justice is in one's own village or town, in the fair interpretation of common law. I am convinced that the law is a citizen's best friend. God save the justices of the peace, I say!" he concluded theatrically, making a joke of his impromptu sermon. Liza regarded him as if he'd gone stark-raving mad. Her mother applauded and laughed.

"Quite so, quite so, Mr. Fairchild." She was smiling as if her entire existence had just been beatified. "I am so glad you are sensible on the subject. I've told Liza how important her forebears were."

"*Please,* Mama, Mr. Fairchild comes from the aristocracy. How much can he be impressed by our simple lives?"

Rosalind ignored her, listing each family member proudly. When she reached the other side of the gallery— her own side—she positively glowed. It was clear by her reverent tones that she considered herself more gently bred than her husband. When they reached one particularly ostentatious portrait done in dark hues and set in a massive gilded frame, she gestured grandly at the picture of a thoughtful young woman with oval eyes, a long nose, and heart-shaped lips who was donned in velvet and furs and a stylish, sugar-bag cap of a previous century.

"And this," she announced proudly, watching Jack closely for his reaction, "is my relative Maria Clementina Sobieska. She was the wife of the exiled King James III.

Maria was the granddaughter of King Jan III of Poland and one of Europe's richest heiresses."

"A very distant relation, Mama," Liza said in a hollow voice.

"Tut, tut, dear, you shouldn't be afraid to boast of your royal blood simply because it is old history. The older the better."

"Very impressive lineage, Mrs. Cranshaw," Jack said, knowing the tour would not end until he'd expressed his praise.

The doors creaked open at the hands of two footmen, and this gave Rosalind cause for even more pride. "Ah, and here comes Lord Barrington! Once our Liza has children with his lordship, the aristocracy won't be so very distant, will it, my dear?"

Jack saw Liza visibly recoil at the sight of Barrington before she rallied. She pulled back her shoulders and tipped up her chin as he had seen her do earlier that morning, and he suspected it was something she'd probably been doing all her life, brave girl that she was.

"Good day, my lord!" Rosalind called to Barrington.

The viscount strode over to them, the beginnings of a scowl on his face. He gave Jack a quick but thorough appraisal and turned to Liza, clearly dismissing Jack as an interloper.

"And who is this?" The viscount waited for an answer, but Liza remained silent.

"My lord," Rosalind offered, "this is Mr. Jack Fairchild, Lord Tutley's grandson."

"Ah, yes," he said, still not smiling, but his eyes lit with interest. "Good to meet you, Fairchild."

"I believe we've played cards at Boodle's together, my lord," Jack said amiably.

He looked down his nose at Jack. "Could have been, could have been. Yes, I think I remember it now. Tutley's heir, eh? What brings you to Cranshaw Park?"

"I'm offering my services to Mr. Cranshaw as a solicitor."

Barrington gaped a moment, then threw back his head and howled with laughter. The unpleasant sound echoed off the high ceiling. Liza and Jack exchanged a meaningful look. When Barrington realized no one else had joined in, he stopped and cleared his throat. "Very amusing, Fairchild. Why are you *really* here?"

"It's true, my lord. I've decided to rusticate and enjoy the pleasures of the country. I'm taking over for Mr. Pedigrew, who has retired. I should be grateful for any work you might throw my way."

The viscount narrowed his cold gray eyes on Jack, as if he still couldn't believe a member of the beau monde would humiliate himself in such a fashion.

"You're serious," he said at last.

"Quite," Jack replied crisply.

Barrington's puggish features turned smug. "Very well. We could use a solicitor now that Pedigrew is retired. Cranshaw has taken me into his business."

"How fortunate for you," Jack said smoothly.

"I'll see to it that Cranshaw hires you in the morning. He trusts my judgment implicitly."

This last statement sounded more like a warning than a boast.

"We'll be a very tightly knit family once Liza and his lordship are married," Rosalind said. "Mr. Fairchild, I still must repay you for rescuing Celia. Will you please join us tomorrow evening? We're having a party for our tenants and neighbors. It will be a small affair. Only seventy or so. We would be delighted to have you as our special guest. We will gather for a small meal *en famille* before the festivities begin. Let us say five o'clock?"

"I would be delighted, ma'am." Jack sketched a half bow, then turned to see the viscount grinning at him with malicious glee.

Jack knew precisely what he was thinking. The viscount was only too happy to humble Jack with employment. It was a way to control him, to make sure that the only other blue blood in Middledale didn't steal the local heiress before Barrington could take her to the altar himself. If the viscount only knew just how financially desperate Jack was he'd be less sanguine about the arrangement. For Jack had little to lose, and he was increasingly willing to do whatever it took to protect Liza Cranshaw from the ignoble nobleman she was determined to marry.

Seven

Liza wasn't sure whether to gnash her teeth over Jack Fairchild's emergence into her life or to celebrate. He was certainly a wild card, and that at least injected an element of unpredictability into what had heretofore been entirely a losing game. And in spite of his unconventional means of nosing into her affairs, Liza sensed he was concerned for her welfare, although she was unsure of the true reason. Her parents couldn't see Lord Barrington's deficits because Liza had been careful not to expose them. Only Jack Fairchild seemed to know what a wastrel she was about to marry. The only thing he didn't know, and couldn't know, was why.

Jack's willingness to call a spade a spade would create untold complications in her life. But he'd also unwittingly given her a vague hope of reprieve. His comments about the importance of law had her rethinking her advice to a local chandler.

Jacob Davis had lost his home and shop six months

earlier in a suspicious fire. Liza was convinced that Lord
Barrington had something to do with it, though she had
no proof and no notion of a possible motive. If she could
somehow prove the viscount's guilt in the case, she could
free herself from her promise of marriage without threat
of retribution.

With that hope in mind, Liza made a herculean effort
to see Mr. Davis secretly. She arranged a rendezvous
through her abigail and then waited until just before the
party to sneak out of the house. Shortly before four, dozens of servants were preparing the great lawn and garden
for the outdoor gathering, festooning the area with banners and ribbons and torches. The musicians were gathering on the terrace, and the majordomo was fluttering
around giving orders. It was a happy chaos, for this affair
was a cherished event that would be talked about for a
twelve-month afterward by the locals.

Liza would be missed as soon as the gentlemen arrived,
but in this chaos her mother would be too distracted to
care for long. And just in case it took Liza longer to return
than she anticipated, she had prepared an excuse to be
delivered by Celia, who'd been sworn to secrecy.

Liza made her escape through the kitchen and hurried
through the outer edge of the garden unnoticed. The
quickest way to reach her destination was over Birch
Road, which cut through a hill in the deer park. Though
the road was too visible for her comfort, taking that route
would save her at least a half hour. With any luck, she'd
be back at the house before too long.

Liza walked briskly, careful not to tear the skirt of her
evening gown on any brambles, until she reached the
road. Pausing to catch her breath, she rushed up the embankment, intending to hurry over the top. Instead, she

ran straight into the path of an oncoming carriage.

She saw the whites of the coachman's widened eyes as he frantically yanked the reins. "Whoa!" he cried out.

The startled horses whinnied and reared their heads. Liza gasped and wheeled back just in time to miss a whirring spoked wheel. She teetered on the edge of the road for a heart-thumping moment, then fell backward, rolling down the embankment.

"Miss Cranshaw!" a voice cried out. "Stop, for God's sake! Stop the carriage."

"Hold, sir," came another voice. "I'm doing my best. Whoa! I've got it. There, there, steady, steady. Very good, sir."

"Miss Cranshaw!"

From the grassy bottom of the hill, where she'd come to a stop with a rib-rattling thud, Liza recognized Jack Fairchild's voice. Relief coursed through her body when she realized that it could have been Lord Barrington instead. She raised herself up from her cushion of grass just in time to see him hurtling in graceful sidesteps down the hill.

"Good God, Miss Cranshaw. Are you hurt? Were you injured?" he asked once he reached her.

"No," she replied with a short laugh, sitting up and straightening her skewed straw bonnet. "Only my pride. Now we've both suffered embarrassment in one another's presence, haven't we?"

He propped one leg slightly up the hillside to balance, his lean leg taut with the effort. Before taking his proffered hand, she dusted off her gown and glanced at him. He was dressed formally in a dark-green tailed coat with a white quilting Marseilles waistcoat and white kerseymere breeches, white stockings, and black buckled shoes.

He was elegance personified, but his normally charming demeanor had been shaken.

"Really, Mr. Fairchild, I am not in the least injured." She loved saying that, for no one ever assumed Liza was hurt or in need or in want of anything. She was too damned capable for her own good. Seeing his worried frown warmed her immensely.

"Miss Cranshaw, let me help you."

"If you insist, sir, but I am quite well, I assure you." She straightened her gown over her ankles, then accepted his outstretched hand. His broad palm easily encompassed her blue glove. The now-familiar charge between them flared like one of the fireworks that would be set off later that night at the party. She felt the *oomph* of explosion in her palm and the tingle echoed in other parts of her body. He pulled her to a stand and they remained close, inches apart. *Step back,* a voice inside her urged, but she ignored it.

"My coachman did not see you come up on the road. Are you hurt?" he asked, looking her over. Amazingly, her blue silk taffeta gown had not torn in the tumble, protected as it was by her long cloak. "Please, forgive me."

"No, it is I who must beg forgiveness." She rallied all her willpower to pull her hand from his. It was unconscionable that she should be so forward with him under any circumstances, but especially when she was nearly engaged. Worse yet, he would make her late for her appointment. She had to speak with Jacob Davis and didn't want him to leave, thinking she'd not shown up. "I did not hear your carriage. Do not worry, and please do not mention a word of this at the house. I must be going."

"No, wait." He looked at the manse in the distance.

"Let me drive you back. It would be my pleasure, a way to repay you for my behavior over the last two days."

She smiled wryly. "I would love to debate the merits of your behavior, Mr. Fairchild, but I am on my way to visit someone in desperate need, and no one must know about it. Please, don't tell a soul."

"Then I will take you in my coach to your destination. No one need know."

"You cannot get there by coach. Go visit with my family, Mr. Fairchild. I will join you soon." She turned to go, but pain shot up her leg like a burning hot poker. "Oh!"

She staggered back, losing her balance, and she nearly collapsed into his arms. She grabbed his arm for purchase and he tightened his hold on her.

"See, you are injured. I can't let you continue alone."

"I do not need your help, sir." She looked up with irritation, then realized how intimate they had become. His fingers on her exposed arm were like twigs of lightning, pulsing some sort of hypnotic rhythm into her flesh. It was so powerful a feeling that she scarcely noticed the pain in her ankle. Realizing just how dangerous a man he was, and just how wanton she would be if given a chance, she carefully extricated herself from his hold and hugged her arms self-consciously.

"I'm perfectly capable of continuing."

She started off again, hobbling with each painful step. But soon she had to stop, for she'd really given her ankle a good twist, and she could no longer deny it.

"Look here, Miss Cranshaw, there is no question that I'm going to help you." He swooped her unceremoniously into his arms.

"Oh, good Lord!" she cried.

He merely laughed. "I was looking for an excuse to do that."

"Put me down at once!"

"And make you late for your appointment? You'll never get there in time with that ankle. Now why don't you forget that you're a proper young lady and be practical about this. Where are you going?"

"Into the woods."

"Which direction?"

"Over there." She pointed to the top of the road.

He strode up the hill without becoming winded and instructed his driver to pull over to a feeder road and wait for him. Then he marched off in the direction Liza had pointed.

"You are an incorrigible rogue," she protested. "If you're going to be a ghastly beast about this, I'll let you take me to the edge of the small ravine. But you must drop me there and never look back."

"How dramatic," he said, his eyes twinkling down at her. "Who are you going to visit, Miss Cranshaw?"

"I cannot tell you."

He was silent a moment, then in a neutral tone asked, "Does Lord Barrington know where you're going?"

She froze. In the potent silence that followed, leaves crunched under his feet. Birds twittered in branches overhead. Sunlight dappled her eyes with hypnotic heat through the canopy of branches. She came to the queasy conclusion that there was no point trying to fool Jack Fairchild about anything. He was the sort of man a woman could be frank with—someone who was used to keeping female confidences, a trait that was responsible for a great measure of his success as a rake, she was certain.

"No," she said hollowly. "Lord Barrington does not know. He would try to stop me if he did."

"You don't love him," Jack said matter-of-factly.

She squeezed her eyes closed.

"In fact, you hate him."

She remained silent.

"Don't marry him. He's a complete ass. Damnation, why do I keep saying these things?"

"Because you're cruel."

"I've got to be more subtle."

"I shouldn't think you were very well acquainted with subtlety." She felt sick to her stomach, and was just about to struggle from his arms when he stopped beneath a giant oak tree that hid them from the lowering sun. When he released her and her feet touched the ground, she winced. He gently leaned her against the trunk of the tree.

"Keep your weight off this ankle. You're still hurting." He knelt before her and picked up her foot. "Let me have a closer look."

She looked at him, aghast. "You can't do that!"

"What?" He looked up, his fine black brows drawing together in a frown.

"You can't touch my ankle."

"Why not?"

"It's not done."

"It is when someone twists a foot. Oh, come, Miss Cranshaw, do you think I'm trying to seduce you?"

Her toes curled with mortification, for part of her had hoped he was. "Of course not. Go ahead. But be quick about it."

She looked down diffidently at his thick, dark waves of hair, thinking how delightful it would be to run her fingers through it, to stroke his face and pull him into her wanton arms. Instead, she dug her gloved fingers into the bark of the tree.

"Tell me when it hurts." He cradled her foot in his hand and gently tugged off her white kid slipper. The gesture was so intimate it felt as if he'd just lowered her drawers. Her head clunked back against the tree as she stifled a hiss. Cool air seeped through her silk stocking and curled around her toes. Liza felt naked, and utterly scandalous.

"You really shouldn't, Mr. Fairchild."

"Shouldn't make sure you're not injured before I leave you alone in the woods?" was his even reply. "Nonsense. It's no more care than I would give a lame horse."

"Then be sure to check my teeth when you're done down there."

He chuckled softly. "Try twisting your foot from side to side."

Eager to be done with it, she jerked her foot at his command, then cried out in pain.

"You see? You are injured," he murmured. He looked up, a dangerous concern itched on his face. "I am worried for you."

"Don't be," she replied in a high, thin voice. "It was a slight twist."

"That's not what worries me."

His fingers dug into the arch of her foot, manipulating the muscles. She groaned and shivered. "That feels too good."

"Your muscles have been strained." He massaged the arch with one hand while manipulating her heel with the other, digging into the soft padded flesh. Every muscle in her body loosened and wobbled. Liza felt herself sliding down the tree trunk and bolstered her other leg.

"I am right about your regard for the viscount, am I not?" he asked carefully.

She had to shake her head to clear her pleasure-soaked brain. "What?"

"About the viscount. You loathe him, don't you?"

"Yes." She refused to elaborate any further.

"And you will not change your mind about marrying him?"

"No."

He heaved a sigh, then looked up sadly. "Then God bless you, Miss Cranshaw, for you shall need it."

He trailed his fingers from her arch to the ball of her foot and softly pinched the spaces between her toes.

Liza bit her lower lip and breathed hard. "Where did you learn to do that?" she rasped, looking down at him as if he were an exotic turban-bearing alchemist from Persia.

His eyes gleamed with challenge. "I do not really think you want me to answer that, do you?"

She laughed, relieved to be reminded of his history with women. It put everything into perspective. This was not a special moment. This was more an automatic reflex—something he would have done for any woman.

"Now try to put some weight on it." He put her slipper back on. The leather slid sensuously over silk. She shifted her weight, and it indeed felt better.

"Your magic hands worked," she said lightly. "Your practice with other women has put you in good stead with me."

He rose and gazed at her steadily. "You see, you should trust me. I will never hurt you, Miss Cranshaw. I'm like an old tiger who has lost his teeth. All growl and no bite."

She narrowed her eyes on him, remembering the last time they'd been alone eight years ago. "Yes, but you still have your claws."

Eight

N o sooner had Liza walked away from Jack than she saw Jacob Davis on the horizon. She shivered to think how close their paths had come to crossing. What would have happened if anyone had seen her behave so recklessly with Mr. Fairchild? In truth, it would matter little. Lord Barrington was determined to get his hands on her father's money regardless of Liza's reputation. She was far more concerned about Jack finding out about Mr. Davis.

She hurried toward the chandler, who hadn't seen her yet. His long, gray mat of hair blew in the wind. He wore a tattered jerkin and breeches that were as brown as his dirtied face.

When he at last spotted her, he strode to her side, then fell to his knees, kissing her glove.

"Oh, Miss Cranshaw, God bless you. Were it not for you, my family . . ." The words choked off in his throat and tears fell down his dusty cheeks. Tears welled in

Liza's eyes as well. When he saw them, he shook his head ruefully. "Beg your pardon, miss. I shouldn't carry on so. I'm so grateful, Miss Cranshaw."

"I know, Mr. Davis." She squeezed his hand, tugging gently. "Please, stand up. You owe me nothing. I have done so little."

And there would be littler still that she could do once her engagement was announced. The viscount would consider her his property then and would carefully scrutinize her actions. Barrington hated her charity work. He considered direct contact with the poor beneath a future viscountess.

"It may seem little to you, Miss Cranshaw, but you've given me hope."

Hope. Was that a wise gift when in reality there truly was nothing but despair for his family? Davis had been a chandler in Middledale during Liza's childhood. She had played with his daughter, Annabelle, and held her in great affection. When they grew older, however, Bartholomew Cranshaw had discouraged the friendship. He had risen in rank and considered himself a member of the upper gentry and too good to be social acquaintances with a man like Davis.

Liza had never adopted such attitudes, and so she'd been eager to help the Davis family. Recently released from debtor's prison in London, Jacob was afraid that the parish beadle would find a reason to send him back to prison. And so he'd refused to show himself to anyone but Liza.

"Mr. Davis, this is the last bit of money I can give you. After my engagement is announced, I cannot say whether I'll be free to meet with you again." She handed him a bag of coins. He hesitated a moment, then took it reverently in his calloused hands. "Of course, you can continue to live in the deer park, as along as Father doesn't see you, but I urge you to go to Reverend Stillwell. He's a good man. He will make sure the parish authorities give you food and money until you can find work."

Jacob's worn face twisted with wrinkles. "How can I know it's safe? What if they hand me over to the sheriff?"

"It won't happen, Mr. Davis. Your debts have been cleared. There is enough money in the parish to help you get back on your feet. I know because Father just made a donation. In the meantime, I have met a solicitor who just might help us find out who forced you out of your home and business."

His eyes focused on her with burning intensity. "A solicitor? Would he help me?"

Jacob Davis loved his family, but he now lived for one purpose only—vindication. He did not seem to see how his family suffered, living in the woods.

"That would be a right good deed, miss. I could never find a solicitor to help in London. There was one who was said to help those in need. A Mr. Fairchild. But I never had the privilege of meeting him."

"Mr. Fairchild? Jack Fairchild?" Liza's skin turned hot and cold all at once. "You say Mr. Fairchild helped those in prison?"

"Yes, miss. He advised the ones facing trial, and never expecting so much as a copper for his pains."

Liza turned and walked a few paces, then covered her eyes with a hand, hiding the tug of tenderness. What an extraordinary thing to do. What was she going to do with this man? This dangerous and wonderful man who continually exceeded all bounds and challenged all the limitations she'd finally convinced herself to accept.

She lifted her face into a ray of soothing sunlight. The hope Mr. Davis felt began now to flicker in her as well. If Jack Fairchild was already inclined to help the indigent, then how much more might he be willing to help Jacob Davis if she asked him to? For some reason she had not yet discerned, Fairchild had made it his personal mission to prevent her marriage. That had to be the motive for his seductive behavior. It couldn't be mere desire. Not even he would be so craven that he would recklessly seduce the daughter of his most prosperous client simply to satisfy a lustful urge. Precisely why he wanted to foil her marriage plans was the great mystery. Under ordinary circumstances she would assume Mr. Fairchild simply wanted her dowry for himself. But he was an unusual man, and she believed him when he said he would never marry for convenience. What an enigma he was!

Considering his behavior thus far, she knew he would welcome the chance to meet with her again. She could easily lure him into another tête-á-tête and then ask him to help the Davis family.

She turned back to the chandler. "There has been a most remarkable turn of events, Mr. Davis. Jack Fairchild is the very man I spoke of. He is now living in Middledale."

"What? Oh, blessed, blessed day!" Davis said, shaking her hand. "Blessed day! He can help me right the wrongs done to me. How did you find him?"

"It was surely Providence. I will talk to Mr. Fairchild about you at the first opportunity. Meanwhile, you must try to remember everything you can about the events that preceded the fire. The law just may be on our side. Will you do that? Good. I'll send word through my abigail

about our next meeting. Good-bye, Mr. Davis. We'll meet
again very soon, I hope."

Davis nodded. "Very good, Miss Cranshaw."

"Good-bye!"

The Cranshaw family gathered with their guests in the
west parlor. Jack only listened with one ear to the idle
predinner chat. His mind was still in the woods with Liza.
She'd not returned yet, and he grew worried. He shouldn't
have left her alone.

Rosalind Cranshaw sat on the sofa with her older sister,
the silver-haired Mrs. Brumble. Liza's sister, Celia, sat
alone at a gaming table, shuffling cards by herself, stealing curious glances at Jack now and then. Viscount Barrington stood near the fireplace with Mr. Cranshaw. Jack
stood by himself near the terrace doors, glancing out of
them when he could. The others doubtless thought he was
admiring the extravagantly decorated grounds. But in fact
he was looking in the direction of the last place he'd seen
Liza.

She was so present in his mind's eye that he could see
her image more clearly than those gathered here in the
room. She had more presence than any other woman he'd
ever met; a certain gravitas mixed with an intoxicating
innocence. It was a heady combination that left him
shaken. Clearly she was more than his usual damsel in
distress. She wasn't going to be an easy conquest. This
act of charity would cut both ways, and likely as cleanly
as a medieval misericorde plunged in the heart.

"You'll find, Mr. Fairchild," the viscount said, breaking
Jack's reverie, "that the people of Middledale are largely
uncultured, typical of most wayward villages. Cranshaw

has a number of arable pastures in the vicinity, and the yokels are invaluable in working the land."

Jack forced his gaze away from the garden and smiled obliquely. The viscount was pretending that Jack hadn't been raised with every expectation that he would one day have dealings with his own tenants.

"Is that so, my lord?" Jack replied.

"Yes, in fact . . ." As the viscount blathered on, Jack held his gaze, but he returned to the mental portrait he'd painted of the lovely Liza Cranshaw. In addition to her singular qualities, he had also noticed her more earthly attributes. For example, the long, languid curve of her neck to her shoulders, and how her creamy skin flowed like satin down to the swell of her breasts. And how her pink tongue brushed the corner of her mouth when she was nervous, and the delicate white teeth that bit into her plump lower lip afterward.

"I say, Mr. Fairchild, tell me about your experience as a solicitor." The booming voice of Bartholomew Cranshaw cut through his musings.

Cranshaw was a short, stocky man with a double chin, a square nose, and a head of graying blond hair that didn't seem to know which way to fall. He was keen-eyed, even behind a pair of spectacles, and though apparently good-natured, Jack had no doubt that he would be inflexible when it suited him. Anyone who'd made himself as wealthy as Cranshaw had must have a determined nature.

"I spent a great deal of time in Chancery Court, Mr. Cranshaw."

"Mr. Pedigrew spoke highly of you," Cranshaw replied. "He said you could have been a bencher if you'd set your mind to it."

"I daresay I could have." Jack cocked one eyebrow and

grinned. "If I'd known that one day I would have to sully my hands working I'd have seen to it."

"What did he say?" Mrs. Brumble inquired, cupping a hand to her ear, where gray curls spilled from under her cap. "I couldn't quite hear."

Jack could not venture a guess as to her age. If Rosalind Cranshaw was in her forties, her sister was surely in her fifties, but her difficulty in hearing and her lovely silver hair made her seem older. She was not the beauty that her younger sister was, but Mrs. Brumble had a comforting charm about her that warmed the room.

"Not to worry, Patty." Rosalind pressed her sister's hand. "Mr. Fairchild said he might have been a barrister."

"That's nice, dear." Mrs. Brumble smiled sweetly at Jack.

"My sister is deaf in one ear, Mr. Fairchild. You know, Patty, how the men like to talk about business. You needn't pay much attention."

"Well, my dear," Cranshaw said to his wife with gruff affection, "isn't that better than discussing the weather?"

"The weather?" Mrs. Brumble brightened. "It's been dreadfully warm. Why, I went for a walk this morning and—"

"We could use a good solicitor here in town," Lord Barrington cut in. "There's a constant stream of contracts and business that needs to be sorted out without going to London. What say you, Cranshaw?" He spoke like a man on the most intimate terms with his future father-in-law. "Should we let Fairchild handle that nasty little business in Broadway?"

Cranshaw took in a slow breath and studied Jack over the top of his spectacles. He pursed his lips and eyed Jack calculatingly. "Yes. And if you deal with this matter well,

Fairchild, there will be more business for you than you can handle."

The doors to the parlor suddenly opened and Liza swept in, as fresh as a breeze over a windswept moor, and looking as lovely as the purple heather beneath it. Her cheeks were flushed and her vibrant eyes fixed on Jack for a tantalizing moment before moving on.

"There you are, my dear," said Rosalind. "I was starting to worry, though I know punctuality isn't your strong suit."

Bartholomew Cranshaw chuckled. It was clear by his softened features and indulgent smile that he doted on his eldest daughter.

Liza's smile brightened at the sight of him as well. "Good evening, Papa."

She wore the same gown Jack had seen her wearing in the park, but she'd added a Chinese robe. She'd doffed her bonnet and her luxurious raven hair was fastened up and behind her head à la grecque and topped with pearls. Ringlets of hair spilled like coiled ribbons from her temples. Her violet-blue eyes gleamed with a hint of mischief as she glanced at Jack again, but turned brittle when she spied Barrington.

"Where have you been, Liza?" he said in a condescending manner. "You know I don't like to be kept waiting. Nor, I should imagine, does our guest."

"Come, come, Barrington," Cranshaw said good-naturedly. "Surely you know by now that Liza keeps to her own time."

"Really, my lord, was it such a crime?" she asked, tight-lipped, avoiding his gaze.

Nonplussed by these twin rebuttals, Barrington raised his quizzing glass and sniffed. "Now that the settlement is all arranged, I have a right to care about your comings and goings, my dear."

"Arranged, but not yet signed," she replied sweetly.

He went to her side and his gaze flitted possessively over her. "I daresay our guest doesn't like to be kept waiting any more than I do. Isn't that so, Fairchild?"

"I should imagine Miss Cranshaw had something pressing to do," Jack replied.

She flashed him a furtive, grateful look, then hurried to kiss her mother and aunt.

Barrington glared at Jack, then grinned mirthlessly. "Don't give a woman too much of a lead, Fairchild, or she'll buck you like a wild horse."

Cranshaw chuckled. "Lord Barrington is a strong man, Mr. Fairchild. That is why we were so delighted when he offered for our eldest. To own the truth, we were relieved. He is the only man our headstrong daughter would agree to marry!" Cranshaw shook his head. "I don't mind admitting that I am one of the richest men in the country. And now my bloodline will join the ranks of the titled. Lord Barrington is a viscount, you know. His father is the Marquess of Perringford. A very old title."

"Yes," Jack replied, "I am well aware."

Liza must have caught his sardonic edge, for she shot him a sly, conspiratorial smile.

"Your grandfather sits in the House of Lords, I understand, Fairchild?" Cranshaw asked.

Jack gave him a sanguine smile. Clearly the time had come to explain his disposition in life. "Yes, sir. He is Lord Tutley. I must be frank, however, and say that the title will do me little good, for I am quite sure my grandfather will not leave me his fortune. That is why I am determined to succeed on my own. In fact, it would perhaps be in everyone's best interests were I to resign the title to Arthur Paley. He'll very likely inherit the family fortune."

"Arthur!" Cranshaw burst out. "But he's a glover! What would he know about running an estate?"

Jack grinned. "He runs a small farm as well. And one needn't know much when one has the money to hire people who do. It is a peculiar business, I must admit."

Barrington sneered. "Perhaps it's for the best, eh? After all, Mr. Paley's parents did not die under a cloud of scandal like yours did, Fairchild. One has to think of the family's reputation."

Every head in the room jerked toward the viscount as if all were attached to the same puppet string. The shock in the room was palpable. No one could quite fathom his lack of tact, except for Liza's Aunt Patty.

"Sandal, did he say?" Mrs. Brumble nearly shouted, holding a hand to her good ear. "Did his lordship say sandal? I don't understand."

No one said a word. Jack merely smiled. He'd gotten under Barrington's skin sooner than he could have hoped. If he could keep prodding the viscount, the brute might slip and show his true colors to Liza's parents. Liza was watching his reaction closely, and her eyes warmed with admiration when he remained imperturbable.

"Well, I must say, this is all remarkable," Cranshaw sputtered. He was apparently amazed to find anyone who did not hunger after a title as keenly as he. He clapped Jack on the back. "What a singular fellow you are, Fairchild. I admire you. Indeed, I do. I believe in hard work, my boy. Even for the grandson of a nobleman like you. And I'll have plenty of it for you, dear boy. Mark my word."

• • •

When the majordomo announced dinner, Jack was given the honor of escorting Mrs. Cranshaw to the dining room, even though he wasn't the highest-ranking gentleman in the room. Mr. Cranshaw followed, escorting his sister-in-law. Liza accepted the viscount's arm, but was startled when he stopped unexpectedly in the hall. He waited until the others had rounded a corner, then snatched one of her wrists, breathing alcoholic fumes in her face.

"Where were you?" he snarled.

"Whatever do you mean?"

"What kept you so long?"

Liza's chest squeezed tight. She swallowed hard, forcing herself to meet his gaze with a light smile. "I couldn't decide which dress to wear for dinner. Do you approve of my choice? If you do not, sir, of course I will change."

"Don't be absurd." His gray eyes narrowed. "You're lying, Liza. I know where you were. You were in the park, down by the pond. That's where you go, isn't it?"

She frowned, then assumed an incredulous look. "Do be serious, sir."

"I am utterly serious," he said in a low voice. "I don't know why you were there, but I know you were meeting someone."

"What a ridiculous thing to say!"

He tightened his grip and she stifled a wince, saying through clenched teeth, "You're hurting me."

"Good. Perhaps it will make an impression on you. And if it doesn't, then I've taken care of the matter in any event."

Her heart quickened. "What do you mean?"

"I don't know who you're meeting, but whoever it is will find himself in a fix if he dares to show up again."

"What have you done?"

"I've ordered the land agent to set an animal trap near the pond. Go there at your own risk."

"You've ordered the land agent?" she spat at him. "How dare you! We are not married yet. This is my father's estate. You presume too much, sirrah."

"I'll remind you that your father is utterly delighted to have me as a son."

"You can't set a trap there. Celia strolls by the pond almost every day."

"Then tell her to stop. You won't deceive me again, Liza. I promise you."

Nine

ranshaw Park boasted one of the region's finest and most elaborate gardens. It contained a Grecian folly and Baroque water fountains, ponds brimming with lily pads, and knotted plots of colorful flowers and pungent herbs that tickled the nose and pleased the eye. There was even a sophisticated maze of clipped hedges hiding an impressive topiary garden.

Liza's favorite area was the ornate chinoiserie garden. It spanned a pond of murky water filled with orange and yellow carp. Liza often took bread crumbs to feed them from the quaint, arched wooden bridge that led to a pagoda-style gazebo. The area was far enough from the house to be hidden from view, but close enough to escape to quickly. Tonight even that private area had been invaded by merry revelers.

The Cranshaws and members of their dinner party strolled among the guests like visiting royalty. Jack had offered to escort Aunt Patty, and there were more than a few times when he thought the old girl was flirting with him. Perhaps it was just the romance of the torchlit evening, or the gaiety of the half-inebriated guests who could fancy for an evening that they, too, were wealthy. Or perhaps Jack merely imagined the need for love in everyone he saw, young and old alike, even while he denied that need in himself. While he strolled with Mrs. Brumble, he watched and waited for a chance to catch Liza alone.

Liza hovered near her mother while Mrs. Cranshaw received homage from the tenants' wives. But as soon as Liza could slip away, she did. She simply would not be at peace until the trap had been dismantled. The audacity of that loathsome man.

Perhaps he was being more disagreeable than usual because their engagement party was fast approaching. He didn't want to lose the prize so close to the finish line, and he undoubtedly felt threatened by Jack's sudden appearance. What an ugly affair, Liza thought with a shiver of self-reproach. How could she ever have accepted Barrington's offer? Then again, how could she have avoided it?

She found the land agent, Mr. Gorman, near a bed of geraniums bordered with creeping mint. She told him that her father was unhappy to hear that a trap had been set near the pond without his permission. When the flustered land agent said he'd only been following the viscount's orders, she smiled understandingly, and then icily informed him that Lord Barrington wasn't master of the estate. She asked Mr. Gorman to leave the party and dismantle the trap at once, and he did. No one at Cranshaw Park, not even the gruff Mr. Gorman, questioned Liza's authority. Everyone knew her parents doted on her and caved in to her will most of the time.

Lady and the Wolf

"Fiery passion . . . [An] outstanding tale of the Middle Ages."
—*Rendezvous*

"*Lady and the Wolf* mixes the plague, primogeniture, the Spanish Inquisition, witchcraft, jousts, grave robbing and some sizzling sex scenes into a brand-new, best-selling, fourteenth-century romance."
—*Chicago Suburban Times*

"A powerful debut novel that sweeps us into the lives of a medieval family . . . a stunning and poignant climax."
—*Romantic Times*

"Beard is writing tales of love and romance that always have happy endings."
—*Chicago Tribune*

She had just turned the corner of the gravel path around the plot of hyacinths when she saw Jack and Aunt Patty approaching. Her spirit soared at the sight of them. Her aunt hung on his arm as coquettishly as a Society belle, and to his credit, Jack listened as attentively to her as he would a potential conquest.

"Good evening," Liza said, and they both looked up, quick smiles appearing on both their faces.

"There she is," Jack said. "I've been looking for you, Miss Cranshaw."

"You should have let him find you sooner, my dear," Aunt Patty said. She tapped her closed fan on his shoulder and winked audaciously. "He is quite a charming young fellow."

"I know," Liza said dryly. She met Jack's eyes and smiled. "Now if I can only find Celia I'll have all my favorite people in a circle."

Jack raised a brow, appearing shocked to be included in her inner circle.

"Have you seen her, Aunt Patty?"

"What's that, m'dear?" She held up her white glove to her ear.

"Celia," Liza repeated louder. "Have you seen her?"

"Not for some time. I saw her about a half an hour ago. She was walking toward the rose garden."

Liza's mouth turned to dry cotton. Celia always cut through the rose garden when she went to the pond. A vision of her sister caught in a crippling trap flashed in her mind. "Oh, dear Lord. I did not act soon enough."

"Is there something wrong, Miss Cranshaw?"

She looked up at Jack and nodded. It seemed she could always count on him to empathize with her concerns. "Yes, Mr. Fairchild. Just before we went into the dining room, Lord Barrington told me he set a trap by the pond. As soon as I could, I told my father's land agent to remove it, but it may not have been soon enough. Why did she leave the party?"

Liza looked to her befuddled aunt, then scanned the crowd for the best person to send after her sister. Suddenly, a sobering thought occurred to her. A few days ago Celia confided that she'd received some sort of love letter. She'd been very secretive about it and refused to tell Liza anything more than that. What if she was meeting the one who'd sent the letter? The tenants' party would be the perfect time to slip away for a rendezvous. Her parents would never miss her in a crowd like this. That meant she couldn't send just anyone after Celia without creating a scandal.

"I believe my sister has ventured to the pond. I must go after her myself. Will you excuse me?" Liza nodded politely and started away.

"Wait!" Aunt Patty said. "Do not go yourself, dear girl. You can't venture to the pond at night. Send one of the servants."

"No, Auntie, I cannot. This is a private matter. I will be fine. Do not tell Mama where I'm going. She'll only worry."

"I will go with you," Jack said, kissing his elderly companion's hand. "My dear Mrs. Brumble, I will make sure that your niece is safe."

Aunt Patty's cheeks wrinkled like fine lace when she smiled, and her eyes locked conspiratorially with his. "Do you know, Mr. Fairchild, that if I were young enough I'd elope to Gretna Green with you. I suppose it's too much to hope that my niece should take the same notion to mind."

This was too much to bear. Liza turned on her heel and hurried through the garden. Jack followed at a discreet distance. When they were far enough away from the house, he caught up with her and she led him at a clipped pace through open fields toward the fishpond. When she stumbled over a log, he offered his arm, and she took it gratefully, tucking her hand in the crook of his elbow. Half her mind was on Celia, and the other half on Jack's every move. Now and then their legs brushed together, and she savored the sensation as long as it tingled along her skin.

"Thank you for coming, Mr. Fairchild," she said. "I cannot tell you how pleasant it is to have a gentleman's comfort and support."

"I am at your service, my dear Miss Cranshaw."

He was too gracious to mention the obvious—that she should have received this support from Barrington.

"You are probably wondering why I've allowed you to accompany me."

He chuckled. "I am, but I did not want to press my good fortune by raising the subject for debate."

"If Celia has been injured, then Mr. Gorman will need your help. If she isn't injured, then I will need your help keeping the land agent away from a possible rendezvous. I'm not sure which outcome I fear the most."

"I understand," he replied, and she knew that he did. In fact, she couldn't imagine that there would ever be a situation he wouldn't understand. He was the sort of man who could be a woman's best friend as well as a lover.

Liza was out of breath by the time they reached the pond. They stopped in the shadow of a tree when they spotted Mr. Gorman disengaging the trap.

"Thank Heaven Celia wasn't caught in the trap," Liza

whispered. Without being seen, she led Jack discreetly to the other side of the pond, where a bench and stone grotto had been built as shelter from the elements. They stopped to watch and listen, but a black cloud had covered the full moon, and it was hard to see. Liza heard a feminine giggle, followed by the low chuckle of a man. Then the cloud parted and silvery light shone down on Celia entangled in a man's arms.

"Oh, no," she whispered.

Jack went still and frowned in the distance. "Is that your sister?"

"Yes. Mr. Fairchild, I must ask you—"

"No, Miss Cranshaw, you needn't ask a thing. I will be utterly discreet. Go speak with her. I will wait for you here until you see who she is with. No need to make more of this than necessary."

Liza nodded gratefully and crept through the tall marsh grasses, stopping twenty feet away from the grotto. Celia was embraced in the arms of a man Liza couldn't quite recognize. They were kissing passionately. The sight shocked Liza, and she reeled with remorse. This was her fault. And Desiree's.

"Celia?" she called out.

The sixteen-year-old jerked back from the young man, and Liza recognized him at last. "Giles Honeycut!"

Giles's mouth dropped open. "Miss Cranshaw!"

Celia looked utterly mortified. "Liza, what are you doing here?"

"I came to save you from . . . from God knows what. Celia, whatever were you thinking, running off like this?"

"I doubt very much they were thinking at all," came Jack's voice. He came up beside Liza and gripped her elbow to lend moral support. He pilloried Giles with a glowering frown. "Forgive my intrusion, but I now have a stake in the outcome of this tête-à-tête. Giles, I'll have your hide tanned for this."

"Mr. Fairchild, it's not what it would appear."

"I'm sure it's much worse," Liza retorted. "Do you know what my father would do to you, Mr. Honeycut, if he found out about this?"

"Please do not tell him, Liza," Celia begged, tears welling in her eyes.

"I should, simply to make sure this never happens again."

"It won't happen again," Jack declared, thrusting his hands in his pockets. "At least not if Giles wants to keep his position as my clerk."

The younger couple exchanged pained glances.

"Go home, Mr. Honeycut," Liza said.

Giles looked longingly at Celia, then kicked the earth with his toe and stomped off.

"Young scallywag," Jack grumbled as he watched the lusty youth vanish into the night.

"Oh, Liza, I'm sorry! Do you hate me?"

Liza turned to her, her anger melting in a pool of relief. "No, my darling, of course I don't hate you."

Celia ran into her arms. Liza cradled her, unable to hug her close enough. She stroked her hair and kissed her head. "Oh, my darling Celia. What happened here?"

"Nothing. He just kissed me," she sobbed, hot tears spilling onto Liza's breast.

"Celia," Liza said gently, "he could ruin you. You will be ruined if anyone learns you were here with him alone."

"But I love him."

Liza laughed incredulously. "No, you don't. You're too young."

"I'm not!" Celia pulled away and stared defiantly at her. "You don't know because you have never loved anyone yourself."

Liza's ears burned at the condemnation. Lord, if only Mr. Fairchild weren't here.

"You do not know what passion is like, Liza. If you did you would never have agreed to marry Lord Barrington."

Liza reached out and clutched her hands. "I have felt passion. I simply never told you about it."

"When?" Celia shot back, still in tears. "When have you ever?"

When I danced with Jack Fairchild, Liza thought. *When he kissed me and showed me a carnal hunger and a passion I did not want to know I possessed.* But she could not say these things in front of him, and so she wept in frustration. The humiliating tears poured out and she covered her hands, crying for all that might have been and all that would never be.

"Don't weep, Liza. Please, I can't stand it. Please."

Celia's arms went around her, and Liza hugged her fiercely. "Oh, lambkin, I care for you so much."

"And I love you, Liza."

"I cannot stand to see you throw your life away."

"I won't, I promise."

Liza drew back and gripped her shoulders, giving her a gentle shake. "Then you must never meet with Mr. Honeycut here again. Do you understand? Your reputation will be ruined."

"What about your reputation?" Celia said, still sounding aggrieved at being deprived of Giles.

"I don't care a fig about my reputation. My life is over the moment I marry the viscount. Don't you think I know that? What does it matter what people say about me? It is you we must protect. I must take care of you, and Mama, and Papa. I'll do anything for you three. You're all that matters."

Celia dashed her tears with the back of her hands, her innocent face sobering with new wisdom. "Oh, Liza, I've been so selfish. I haven't thought of you at all, and what you've given up for me. Of course, I will do whatever you say. So . . . so you want me to refuse Mr. Honeycut?"

"No, darling. I ask only that you wait. You trust me, don't you, dear heart?" When Celia nodded, she smiled. "As far as I'm concerned, you may marry Mr. Honeycut if you wish, but first you must wait until I am married."

"I wish you wouldn't."

Liza smiled grimly. "I must. It is a fait accompli. When I marry Barrington, Papa will have his precious title in the family."

"But there are other noblemen you could have chosen, Liza. The viscount is so hideous. Why him? Why?"

"I have my reasons." She kissed Celia's forehead. "Leave that to me. Once I'm married to a viscount, Papa won't care who you wed."

"Do you think?" Celia's face lit with wild hope. "Oh, Liza, that would be famous."

"Just give it time, darling. I will marry soon and then you can have your Season. You'll pretend to consider Lord Such-and-Such and Earl Fat-Calf and the marquess of Boredom and then, if Mr. Honeycut makes something of himself, you can run off to Gretna Green with him. By then I will have had an heir, and perhaps even a spare, and Papa will forget all about your egregious choice for a husband."

Celia hung on her every word, and then threw herself

into her sister's arms. "Oh, Liza, I love you. I just wish you could marry a man you loved, too."

Liza squeezed hard and smiled, drawing away and stroking her cheek. "It cannot be done, dearest. Now be smart about this, Celia, will you? If you aren't, you'll end up married to the earl of Bedwald."

Celia shivered, shaking from head to toe. She swallowed a vile taste. "Oh, do not say it! Have you seen him?"

Liza nodded. The earl was an enormous, gelatinous hedonist who was said to have a taste for small boys. Of course, Liza's father never believed the gossip. He was too blinded by his desire to raise his family up from the merchant class through his daughters' marriages.

"I would rather die than marry him," Celia declared with a final shudder.

"I would feel quite the same way. But we won't let that happen. Now go back to the house and act as if nothing happened here."

"Very well." Celia wiped the last of her tears and looked up, noticing Jack for the first time. He stood discreetly at a distance, though she was sure he had heard every word. She regarded Liza speculatively, wondering what her sister was about, letting this stranger have such intimate access to their family secrets. If she lived to be a hundred, Celia was quite sure she'd never understand her splendid older sister. Celia turned and walked back to the house.

Ten

Liza watched her go and moved not at all. An owl hooted overhead, so loud and true a sound it sent a tremor down her spine and a tear down her cheek. Sometimes life was so painfully beautiful she could do naught but weep. Thank God she could still feel. How long would that last, though, once she was Barrington's wife?

She heard Jack's feet brushing through the grass as he came up behind her. She felt his presence. It tingled along her back. She longed to feel his embrace, to take comfort, and yet he was the one who was really to blame for Celia's indiscretion. When Jack touched Liza's arms, she stiffened and turned, stepping back to withdraw from the magnetism he exuded.

"Don't touch me," she said coldly. "Don't ever touch me again."

"Miss Cranshaw—"

"No! Don't say anything. This is your fault. Do you

still not know that? How can one so exquisitely intelligent and sensible as you not know that this is all your fault?"

He frowned at her rising pitch and took another step forward. "How—?"

"She saw you kiss me." Liza flung a hand in the air as if this should be obvious to even a fool. "She saw us kiss and it gave her ideas."

Jack grinned. "I doubt that very much. I'm sure Miss Celia had planned that kiss for some time."

Liza shook her head violently. "No, I unwittingly gave her permission when I allowed you to steal that bold kiss the other day. She idolizes me and saw me acting wantonly."

"You are too hard on yourself, Miss Cranshaw. The fate of your entire family does not, or at least should not, rest on your shoulders! It breaks my heart to think you will sacrifice yourself so that your father can boast a titled grandson."

Liza stood so still she could have been a statue in the moonlight. "Your heart breaks! *Your* heart? Was it your heart that so inspired you that night we danced eight years ago?"

He shifted his weight and folded his hands. "Was that night so terribly important to you?"

"It changed my life."

He said nothing.

She looked up and smiled bitterly. "You do not believe me. You still do not remember, do you?"

"Remember what?"

"Oh, you bloody bastard," she rasped. "Don't you remember *this*?"

She walked the distance to him and gripped his lapels. She tugged him down until their lips met. Her heart skipped a beat. His eyes widened momentarily, then fell shut. She cradled the back of his neck and made him kiss her even deeper, longer, harder. Her tongue gently parted his lips, flickered between his teeth, and plunged into the intimacy of his being. He went rigid. His arms clutched her waist. His shaft pressed hard against her stomach.

"Oh," he groaned and bent her back, taking over, dominating as she had just dominated him. He explored her deeply, nipping her tongue with his teeth, angling his head in his quest for deeper, ever deeper. When it was over, when they finally broke off in a stalemate, he was panting hard. He stood straight and stepped back as recognition dawned. "Oh, gads, I do remember."

"How could you have forgotten?" She shook her head incredulously.

He bent an arm around his waist and rested his other elbow on it, rubbing his eyes remorsefully. "I'm sorry. There have been so many."

"And it was the only kiss I've ever had. If you'd only been somehow less imploring, less consuming of me, I might have easily forgotten it. But it was your fault. It was you who gave so much, and took so much in return, in that one blasted little kiss."

"Tell me, please forgive me, my dear, but tell me, what happened?"

She hugged herself. "It was the second week of my second Season. I knew I shouldn't dance with you, but I managed to accept your invitation in spite of my chaperon's careful scrutiny." Suddenly exhausted, she leaned her head against his chest. He put an arm around her and held her close and the memories came tumbling back so clearly it was as if it had happened yesterday.

By the time her second Season rolled around, seventeen-

year-old Liza had begun to feel like a true member of the
beau monde. She knew precisely what sorts of gowns
would attract the most attention at the balls and soirees,
and she knew which of the young bloods she wanted most
to dance with. She was too strong-headed and excited by
glittering London to feel like a failure simply because she
hadn't made a match during her first Season.

She wasn't expecting much from marriage. Simply a
title, civilized conversation, and children. Good looks
would be splendid, but they were not required. Her father
had impressed on her the importance of marrying well.
This was a duty she did not question, in large part because
it meant so much to her darling Papa. To Liza, the process
of picking a mate was an exciting diversion from the se-
renity of country life. And all had gone well until the
night she first saw Jack Fairchild.

He was younger then, just as dashing and brazen, more
quick to laugh, and always surrounded by the most fashionable young bloods. She saw him at the Carletons' ball.
She was passing by and he looked up from his circle of
friends. His riveting eyes narrowed on her, and he tipped
up his chin in interest, his lips curling in a slight smile.
She looked away immediately, but already she began to
burn from head to toe with excitement. With one look, he
had laid to waste all her plans for a tranquil execution of
duty. With a seductive charisma that was impossible to
define, but easy to recognize, he had drawn her into the
vortex of womanly desire. The devil had tempted her, for
even then he was known for his devilish exploits with
forbidden women. Married women, of all things.

Later, when the dancing had begun, he distracted the
earl of Hilborne's son, sending him off on a goose chase,

simply so he could steal the dance Liza had reserved for the earl's son. Then he deftly escorted her through the hubbub of dancers to the far end of the crowded dance floor, just out of sight of Aunt Patty and her friend, Mrs. Green. Liza had watched in wide-eyed wonder as it all transpired and did nothing to stop the audacious coup, for in truth there was no one with whom she would rather dance than the gorgeous Jack Fairchild. Even though she sensed he was the kind of man who could lead a young lady to ruin.

They'd been introduced the previous week at a crushing soiree so crowded one could scarcely breathe, and so he knew a little of her, but it was clear by his hungry, curious gaze that he wanted to know much more.

"My dear Miss Cranshaw," he said as he circled her with graceful dance steps, "you are the most enchanting and refreshing young belle I've seen in years."

Liza's skin felt like it was on fire. Every word, every flicker of his eyes, every brief touch of his hand on hers in the course of the dance, made her tingle with delight and a strange, fierce hunger.

"I should think you've said that before, sir," she managed to reply. "Perhaps even here tonight to another young lady."

A smile broke over his handsome face, cheeks dimpling deeply. "Oh, la, Miss Cranshaw, you pierce my heart."

"But not with Cupid's arrow, I think. I've heard all about you, sir, and know you reserve the most prodigious amounts of your charm for untouchables, like Mrs. Vertraux."

"Mrs. Vertraux is a good friend."

"I should like to be your good friend," Liza said stupidly, then blushed to the roots of her raven curls, for she'd all but invited an advance with that naively honest statement.

"Ah, but you are the one they call the Untouchable. No one is good enough for Miss Liza Cranshaw. And now I know why. You are bound to surpass everyone's expectations of you, my dear. Do not settle for less than you deserve."

He slanted her a charming grin, and she knew he meant it as a compliment. And so the dance proceeded, with him flirting and her parrying, and all too frequently revealing her raw desire for him, as she wasn't experienced enough to hide it. When the dance ended, they somehow managed to end up on the balcony. It was no accident. Liza felt him tugging her by the hand in such a way that no one could see. She followed, a warning screaming distantly in her ear. *Don't follow. It is doom he leads you to. You can never have him. He will only steal and run, taking the best of you and leaving you wanting. Stop now. Go back while you can.*

But her heart would not listen. She knew only that she wanted this dangerous, forbidden thing he had to offer. With her heart thumping wildly in her chest, she breathlessly followed him to the balcony and stepped behind the half-open door. They were shielded by the drapes. No one could see them. And in that dangerous, transitory privacy he'd ferreted out for them, he kissed her.

At first it was a simple kiss. One that allowed time for a slap on the face if it was to come. But she was frozen, suspended in a swirling spiral of hunger and need and fire and obsession. She had to admit to herself that she'd fallen in love at first sight the week before. Since then she'd dreamt of him, thought of him, imagined what he was like, and generally made much more of him than she might otherwise have made had he not been an enchanting vision just out of reach.

When he felt no resistance, he deepened the kiss and pulled her close with a hand scandalously wrapped around her waist. He was all lean muscles and lithe limbs and firm hands. He seemed to be drawing the very life from her, and giving it back again. He was tender and demanding and arousing as he breathed her in, tongue exploring sensuously in his intoxicating kiss.

He finally drew back, very slowly, as if he could not bear to part. When her eyes fluttered open and focused on him, he was frowning, disconcerted about something.

"What a remarkable thing," he said, sounding wholly shocked.

She'd never known what he meant by that, for just then someone started to come out on the balcony. He stopped the guest from pushing the door open further, and hurried around, engaging the man in conversation. Jack looked back at her once, with a peculiar mix of longing and regret. It was understood that she should linger long enough to make it seem as if she'd been on the balcony alone.

To her knowledge, their forbidden kiss had never been discovered by anyone else. She might have escaped the incident unscathed. Except that she'd learned then just how passionate in nature she was. She felt ashamed, and didn't understand why she was that way until she'd learned of Desiree. But more than that, she felt an absolute certainty that if she couldn't have a man like Jack Fairchild, she would have no man at all.

She smiled wistfully, remembering it all in such clear, sad detail. She looked up at him in the moonlight, thinking how little he had changed since then.

"You managed to pull me out onto the balcony after

our dance, do you remember? When it was over, you leaned down to kiss me. It was going to be a gentle peck, wasn't it?" She studied his solemn expression. He was there again, transformed in time, remembering every heated breath, every flick of the tongue. They gazed at one another, remembering together that fateful kiss.

"Yes, I had meant it only to be a rather innocent kiss, because you were so extraordinarily unique and lovely."

"But as soon as our lips touched, we caught fire."

He smiled, remembering that smoldering interlude. "Yes. I was amazed you had that effect on me."

"On you! What about me? I'd never known a kiss could be that . . . violent."

"In a pleasing way," he amended.

"Of course. That was the problem. I felt utterly . . . transformed."

"Ruined," he said ruefully.

"Yes, but not in the way you might imagine. No one ever saw, Mr. Fairchild. My reputation survived that night."

He frowned. "But you left a few minutes later and I never saw you in Town again. At least not that Season."

"I left of my own volition. And when I came back for a third and final Season in Town, I made sure we never attended the same functions."

She reached out and touched his cheek. The skin over high bones was warm and smooth, save for the stubble of hair that felt like sand. She loved touching him. Loved having that special privilege, adored his look of being entranced by her touch, of needing her without even knowing it. How many times after that kiss had she dreamt of touching him just one more time?

"You spoiled me, Mr. Fairchild. You gave me something so fine, I wanted nothing less in its place."

He took her hand and kissed her gloved palm, then pressed it to his chest. "I am sorry."

"With that kiss I realized that I wanted a man like you. Handsome and kind and passionate and intelligent."

His eyes darkened with irony. "Are you sure you're not talking about another gentleman?"

Charmed by his humility, she gave a short, breathless laugh, wondering what strange convergence of stars had brought them back together. "I knew I could never have you. You'd let the world know you didn't want to marry. The gossips all said you'd be the last to succumb to marriage. You were like this strange god of love who lived by his own rules. And even if you had been so inclined to commit, my parents would never have approved. You had a scandalous reputation. And so I decided then that if I couldn't marry the sort of man I wanted, I wouldn't marry at all."

His face went blank. "No, Liza, say it's not so." He frowned and gripped her forearms. "That couldn't have happened. Not after one little kiss from me. Say it's not so."

She slipped her hand in his and smiled wryly. "Very well. It's not true."

"You're lying to please me. Damn, Liza, but how could that have happened? I scarcely knew you."

"But I knew you." She pulled away, feeling like a loon for having based such an important decision on one evening. "I know it sounds mad, but I believe the heart knows what it wants from the first moment."

She hugged herself and put more space between them, glancing up at the moon. "So you are to blame for this debacle. I would have been happily married long ago if not for you. And Celia would never have seen me succumb to such a frivolous kiss."

"Maybe it wasn't so frivolous," he shot back with a hint of frustration.

She glared at him. "Don't. Don't pretend you feel more than you do."

He held her gaze for a long, dangerous moment, but he was the first to look away. "One kiss from me did not force you to accept an offer from a jackanapes like Barrington. I refuse to accept responsibility for that."

She smiled sadly. "Of course you are right. It is not fair of me to give you so much credit and blame. You are who you are, Jack Fairchild. I never expected more from you. I knew how little you were willing to give a woman of the things that matter most in life."

He pressed a palm to his heart, acting as if he'd been stabbed. "Shall I help you twist the knife further? You know, Miss Cranshaw, you never asked for more of me. In fact, you avoided any future contact with me."

"I was ashamed. And I was just a girl!" she shot back. "I was but seventeen. What did I know about asking things from experienced men of the world?"

Liza sighed wearily. Jack took in a deep breath and stretched his neck as he scanned the starry sky. "I must give you credit, Miss Cranshaw. I have never regretted anything in my life. But you now have me full of remorse. I was too stupid to know then what a prize you were. And I am sorry for it."

She nodded her acceptance of his apology and forced a smile. "Good. Then there just may be hope for you yet. I think we need to prepare you for marriage, Mr. Fairchild. You're long overdue. And remorse is always the first step."

She started walking back to the house, only the slightest limp still evident. "May I visit your office tomorrow?" she called over her shoulder, not caring whether he kept up or not. "I need to ask a favor of you regarding a legal matter."

"Tomorrow I will be visiting my grandfather. Will the next day do as well? How about three o'clock that afternoon?"

"Perfect. I've been expecting a letter from my friend Mrs. Halloway. It will be only natural for me to stop by your office. Perhaps there really will be a letter waiting this time."

Jack was surprised to see a light glowing in the window of his law establishment when he came home. He was quite sure that Harding had gone to bed early, and so it had to be Giles. The nerve of that lad! He didn't even have the decency to slink off like a chastised hound. When Jack shoved open the door, the clerk rose nervously from his usual place on the couch.

"You're back," Giles said stupidly.

Jack glared at him and tossed his hat on the front desk. Then he placed his cane down and tugged off his gloves, finger by finger, looking at Giles all the while as if he were the most despicable creature who'd ever walked the earth.

"Why are you still here? Have you no shame?"

"I thought you'd be proud of me, sir," Giles returned petulantly. "You have quite a reputation in such matters, you know. Perhaps I've decided to walk in your footsteps."

Jack turned a look of disbelief to the clerk. He raised a forefinger, wagging it in the air as he struggled to find the perfect rebuke. But then he realized that Giles was perfectly on the mark. The young clerk had done nothing that Jack himself hadn't done a thousand times over.

"Look, lad, I am no more proud of myself tonight than I am of you. Now get the hell out of here while I drink myself into a stupor."

That took the wind out of the clerk's sails. "Aren't you going to give me a tongue lashing?"

"Why bother?" Jack said wearily as he loosened his cravat. "Words mean nothing to a young man in his prime. You'll listen to my lecture then follow your cock right back to the Cranshaws' house. But if you're smart, you'll keep it tucked safely in your trousers."

"You're not being fair! You make this sound like a tumble in the hay with a dairymaid. I love Miss Celia."

"Pshaw! You don't know the meaning of love. You're in lust!"

"I am not a London rogue, sir. I have a heart. I have a sense of responsibility to those with whom I trifle."

"And I don't?" Jack nearly shouted. "Is that what you're implying?"

Giles glowered and bit his lower lip, but said nothing.

"I see you've heard plenty about me already. Don't blame me, young man, because you've done nothing to prepare yourself for a bright future. You have to make something of yourself before you can have a lady like Celia Cranshaw. I see too much of me in you, Giles Honeycut. You're not thinking about how difficult life can be. Do you want to amount to something, or do you want to spend the rest of your life in the suds?"

"Of course I want to be a gentleman."

"Then button up your inexpressibles, sir, and keep them buttoned until the time is right to make your move. And then move! Don't let it pass you by, lad. Don't waste your life avoiding the one thing everyone wants most in life."

Giles frowned. "You mean love, sir?"

Jack laughed morosely. "Is that what I mean? I was speaking about money," he said unconvincingly. He rubbed the back of his neck and poured himself a brandy. "Unless you're prepared to work hard to become a solicitor, I have no use for you, do you understand?"

Giles scowled at him.

"Don't give me that look. Yes, I need you. But I'd rather give you up than watch you kick up a lark and never have a feather of your own to fly with. I'd fire you and watch myself go under all the quicker rather than watch you fail. I won't allow it."

Giles blinked twice. "Very well."

"Now go home and think about what I've said. If you're willing to apply yourself like a gentleman, then come back tomorrow and never, ever mention Miss Celia again. Is that understood?"

"Yes," Giles said quietly and retrieved his hat.

Jack watched him go, then sagged in a chair, feeling old and sad and worn out. God, if only he could be that young again, there was so much he'd do differently. If only he could be on that balcony again with Liza.

He put his thumbs in the corners of his eyes and pressed hard. Hell. Damnation. Hell. There was only one thing left to do. He had to offer for her. He had to marry Liza Cranshaw. It was the only way out for her, and the only honorable thing for Jack to do. Never mind that the very notion of marriage made him break out in a cold sweat and short of breath. And never mind that she would refuse him. He could never live with himself if he thought that his careless behavior had led Liza to making choices that ended with marriage to Lord Barrington. The only way to keep her from marrying that oaf was for Jack to take her for himself.

He knew she would never agree to breaking off the engagement. She was clearly determined for unknown reasons. Therefore, Jack might have to resort to old tactics and seduce her. He might have to make love to her so completely, so intoxicatingly, that in her dizzy ecstasy desire could finally prevail over cold logic.

Hell, he didn't want to. He now understood fully the inkling that had startled him eight years ago on the balcony. That Liza Cranshaw deserved more than a thoughtless kiss. More, even, than one night of pleasure. She was the kind of extraordinary woman—passionate, wise, intelligent, vulnerable—who deserved to be pleasured devotedly every night for the rest of her life. Now if he could only think about marriage without collapsing into a fit of vapors!

Eleven

iza Cranshaw was very much on Jack's mind the next morning during his two-hour journey with his cousin Arthur to Tutley Castle. He had the uneasy feeling that he still had to settle with her over that blasted kiss. Even if he kidnapped her and forced her into marriage, he still wouldn't be at peace until he heard her say she'd forgiven him. She'd accepted his apology, but it wasn't the same as being forgiven.

Forgiveness. Hell, what a messy process that was. He hated to ask for it, and wasn't very good at giving it. Fortunately, he suspected Liza would be much more at ease with forgiveness than he. She was that kind of woman. The kind who made a man better just by being in her presence.

Jack could scarcely fathom the depth of Liza's sense of responsibility to her family, her determined grace in the face of her natural passion. She gave so much and expected so little in return. It made him want to give her

the world, and this at a time when his own world was
about to crumble to dust. And compared to his feelings
about his own family! She was a better person than him,
that's all there was to it.

Thoughts of Liza began to fade from his mind, though,
when he started to recognize familiar terrain. Arthur eagerly gave him a running commentary about the scenery
as it passed, talking about how this cottage or that had
fallen to ruin since Jack had last been here, how well or
poorly the crops had been in recent years, how many
sheep the estate now boasted, and how grand it would be
if Jack and his grandfather could reconcile. The conversation always came back to that.

But soon all conversation ceased when the grand castle
loomed in the distance, sitting in all its elegant glory on
a hill green with well-manicured grass. Jack's heart rose
in his throat, and no jostling or pitching to and fro by the
carriage as its great, round wheels rumbled over the rutted
road could dislodge it.

Tutley Castle was, by anyone's account, a magnificent
holding, as elegant as it was large. It had been built in
the Restoration by the first Baron Tutley, who had striven
to build a monument to his own ambition so grand that
he'd died before it could be completed. There were more
than twenty-five bedrooms and countless other chambers
that the present baron often would not see for a year or
more at a stretch, so numerous and ponderous were they.
Especially to a man like Richard Hastwood, Baron Tutley,
who preferred the sunny outdoors to the chill of a poorly
heated stone castle.

The very sight of it brought forth a gushing river of
emotions Jack had sworn he would not feel. He said nothing until he found himself at the front door.

"Why am I doing this?" he muttered as they waited for the door to be opened. He rocked on his heels, his hands locked in a stranglehold behind his back. "Why did I let you talk me into this?"

"Because," Arthur replied, "whether you realize it or not you are a man of conscience. And men of conscience always see to their family members in times of illness."

"Grandfather is not ill," Jack groused, tugging nervously at his cravat. "The old goat will live to be a hundred. He's feigning for attention. And that's precisely what he's getting."

"You don't know," Arthur replied patiently. "You haven't seen him in ten years."

"I wish it would be another ten years," Jack grumbled, but silenced himself when the door opened at the hands of the butler. Before him stood the ancient, seemingly immortal, Kirby. He'd been the butler for as long as Jack could remember, and he looked as if he were already a hundred himself.

"Master Jack," Kirby said in a hoarse and worn-out voice. His beaming smile revealed few teeth and his eyes were clouded with white rings and sentiment. "Well, well, well. What do you know? I told his lordship you would come."

"As if he cared," Jack murmured out of the side of his mouth for Arthur's benefit.

Ignoring him, Arthur said, "Is he up to seeing us today?"

"Yes, yes," Kirby said, opening the door widely. "I daresay he will be, Master Arthur. If you do not mind, sirs, it would be better if I do not announce you first."

"I quite agree, Kirby," Arthur said conspiratorially.

Kirby stepped back and allowed the men to enter. The

cool, stony smell of history wrapped itself around Jack, awaking a longing for this place he thought he'd hated so. The entrance hall was tall and cavernous and their voices echoed and disappeared in a wave of insignificance.

"You know, Master Jack," Kirby said as he led them through an enormous gallery and down a long corridor to the baron's quarters, "you look more like your father than ever."

"I take that as a compliment, Kirby. But I can only hope for the sake of this visit that your eyes deceive you. I doubt Grandpapa cares any more for the memory of my father than he did for the actuality of him."

As Jack had grown up and begun to look more and more like a Fairchild, the baron's reaction to him had changed. It wasn't long before he could not regard Jack without a sneer of distaste. Jack steeled himself now in anticipation of it, and he was not disappointed.

"What's this?" the old man snapped when they entered his bedroom. He lay in a giant Elizabethan bed hung with scarlet and blue silk, and whose posts, which rose to enormous heights, were carved in the likeness of acanthus leaves and berries. He looked very small in such a large bed, and Jack felt a twinge of unexpected empathy. Even an old fearless bastard like the baron couldn't stave off time.

"Kirby, who's this? Ah, Arthur! My dear boy, Arthur. And who's this? Good God, is it Fairchild?"

"Yes, my lord," Kirby said placatingly. He went to his employer's side and fluffed his pillow. "It's Master Jack come to pay his respects, your lordship."

"Respect," the old man spat. He squeezed his eyes shut

and his nose, which was more beaked than ever, flared. "The bloody hell he has."

"My lord," Arthur interjected, "Jack has come a long way to see you."

"What does he want? Money? Is that it? Well, he won't get it from me." The old man balled his gnarled fingers into fists.

"To hell with your money, sir," Jack said smoothly and stopped at the foot of the bed. "I came to see if you were still the cantankerous old man I remember. And I see that you are."

Jack smiled perfunctorily and focused on his grandfather's eyes. They were sharp with blue venom. It was somehow comforting. Jack would rather deal with the old man's hatred than any belated sentimentality. As long as the baron hated him, Jack knew how to respond.

"Your parents squandered your financial security, young man. Do you still defend them? I trust you've come to beg my forgiveness and to tell me I was right all along."

Jack looked down at his polished boots, contemplating this expectation. The journey from Middledale had given him time to review his thoughts on the matter. After his confrontation with Giles, Jack was willing to entertain the notion that he had made a mess of his own life. Perhaps his grandfather was right about that. And because of the choices Jack had made, he was very much on his own, in every sense of the word. He had no loving family, no trust funds, no inheritance. And no one to love. But neither did he have to live with the burdensome knowledge that his parents were desperately unhappy.

"My parents are free, my lord," Jack said. "I do not begrudge them that. My only regret is that my mother did not receive her father's blessing before she died. Her only crime, you see, was being faithful to the man you wanted her to marry, with no thought to her happiness. And in the end you abandoned her."

"Don't blame me for that. Your father—"

"My father," Jack cut in sharply, "was faithful to my mother to the bitter end. He simply loathed her, and she him. You cannot begrudge two people who should never have married in the first place."

"They weren't the first couple to wed unhappily, and they won't be the last. They were too sentimental. And you're just like your father."

"Me? Sentimental?" Jack snorted a laugh. "I should like the ladies of London to hear that."

"Now, now, my lord," Arthur interjected. "Won't you join us for a cup of tea?"

The old man sank back wearily onto his pillow. "I am too ill."

"Kirby says you are doing much better this week. Come along, then. I will help you."

Arthur went to the bed and helped the baron climb out. Arthur had always been the peacemaker in the family. And even though Lord Tutley treated him with scarcely more dignity than he would a servant, Arthur had been as faithful to him as a son.

He's a bloody saint, Jack thought as he watched the younger man patiently help the older man lower first one thin leg and then the other, hoist him up, and then tie a robe around his alarmingly thin waist.

So it was true. Richard Hastwood didn't have long to live. The realization was quite shocking. Jack's stomach pitched unexpectedly. When Jack became Baron Tutley, though he might remain poor as a church mouse, he could not be imprisoned for his debts. Therefore, he should be glad that the Grim Reaper stood in wait for the old man. But he wasn't. He was unaccountably shaken.

Jack followed a few paces behind as Arthur led the old man from his large bedroom to an even larger sitting room. Here they were greeted by a crackling fire and a cozy mixture of medieval decor and elegant modern furniture. There was a charming blue Chippendale sofa near the hearth, and two upright Hepplewhite chairs.

Their boots clicked against the stone floor, the sound echoing softly in the rafters high above them, where ancient banners hung in dusty silence.

Once they took their places by the fire, a covey of footmen appeared, seemingly from nowhere, producing a Chinese teapoy and a tray of sweet cakes.

Jack watched, feeling out of sorts, as the efficient servants with their powdered white hair silently bustled about. They knew Lord Tutley would whack them with a cane or, at the very least, shout in displeasure if they failed to meet his expectations. So little did meet his high standards. That was why he would die alone, Jack thought. For the first time, perhaps ever, a chill crept over him at the thought of dying without someone to hold. That was the first and only good reason he had ever discovered for marriage, to stave off the solitude of death.

"Sir, Jack is living in Middledale now," Arthur said with amiable determination to rescue the visit. "He is in riding distance now. Perhaps you can reacquaint yourselves."

"Harumph," the old man said, accepting a cup and saucer with shaking hands.

Jack swallowed the same negative response.

"Why are you here, young man?" Lord Tutley inquired

gruffly, his sharp eyes burrowing into Jack.

"Frankly, Grandfather, I came at Arthur's bidding. He is an incorrigible optimist and hoped that you and I might reconcile. I should think it's obvious to us both that that is impossible. But while I'm here, I want to say that, for what it matters, I thoroughly hope that you will leave your fortune to Arthur and his family. They deserve it. And need it. Whatever your anger at me may be, sir, I hope you will not make Arthur suffer for his distant relation to me."

"Jack, that is quite unnecessary." Arthur put his cup in its saucer.

"I should hope it's not necessary," Jack replied.

"Do you mean to tell me what to do with my own money, young man?"

"No, sir. I simply want to make sure that you don't think I would have it if you offered it simply because I was the oldest male descendant."

"Jack!" Arthur choked out.

"And how will you live now that your parents have squandered your future?"

Jack sipped his tea. His heart beat in his throat, no matter how slowly he swallowed the astringent liquid. He looked up and answered frankly, "I will make it on my own, sir."

"No one makes it on their own, young pup. No one who is anyone. You need your family to survive in the beau monde."

"Perhaps you are right," Jack replied.

Arthur sighed, but his relief was short-lived.

"Perhaps that is what killed my mother. She was abandoned by the father who forced her into a marriage that never should have been."

"I did not abandon her!" The old man lifted his cane and brought it down with a resounding crack on a round mahogany table. It was a wonder the slender rod didn't splinter in two. "She and that wastrel of a husband refused to follow my advice. That led to their ruination."

"The world is not your stage, Grandfather. You are not a god to decide the course of everyone's fate."

"If I were a god, a just god, you would never have been born. If not for you, your mother might have divorced her worthless husband when she was young and made a better match. I would have lived with the scandal to see her happy again."

Jack shuddered, but willed himself not to show it.

"I'm sorry," Arthur whispered to him. Then more loudly, "My lord, Jack means to make a success of himself in Middledale. Perhaps you have some connections so that Jack might prove himself."

"I need no help, Arthur." Jack rose and put his cup on the table, straightening his trousers and tugging on his waistcoat. "It was as much a pleasure seeing you as ever, my lord. I should have thought that the approach of death would make you reconsider the way you try to strangle all self-determination from those you purport to love. But I see you fear not even death. You will die a lonely old man. And for once I can honestly say I pity you."

He turned abruptly and strode toward the door, his footsteps echoing loudly up to the rafter and shields once born by his too-proud family.

"I don't want your pity! Don't you ever come back here again. Do you hear?"

Jack did indeed. He heard loudly and clearly. This, he was quite sure, would be the last time he would ever see Lord Tutley.

Twelve

"I say, Mr. Honeycut," Harding said shortly before three the next day, "would you care to join me at the Sickle and the Boar for a light meal?"

From his desk, Giles looked up with a frown and dipped his quill in his inkpot. "I really must decline, Mr. Harding, I have work to do."

Silence followed this profound declaration. Harding, who'd been shuffling papers, stopped and frowned at him. "Did you say you have work to do? But you've been slaving away all afternoon. I didn't think you had such dedication in you, dear boy."

Giles looked up with uncharacteristic remorse. "All that is going to change, Mr. Harding. You're going to see a new Giles Honeycut from this point forward."

"Really?" Harding rose, tugged on his coat, and sniffed. "What a shame. I was just beginning to think I might enjoy the leisure of country life. You were going to be my shining example of lethargy."

"Do not jest, sir." Giles carefully blotted his letter. "I am not proud of my work habits. Especially now that I realize what it takes to succeed in life." He frowned. "Have you ever been in love, Mr. Harding?"

The secretary's puffy cheeks twitched as if he'd just been struck with indigestion. "Good God, no. I learned long ago that women don't set their caps at fat men with thin pockets. So I gave up any hopes of love early on. I highly recommend such an approach to you. There's less heartache that way. Besides, as you'll soon learn from observing Mr. Fairchild, appealing to the fairer sex carries its own special burden."

Giles nodded sagely. "I believe I understand completely. I'm going to make something of myself, Mr. Harding, and that means I won't have time to indulge in affairs of the heart. But I don't seem to quite have what it takes, do I?"

Harding frowned sympathetically. "All you need is a good tailor. Would you like me to instruct yours on the latest fashions from London?"

Giles's face lit up. "Would you? That just might do it." He grinned and reached for his coat. "I avow, Mr. Fairchild will be pleased if I dress more like a gentleman."

Giles opened the door, his mood as bright as the sun on the pavement. "And since you're going to help me with my clothing, I could teach you a thing or two about charming the ladies."

Harding stood in the doorway and said, "Remember, lad, I've worked for Mr. Fairchild for years. I've seen the best in action, and I assure you, savoir faire is not contagious. I wouldn't be able to charm a bird from a tree."

"Oh, it just takes practice, Mr. Harding." He tipped his chin in the direction of a young woman off in the distance.

"Look over there. Here comes a lady now. If you turn your calf just so, I avow she'll take notice whether she wants to or not. But watch the eyes. She won't turn her head. It will be just a quick glance."

"Oh, come, Mr. Honeycut, this is absurd."

"Come on, then." Giles squatted down and forced Harding to turn out his foot. He stood up again to approve of his work. "That's it, sir. Now stand here and watch her succumb to your charms."

Harding reddened, but he kept his foot in place. He tugged at his collar and grimaced nervously. "How long do I have to keep my foot twisted in this unnatural position?"

"Until she walks by. Yes, I can almost make her out now. Oh, a comely lady at that." Giles squinted at the approaching figure. "Why she's—" Giles stopped midsentence and gulped hard. "Oh, good God, she's Liza Cranshaw."

"What?" Harding yanked his foot back and stared at the object of Giles's horror. Then his heart nearly stopped in his chest when he recognized who she really was. "Oh, sink me!"

"Oh, hide me!" Giles scrambled inside and nearly shut the door in Harding's face.

The secretary hurried after him and closed it with a bang. "That's Miss Cranshaw? Are you quite certain?"

"Yes! And if she sees me she'll put me in the stocks. She'll have me hanging high from Cranshaw Park."

"Good Lord, Mr. Honeycut, whatever did you do?"

"Never you mind, sir," Giles said, looking for a good nook or cranny in which to cram himself. "But Mr. Fairchild knows how much trouble I'll be in if Miss Cranshaw gets me alone in a room."

"Good Lord! She sounds like a virago. Do you realize, Mr. Honeycut, that the woman coming down the sidewalk now is the same one who nearly ran over us in the carriage? And you're telling me she's Bartholomew Cranshaw's daughter? The one whose letter Mr. Fairchild read?"

"Yes!" Giles began to pace like a caged animal. "How can I escape?"

"Oh, Lord!" Harding lamented. "Mr. Fairchild fell in love with her at first sight. I know it. And now she's coming to see him! That means trouble. It won't be long before she falls in love with him, if she hasn't already. Then Mr. Fairchild will be called out by Lord Barrington and . . . oh, what a muddle! He'll be ruined financially . . . again!"

Giles stopped his worried pacing and gave the secretary a befuddled look. "What did you say? I didn't quite follow."

"No, you wouldn't, would you?" Harding said irritably, taking up the pacing for him. "I'll tell you what, Mr. Honeycut. I have a way to solve both our predicaments. You go into Mr. Fairchild's inner sanctum right now and tell him you have urgent business. Make something up if you must. Just keep him occupied until I can find a way to get rid of her."

The door began to open and Giles nearly threw himself headlong into Jack's chamber. "Right, then, jolly good, Mr. Harding."

The secretary had just enough time to tug down on his waistcoat, turn, and assume a diplomatic smile when Liza entered, followed by an elderly woman.

"Good day," Harding said amiably. "May I help you, miss?"

"Yes, you may, good sir. I have come to see Mr. Fairchild about a legal matter."

Harding raised his brows. "Is that so?"

"I'm Miss Cranshaw, and this is my aunt, Mrs. Brumble."

Harding bowed. "A pleasure, I'm sure. But I fear there has been some mistake. Mr. Fairchild is not in. He's—"

"Harding!" Jack barked, poking his head out the door. "What is going on here? Why, Miss Cranshaw, how good to see you."

"Ahem," the secretary muttered, reddening like a suddenly ripe strawberry, adding sheepishly, "I did not realize you were in, sir."

Jack opened the door more fully and crossed his arms, skewering Harding with a look that was only slightly ameliorated by his breathtakingly graceful features. "Is that so?"

Harding smiled lamely at Liza. "Indeed. Miss Cranshaw is here to see you, sir. Would you care for tea, miss?"

"That would be lovely, thank you," Liza replied.

Jack watched his secretary bustle upstairs to ask the housekeeper for tea just as Giles made a hasty exit out the back door. When all the mayhem had ceased, Jack welcomed the ladies into his office. Liza looked stunning as usual. She wore a soft green straw hat tied with a ribbon around her chin and a simple striped green high-waisted gown with a beautiful India shawl over the dress. A soft white ruffle lined her bosom, and she set down her closed parasol as she helped her aunt settle in a chair.

She was her usual attentive and efficient self, oblivious to her own graceful beauty. The only thing that gave away any unease was the quiver in her eyes whenever he caught her gaze. It was as if his looks, his mere presence, was like a stab in her heart. It saddened him, and he wished he could make it up to her somehow. This sadness, this deep sense of cause and effect, troubled him. It was a damned vulnerable feeling, and he didn't like it a bit.

"Mr. Fairchild," she said as she helped Mrs. Brumble into the chair, "how different the place is now that Mr. Pedigrew is gone."

"I hope improved, or at least equal to its past glory. May I fetch you some water? The tea will be along soon."

"No, thank you. The differences are subtle but distinct," Liza said, sitting to her aunt's left. There remained an available chair to Liza's left, and Jack eyed it covetously. He could sit comfortably behind his desk, but she was like the moon drawing the ocean near. Whenever they were together, he felt that unseen tugging, the longing to be near her, especially after their frank confessions by the pond.

"There is more sunlight now." She fixed him with a light smile. "When old Mr. Pedigrew practiced law here, his chambers always smelled of old documents. Now I detect the scent of flowers, and boot polish."

She laughed lightly, and the sound was music to Jack's ears. If she could laugh that sweetly, perhaps he had not entirely ruined her. He sighed, trying not to look as besotted as he felt. He admired her pluck enormously. She showed not a jot of awareness. It was as if they'd never kissed, as if he'd never seen her cry. Had he imagined it? Had he imagined such passion from such a decorous lady?

"And what do you think of the changes in these rooms, Mrs. Brumble?" he asked, trying to keep things carefree.

"What, dear boy?" The silver-haired lady held a hand to her ear.

"What do you think of Mr. Fairchild's establishment?" Liza repeated loudly near her ear.

"Oh, lovely," she said and eyed Jack impishly. "And such a charming man, that Mr. Fairchild, wouldn't you agree, m'dear?"

Liza's pretty cheeks turned rosy. He looked fully at her and she grinned wryly in spite of her embarrassment. He had the sudden urge to tell her a bit of bawdy humor. She'd probably laugh. She was probably the kind of woman who would be free enough to laugh while making love. He hardened at the thought of it.

While Mrs. Brumble prattled on with generic superlatives about Jack and his law office and his furniture and the weather, Jack admired the beauty of both women, for Aunt Patty had a timeless grace about her. There was no question that the Cranshaw women had a bone-deep elegance.

"Miss Cranshaw," he said when he could finally get a word in edgewise, "what a pleasure to receive you. I hope my secretary wasn't too off-putting."

"Not in the least."

He sat down next to Liza, difficult as it was, considering his state of arousal. When she gave him an intimate look, he glanced surreptitiously at Aunt Patty. She'd begun stitching on a small sampler she'd plucked from her reticule.

"I know what you're thinking," Liza said softly, her sultry voice seeping down his collar. "You needn't worry about my aunt. She can't hear a thing out of her left ear unless you practically shout. As long as she remains to my right, we will have as much privacy as we might expect. I couldn't come without a chaperon."

"Of course not. What can I do to help you?" He half

turned toward her, propping his right arm on the back of his chair. "I think you know by now that I am willing to go beyond the call of duty."

She sighed, releasing all the nervousness she'd been penting up. "Oh, there is no use pretending with you, Mr. Fairchild. If I don't speak frankly, you'll simply ravish me in public and embarrass me into some new confession of my utmost secrets."

He grinned and studied her lovely lips, wishing he could nibble on them here and now. It was as if their airing their grievances had brought them even closer together.

"I am not that incorrigible, am I?"

She rolled her eyes in his direction and her cheeks dimpled in a tolerant smile. "You do not really want me to answer that, do you?"

He barked out a laugh. "Go on, Miss Cranshaw. I promise I won't interrupt again."

She regarded him warmly. "I scarcely slept all night, and after much thought I have concluded that you are the only one who can help me. You see, I know all about you now."

Uneasy, Jack raised a brow. "I thought you knew all about me already. What else have you heard?"

She twisted in her seat until they were almost face-to-face. He could smell the scent of lavender sweet water. Did her sheets smell of them, too, where her silky skin touched linen? Had she washed her shiny, dark hair in it? Or had she dabbed it behind her ears, at the pulse of her creamy throat, or between her ample, pretty breasts, which stood rounded above her collar?

"I now know how good-hearted you are," she said, something new and disconcerting in her eyes. Good Lord, was it admiration? "I've heard about your kindness to those in need. So you are far more than an incorrigible rake."

She gave him a tiny, knowing smile. Jack's mouth rippled with ambivalence. He could tell her compliments were leading somewhere he didn't want to go.

"I see. Well, I am at your service, I assure you. However, I have given up on most of my good works. You are the one I want to help at present, Miss Cranshaw. You alone."

She smiled brightly. "Well, then you *will* help me. You see, Mr. Fairchild, I am trying to aid a good man who has fallen on hard times. I know you can understand my desire to do so."

Jack folded his hands and frowned. "Go on."

"His name is Jacob Davis. He was the town chandler until his shop was burned intentionally. I am sure it was arson, though he's been unable to prove it. He was able to buy his way out of debtor's prison recently, but he is determined to find justice. Unfortunately, he no longer trusts anyone except for me, because I was a friend to his daughter when we were young. He's afraid of being thrown back into prison."

Jack leaned back and surveyed her with a jaded air. He felt for the man, but he tried not to show it. "I see."

"Will you help him?"

She clutched the arm of her chair with both hands and looked up at him as if he were a miracle worker. The look in her eyes was pure honey. The finest claret. And as addictive as opium. He knew how self-possessed and capable and reluctant to depend on anyone else she was. Therefore, having her look at him with those expectant eyes filled him with pride, made him feel ten feet tall, and made him want to go to the ends of the earth to fulfill her every wish. *Yes,* he wanted to shout. *Yes, yes, of course I'll help you.*

"No, Miss Cranshaw," he answered instead. "I am afraid I cannot do it."

Her luminescent eyes dulled momentarily. "Why not?"

Jack scratched the side of his cheek where he'd nicked himself shaving that morning. He should have known then that this would be a miserable day. "Let me make an assumption here. You've heard that I will take any and every indigent client from here to the Thames with no thought to the size of my own pocket, is that it?"

She blinked in dismay. "Why, no, I've heard only that you helped men unjustly imprisoned for their debts. I admire that enormously."

"That was in the past." He rose and began to pace. "I came to Middledale to make my fortune. I don't mind admitting my intentions were purely mercenary."

"But there is no one else who can help me as you can. You know how to investigate these sorts of things, since arson makes this a legal matter. You yourself said the law, locally applied, is of the utmost importance. If you take this case, you'll have a professional duty to maintain confidentiality, which means Mr. Davis will trust you. Please, Mr. Fairchild, if you have been moved by tragedy before you can be so moved again."

"But I don't want to be!" he argued querulously. "I—"

He was cut off by a knock on the door.

"Come in!" he barked, and Harding entered carrying a tea tray. "Put it on the table, pour three cups, please, and go."

Harding assumed a wounded look. "Of course, sir."

Damned, impertinent secretary, Jack thought. It seemed everyone expected perfect equanimity from him, perfect charm and ease. Everyone wanted a miracle from him. But even he had his limits. If he started taking charity cases again, he'd never earn a farthing. He had to think, think. How could he help her and still help himself?

Harding gave each of them a cup of tea and departed. Jack held his saucer and sipped thoughtfully, staking out the safe territory in front of his desk. As he sipped, he glanced at Liza from the corner of his eye and realized her hopeful gaze had never left him. He felt like a trapped animal. He was trapped. Caged by a good woman's esteem.

"Miss Cranshaw, I do not mean to seem impatient or callous, it is simply that I cannot do this. I don't mind admitting I need to make money or face my own peril."

"Surely not, Mr. Fairchild. You cannot compare your needs to that of this poor chandler."

"No, of course not. Nevertheless—"

"I'll pay you. I'll come up with the money somehow."

"You couldn't possibly pay me enough, I fear. This isn't simply an isolated case. You see, I am determined to change everything about my life. I can no longer afford charity."

She digested this, her eyes darting back and forth between his. "Would it make any difference if I were to tell you that I believe that solving Mr. Davis's problem might very well solve my own?"

He looked up, caught off guard. He put his hands in his pockets and shrugged. "What are you saying?"

"That I believe Lord Barrington may have had something to do with Mr. Davis's demise." She glanced surreptitiously at her aunt, who was dozing. "I dare not say more until you assess the situation."

Jack felt his resolve and restraint fall off him like scales of armor after a heated battle. She was offering him the one thing he could not resist—proof of wrongdoing against the man he didn't want her to marry. The wily little vixen. He gave her a half smile of grudging admiration.

"I know what you're doing, Miss Cranshaw."

"What am I doing, Mr. Fairchild?"

"You are making it impossible for me to refuse."

She smiled brightly. "Am I?"

He shook his head ruefully and sank onto the edge of his desk, crossing his arms, feeling manipulated and irritated. "Yes, damn it. You are."

He only hoped she would be grateful enough to kiss him again. It didn't take much to envision even more than passionate kisses—wild lovemaking, skin on skin, and lots of groaning. His trousers were too tight again, and he turned to look out the back window so she would not see.

"Very well, Miss Cranshaw. I will hear Mr. Davis's account of his tragedy. If there is any way I can help, I will."

She put her cup down immediately and sprang to her feet. "Oh, Mr. Fairchild, you're restoring my faith in humanity."

He tossed an amused look over his shoulder. "Is that good?"

She hurried around the table to his side, and for a heart-stopping moment he thought she would embrace him. She stopped and rocked back on her heels at the last moment, then smiled splendidly and offered her hand. Not just two fingers, but her whole hand. When he took it in his own, she squeezed hard.

"We'll meet him tomorrow for a picnic. Oh, Mr. Fairchild, I will never forget this," she whispered as he kissed her knuckles.

He smiled sardonically. "I fear neither will I."

She laughed, eyes beaming. "You are so wonderfully cynical, sir."

"I try." He reluctantly released her hand and she went to her aunt, gently shaking her awake.

"Time to go, Aunt Patty."

"What? Oh, very well, dear."

"Before you leave," Jack added, "I want to paint an accurate picture of what this case will mean to me."

"Yes?"

"If I take on Mr. Davis's case, as you have requested, that will leave me less time to work for your father, less time to make money, less time to pay back a three-thousand-pound debt my father owed. That means I will in all likelihood land in debtor's prison before the month is out."

She stood straight as an arrow and frowned. "Are you truly that desperate?"

"Most certainly." He smiled charmingly. "Not a pretty picture, is it?"

She shook her head and sank into her chair. "I did not know your finances were so pressing."

"They are indeed. However, I do believe I can help you. And I am willing to sacrifice my time, even at the risk of my own peril. However . . ."

He paused for dramatic effect, shrugged, took a sip of tea, and returned to his chair, sitting nonchalantly.

"However what?" she asked from the edge of her seat.

He inhaled her luscious scent again. "However, if I take the case, I will expect full compensation."

Her eyes clouded with disappointment. "I can't possibly come up with three thousand pounds."

He licked his lips and delicately placed his cup in his saucer, giving her a sidelong glance. "I do not want money from you, Miss Cranshaw."

"Then how about my jewels? You can have those."

"No, I wouldn't dream of it."

Her frown deepened with every word. "Then what is it you want?"

He tipped his head back, staring distractedly at the dark beams and white plaster overhead. His skin chilled and his heart ached. Now was the time. He had to do it.

"I . . ." He cleared his throat and looked directly at her. "I would like to ask—no, beg—for your . . . forgiveness."

Her mouth parted and she blinked several times. "My forgiveness."

He nodded, a wave of guilt washing over him. And it wasn't just guilt for what he had done to her, but for all the triflings and glib words and brief embraces he'd given other women over the course of his lifetime.

"I want your forgiveness," he said more forcefully. "In fact, I do not think I can live with myself without it. Can you forgive me, dearest lady?"

She looked down at her hands neatly folded in her lap. Her head lowered, and he sank with disappointment. She was going to refuse him.

"Yes, of course," she surprised him by saying a moment later. "I do forgive you."

He looked away quickly, lest she see moisture in his eyes. He cleared a lump from his throat and shuffled some papers. "Capital," he muttered. "That is capital."

"I do believe you are a wiser man now. I only wish that the man you are now was the one who kissed me back then."

He blinked rapidly, then shook his head wonderingly and smiled. "What a kind thing to say, Miss Cranshaw. You are too dear by half."

"And you, sir, are a wonderful man. You simply don't know it yet. Now, shall we prepare for our visit to Mr. Davis?"

He nodded, smiling like a giddy fool, feeling a thousand pounds lighter. Perhaps this thing called forgiveness wasn't so hard after all.

Thirteen

That night as Liza lay in bed, she had a vague understanding that something tremendously important had happened at Jack Fairchild's office. Having his help with Jacob Davis might very well be the key to her freedom from the viscount. But more than that, granting forgiveness had freed her of a burden she didn't know she'd been carrying. She was at peace. She felt at one with Jack. And she didn't even realize how thoroughly at one until she fell asleep.

Deep in her dreams, he came to her. The wind was blowing through his hair, billowing the skirt of his robe. He wore nothing beneath it, and she saw his flesh gleaming in moonlight. Sweat coated his skin, undulating down the muscles that patterned along his sleek torso. Then, in the strange way of dreams he was beside her, naked, whispering her name in a way she couldn't possibly resist. Loneliness was gone. When his hungry fingers caressed her breasts, she arched to meet him, shivering deep in a place she didn't know existed.

"Liza." His voice was a wave crashing onto shore. "It was you all along. Where have you been? I've been looking for you."

A bittersweet feeling strangled her, and she couldn't reply. She could only clutch his arms. *I'm here, Jack. I've been here all along. I thought you were gone.*

"Where were you?" he repeated, then began to make love to her. His hands were everywhere, stroking and teasing, lifting up to some incredible ladder of ecstasy. He was like a storm overtaking everything in its path, or an amorous creature whose sole function was to give pleasure, and soon she felt a throbbing between her legs. It was a shaking pulse so intensely pleasurable, and so often repeated, that she woke up crying out with passion.

"Oh, Jack!" She sat up in bed, still aching and throbbing between her legs. Sweat dripped between her breasts. Her hair was matted to her forehead. She panted, unsure how to cope with so much pleasure. And then, when she realized it was only a dream and a hollow longing replaced her shivering desire, she wondered how to make it happen for real.

She swabbed her moist hair away from her temples while her pulse beat like a bird's wings in her throat. Then she sank back onto her pillow, knowing with certainty what had to be done.

She would seduce Jack Fairchild. Once she'd had him, she could die happy. But she had to have him. He wouldn't have to look for her anymore. She would claim the pleasure she desperately craved while there was still time.

Shortly before noon Jack Fairchild and Clayton Harding carried picnic baskets across a field in the far reaches of

Cranshaw Park. Liza and her aunt Patty walked ahead at a leisurely pace, leading the way through a meadow that led to an old churchyard.

It was one of those perfect summer days when the sun was baking hot, the breeze was refreshingly cool, and the cloudless sky was an extraordinary periwinkle blue. But Jack's appreciation of nature could not hold a candle to his awareness of Liza.

He watched her walk just ahead of him with willowy grace, arm-in-arm with her aunt. Their gowns brushed through tall, green grass with white tassels. Summer grassland butterflies flitted at their feet, delicate, whimsical escorts. Jack smiled at the pastoral scene, knowing this outdoor venture was merely camouflage for their interview with Mr. Davis. After sleeping on it a night, Jack was eager to speak with the chandler. If he could find a legal way to extricate Liza from Barrington's blackmail scheme, then Jack wouldn't have to seduce her into reason. The more he got to know Liza, the more honorable he wanted to be. He was just beginning to think his new resolutions might work.

"I should be in the office," Harding said, his words coming between labored breaths of air.

"Nonsense," Jack replied. "You need more walks. Look at you, Harding, you can barely carry a basket of bread and wine without falling into a fit of apoplexy."

"I say, sir, that's unfair. I have the heaviest basket. And I take exception to the notion that Mrs. Brumble will be a good companion while you and Miss Cranshaw slip away on personal business. She's a bit stricken in years."

"Harding, I should think you'd know better. You can't be fooled by a little snow on the chimney. Liza tells me her aunt is only fifty-seven. She's your senior only by a few years. Just because her hair is silver doesn't mean her heart isn't ripe as a red berry and ready to pluck. Besides, she's deaf in one ear. It was a childhood accident, not old age, that has partially robbed her hearing. Speak on her left side and you can complain incessantly about the country and all she'll do is nod, pretending to have understood you. That arrangement will suit you, won't it, old chap?"

Harding sneezed in response. "Bloody flora and fauna," he grumbled, sneezing again.

When they reached the old abandoned church, Liza led them to the graveyard, where headstones had tumbled over like sleeping angels, and weeds choked memories of the dead.

"Here we are," she said.

She turned and smiled at the men, but the warm look in her eyes she saved for Jack alone. Her gaze lingered, scorching him with its intensity. His heart skipped a beat, and he recognized something he'd seen in many women before, but never in Liza—pure, raw desire. Audacious sexual need. His mouth went dry, and he began to ponder the possibilities. Perhaps a stolen kiss might cap off the day after all.

He was beginning to feel as if he'd known Liza a long time, as if she were an old and dear friend, or a mistress who knew his every mood and whim.

"Shall I throw down the blanket?" Harding inquired, readily dropping his basket.

With Mrs. Brumble pointing him here and there, the secretary set out the picnic delectables under the shade of an oak tree. Liza helped her aunt to the ground, then looked at Jack. Her sultry come-hither eyes flickered over his lips, and she smiled coyly.

"Shall we see if we can pick some fresh berries, Mr. Fairchild?"

He stifled a smile, wondering what the devil she was about. "I own that I'd be delighted to engage in such an adventure. Mrs. Brumble, would you care to join us?" he asked, but only because he knew the answer would be no.

"What did he say?" she asked Harding. "Coin us?"

"Join us, he said, ma'am. Would you like to pick berries with them?" Harding replied loudly.

"No, upon my word, I'm exhausted already. You two go on and stay nearby, won't you, m'dear?"

"Of course, ma'am," Jack replied, holding out his arm for Liza to cling to. "I will be a perfect gentleman."

His assurance was wasted on Mrs. Brumble, for she was already listening with rapt attention to Harding's complaints.

"Are you certain Aunt Patty won't return home with a bad report about our improper absence together?" Jack said when they were out of earshot.

"Quite certain," Liza said. "And Lord Barrington left unexpectedly this morning. He told my father that he wouldn't be back until late tonight. So there was no need to go to elaborate lengths to explain away a picnic with you. As long as I have a chaperon, my parents don't care. It was only Barrington I was worried about. Of course, he has no right to track my comings and goings, but he does it nonetheless. Lord, it feels wonderful to have him away from the house. He stays with an old family friend a mile down the road when he's in the Cotswolds, so he's a frequent visitor to Cranshaw Park. I feel free for the first time in months."

She gave Jack the first truly joyful smile he'd seen from her. He was dazzled by it.

He pressed his right hand onto hers, which was tucked in the nook of his left arm. The touch of her sent a charge up his arm, and honorable thoughts vanished. He wanted to take her here and now, to lie down in a field of daisies and let the breeze flow over their naked bodies, to sweat together in the sun, to groan with the wind. He wanted more than physical release with Liza. He wanted to make love to her, to cherish her, to make her scream with pleasure. But he would not. He was a new man. At least that's what he kept telling himself.

They fell into silent accord as they approached a little stone cottage nestled in a forgotten apple orchard. The sun beat down warmly on them. Jack couldn't remember ever feeling this fit and invigorated and contented all at the same time.

"Tell me, Miss Cranshaw, does your friend Mrs. Halloway approve of Lord Barrington?"

"No," was Liza's immediate reply. "She thinks he is contemptible."

"So she encouraged you to avoid marriage to him?"

"No," she said sadly. "She understood my reasons and agreed that marriage was the only recourse. I wish she would write to me soon."

Jack sighed, feeling for her. "Perhaps she will," he murmured. "Perhaps she will."

When they arrived at the stone cottage, bees were flitting around the old orchard, which consisted of a dozen rows of apple trees that had long since gone wild. New fruit was budding on neglected branches, and the old fruit rotted beneath their feet. They walked up a stone path to the front door. Liza knocked and the wooden door flew open immediately.

"You're here" was the blunt greeting from the man who stood in the doorway.

When Jack's eyes adjusted to the relative darkness of the room and he was able to make out the man's features, he nearly gave a start. Davis was a gaunt man with haunted eyes and matted hair, which was caked with burrs and straw. Jack had seen the worst sort of misfortune and knew what a physical toll poverty could take on a man, but he was taken aback to realize that the beautiful Liza Cranshaw had taken such great pains to continue her association with this poor, unkempt creature.

She made introductions with admirable poise and led Jack into the cozy quarters. Though the floor was made of packed earth, it nevertheless was covered with a relatively new rug that lay before a charming fireplace. There was a small table, a couple of chairs, a bed, and windows with curtains. Light streamed in brightly, revealing a row of dried flower bouquets that hung from the ceiling. A bouquet of dried trillium and pink roses sat in a vase on the table.

"This is my little hideaway," Liza said, dusting off a few chairs that stood around a rough-hewn table. "No one comes here because this is no longer my father's property. It was purchased by Lord Halifax, but he hasn't visited Middledale in fifteen years. I used to sneak here as a child when I ran away from home. I offered to let Mr. Davis have it, but on a clear day you can see it from the opposite hill, and he was afraid someone would find out he'd returned to Middledale, so he's been sleeping in the woods with his family. Mr. Davis," Liza said anxiously, "won't you please have a seat and tell Mr. Fairchild all about your troubles?"

Liza sat down first, then Davis took the seat next to

her. Jack sat down opposite them and listened carefully as the chandler told his story.

"You see, Mr. Fairchild, a man approached me about buying my shop six months ago. I told him that I had no intention of selling no matter the price. I'll be bound he was none too pleased by that." Davis folded his bony hands together and stared angrily into space. "I could see that. If I'd known then like I do now what my refusal would signify, I might have sold the place. But Middledale was my home, and I said I ain't leaving. A few days later, I found a note nailed to my door. The note said I had better leave town and never come back or I would regret it. Two days later, I got me another such note. Then that blackguard came back and asked to buy my place again. I stood my ground, suspecting that maybe he was the one who'd threatened me, trying to scare me into selling. That night, the place went up in flames."

Jacob Davis fell silent. He folded his dirt-caked fingers together and tried to still his quivering lower lip.

"Lost everything, I did. I couldn't pay off my debts. I near went addle-brained when I ended up in debtor's prison in London. My girl and my wife lived in a slum nearby. Thank God a cousin died, leaving me the money to get out. It nearly killed me, Mr. Fairchild. Do you know what Fleet Prison is like?"

"I have a fair idea," Jack softly replied.

"You can't really know what it's like until you're in there yourself."

"Pray God I never find out."

"I swore when I was in there I'd get revenge on the blood what did this to me."

Jack cocked his head. "What makes you think he was a nobleman?"

"Because the lad who threatened me said that 'his lord-ship' would be none too pleased by my refusal. Another chap, apparently an accomplice, called him Rodge."

"Mr. Rodge?" Jack asked, intrigued.

"No, just Rodge."

"Roger," Liza said quietly.

Jack looked at her a long moment, wondering at her certainty, then listened to the chandler further detail his family's suffering.

"Well, Mr. Fairchild?" Davis said in conclusion, "can you help me find out who did this to me?"

Liza leaned forward expectantly. "Will you take the case?"

He looked at Liza, struck by her nerve and resource-fulness, then at her friend, and rose from his seat, shoving himself up from the table like an old man. He leaned on it, shaking his head. "You want revenge, Mr. Davis, not justice."

"Isn't it the same thing?" Davis shot back.

"Not always. You're free from prison. I suggest you go on with your life."

"How can I when everything I owned is gone?"

Jack had no answer for this. These matters were never clear-cut. But Jack knew one thing. If he ever stopped trying to use the law to defend the helpless, he would no longer respect himself enough to call himself a solicitor.

"Very well, Mr. Davis. I will take your case. I cannot guarantee I will succeed in finding the man you want, but I can make sure you don't end up back in prison unnec-essarily."

"Oh, thank'ee, sir." Jacob seized his hand and pumped it joyfully. "Thank'ee."

"Do not thank me yet," Jack said, patting him on the

back and extricating his hand. "Do you have any idea why you received these threatening notes, telling you to leave town?"

Jacob shook his head. "Nay, sir. I thought the man wanted my property, a nice little piece of land in town, perfect for a shop."

"But the building was burned and whoever bought the property hasn't done anything with it," Jack surmised.

"Right, sir."

"Who bought it?"

"I don't know, sir. The bailiff sold it off to pay some of my debts, but I don't want to talk to the authorities for fear they'll find some other hidden debt and I'll end up back in prison."

Jack leaned back and stroked his chin. "It would be my guess that the man who first offered to buy your property did so simply to get you out of town, and once you were gone his goal was accomplished and someone else bought the property instead."

Liza and Jacob exchanged glances. Jacob looked back at Jack with admiration. "That could be, sir. That could very will be."

"There must be some other reason he wanted you gone. Have you talked to your wife and daughter about this, Mr. Davis? Do they have any idea why anyone would want you to leave town?"

Davis shook his head. "Nay, sir. My wife is as befuddled as I am. And my daughter, Annabelle, why, she keeps to herself. Especially after living in London."

"I'll see what I can do. Go back to your family, Mr. Davis, and ask them once again what preceded these problems—any altercations, any contact with strangers. Let me know what you find out."

"Very good, sir. I'll go at once. Thank'ee, Miss Cranshaw."

Liza showed him to the door and wished him well, following him a few paces out on the stone walkway. She watched him disappear through the orchard branches, then turned back to the cottage entrance, her heart pounding so fast she could scarcely breathe. The time had come. It was unlikely she would ever have this opportunity, this privacy, again. While she had every reason to hope that Jack could save her, there was no guarantee. Jack still did not know the price that Barrington was prepared to make her pay. She would give in to her desires now, because now might be all they would ever have.

She pushed open the door and found him sitting in a chair, lost in thought, leaning his cheek on one upraised fist, one lean, booted calf swung over the other knee. When his eyes found her, they crinkled warmly.

She loved that warmth in him, she thought as she closed the door and leaned against it. She loved his ability to see the best and understand the worst in everyone he knew. She could not regard him without melting inside. Presently he regarded her like an artist trying to decide precisely how to frame his subject.

"What is it, Mr. Fairchild?" she asked, wondering how she would get from here to there without looking like a scheming trollop. How in bloody hell was she going to initiate this?

"Tell me about Rodge."

She grinned. "You're a smart one. You have it all figured out, haven't you?"

"Not quite everything."

"Rodge is Lord Barrington's man of affairs." Remembering her dream, allowing it to fuel her courage, she did not remain a safe distance away. She went to his side and looked down at him, not hiding the smoky hunger in her eyes. Her hand tingled at her side, aching to caress his handsome cheek. "Roger Cradich comes and goes, but he was clearly in Middledale the night of the fire. I didn't want to say it in front of Mr. Davis."

He tilted his head back to regard her, then took her hand in his. Fire burned through her fingertips. Did he know what she had in mind? Did he want her? Surely, he did. Lord, she prayed he did.

"That means Lord Barrington is responsible for the fire," Jack said, still regarding her steadily as he gripped her hand.

She nodded, moving forward until his shoulder touched her ribs. His eyes widened almost imperceptibly. Her breath came shallow again. She wanted his lips. She needed them.

"And if we can prove it was a case of arson," he continued as if nothing untoward had occurred, "then you can cry off without him suing for breach of promise."

"That is my dearest hope." Her free hand raised, seemingly of its own accord, and smoothed through his hair. A wave of tenderness and hot desire surged up her arm. Her glove-clad fingers spread over his scalp, tugging through the waves. He pulled on the hand he still held, and she readily sank into his lap, placing an arm around his shoulders. She could feel his breath on her bosom, could feel the heat wafting from his body. She could see the hunger in his dark eyes, could smell his manly scent. His lips were so close. Oh, so close.

"What are you doing?" he asked pointedly, amusement dancing in his eyes.

He was going to make her say it, devil take him. She

swallowed hard and nuzzled her lips against his temple. His skin was hot silk on her mouth. Desire and fear made her heart thunder in her breast. "I'm trying to seduce you."

When she pulled away, she felt his breath fan her shoulder, sensed his eyes taking measure of her bosom with the wary distance of a reformed sinner. He wanted her! Oh, thank God. Knowing it would make this so much easier.

"Liza," he said softly, his intelligent eyes rising to meet hers. "I need for you to tell me why you agreed to marry such a scoundrel."

She blinked in surprise. "Why?"

"I have my reasons." He gave her a smoldering smile. "I need to know as much as I can about the woman who is so determined to take my virtue."

He reached up and curled a strand of hair around her ear. A shiver coursed down her neck. The lightest touch from him had the power to utterly undo her.

"Tell me, Liza."

He was trying to seduce her into revealing her secret. She shook her head impatiently. "I cannot tell you that, Mr. Fairchild."

"Oh, for God's sake, can't we Christian-name each other? Don't we know each other well enough by now?"

She leaned into his chest, savoring his warmth, and smiled wryly. "Very well. I cannot tell you . . . Jack."

He studied her, perceptively scanning her features, then thoughtfully ran a finger over his upper lip. The motion rustled against the whiskers just edging at the surface of his skin. "He's threatening you, isn't he?"

She frowned as her heart went from a trot to a full gallop. Lord, how did he know that? And how much more did he know? She had to remain calm. He was guessing, and she mustn't confirm anything he said. She recovered her composure and looked straight ahead, giving nothing away.

"What is he threatening? Does he have something to hold over you, Liza? Tell me, darling. I need to know."

She said nothing, merely blinked stoically.

"What could he possibly hold over you? If I knew I could help you."

Frustration made his voice scratchy and thin. He cared so much. Knowing that he was more concerned about her situation than about satisfying his own needs enabled her to trust him. Confidence finally settled over her. She turned to him and stroked his face with her hand. It still amazed her that she could know such intimacy with this extraordinary man.

"You don't need to know anything more about me than you already do, Jack. You simply need to find proof against the viscount." She added in a sensual whisper. "And there is one other thing you positively must do."

She brushed her lips seductively across one cheek, caressing his mouth, nuzzling and inhaling his breath. It smelled of mint and his own unique, delicious scent.

"Don't do that, Liza," he said warningly.

"I must, Jack. For you are being unmercifully hard to seduce. I have no idea what I'm doing, and yet I must forge ahead or face the possibility of never, ever . . . knowing you. And I simply can't bear that thought."

She loosened his cravat, caressing his face with her eyes. He tipped his chin up so she could more easily loosen his collar.

"You know precisely what to do, my dear," he murmured in a strained voice. "Instinct is your teacher."

"Instinct tells me to kiss you," she murmured. She tilted

her head and touched her mouth to his, brushing his lips, looking him in the eye, making love to his mind as she toyed with his self-control. She would be acting like a hopelessly shy virgin if she had not waited so long for this moment. Eight years. All she had to do was reenact her dream.

She took off her gloves and then kissed him again. His mouth parted with only the slightest urging from her. It was a slow, wet, and lingering kiss. Her tongue tingled as it danced with his. She made love to him, loved him, with nothing but this kiss. But then he ended it by drawing back. He frowned, and her heart tumbled with disappointment. Hadn't she pleased him?

"What is wrong?"

"We can't do this," he said hoarsely.

"Why not?" She could feel his desire pressing like a rod against her hip. He wanted her. She was sure of it.

He gripped both her upper arms firmly and put space between them. "You don't understand. Soon I won't be able to stop myself. Liza, there will be no going back."

She lifted a brow. "No, you're the one who doesn't understand. I don't want you to stop."

He went still and nodded, realizing her intent. "You know the risks."

"I know them all. I'm not that naive. Damn the consequences to hell, I say. Jack, one night of pleasure. Don't I deserve that much at least?"

Sadness flitted over his face, but it was quickly replaced by a look of sexual hunger. He stretched his hand wide like a musician carefully preparing to stroke the keys of a pianoforte, raised his palm and settled it just so on her breasts. Liquid heat spread over her bosom. She shut her eyes as his fingers rubbed her skin and molded around the swell and cleavage nestled against her low-cut gown. Ah, yes, this was what she'd been waiting for. God, could one touch do so much? She arched her back to press her bosom more fully into his hand.

"You are so lovely," he whispered, tilting his head the other way to look closely at her profile. Her breasts rose and fell faster as her breath quickened. He moved his hand under the swell, sliding into her gown, and squeezed one rounded mound, finding the nipple that had hardened beneath the fabric. He pinched it softly, and she hissed in a breath. She tightened her grip around his shoulder.

"I want to make love to you, Liza." He kissed her cheek, and she leaned into him, her lips parting with a groan. He nuzzled her ear, whispering, "I want you. I want every part of you, and not just for one night."

Joy buoyed her up out of her sea of hunger, and she smiled, then gasped in shock a moment later when he kissed her ear, his tongue delving inside the tiny hole. She frowned at the shocking sensuality, then shivered with pleasure and shook violently. He pulled back and bit the lace edge of her collar, pulling it down with his teeth until her shoulder was exposed, all creamy smooth and white. He kissed her there, too, then looked up with a frown.

"Are you sure you want this, Liza?"

She stiffened her spine and looked down at him as if he were mad and bound for Bedlam. "Lord, yes!"

"I won't do this unless you want me very, very much."

"Yes, Jack. I want you very, very much."

He'd unleashed something wild in her, and she wanted to make sure it didn't end here. She kissed him, letting her tongue dart into his mouth. Something between them snapped, the taut cord upon which they'd been walking such a fine line. They fell into an abyss of intimate knowledge, and control crumbled like brittle shackles. She was all heat and abandonment, kissing him with a passion she didn't know she possessed.

He gripped her hips and leaned her over, supporting her with an arm as he consumed her. Then he stopped abruptly, catching himself, and his head dropped as he sighed with frustration.

"God, Liza, I've never wanted anyone this much before. But I can't do it yet. Not until I tell you something you need to know."

She sat up, amazed at his herculean self-control and sobered by his deep frown. "What is it, Jack?"

He wrapped his arms around her as if he were going to tell her a bedtime story. "Once upon a time, there was a man named Lord Robert Barrington. He was a viscount who lived a squalid, unprincipled life and in the process spawned a couple of by-blows. They live like urchins in the streets of London with their mothers, half crazed for want of food and a name to call their own."

Their eyes met, only inches apart. "How do you know this?" she whispered.

"I've spent a great deal of time helping clients in prison. One hears these things in cold, dark cells and filthy alleys."

"I thought all noblemen spawned side-slips."

"Often that is the case. With Barrington, however, it wasn't a matter of an indiscretion or two with an ambitious servant. He frequented doxies. And there is some question whether he ever paid for services rendered or whether he took his pleasure against their will."

Liza's head began to pound. "Do you mean . . . do you mean he . . . he raped them?"

"There is a suggestion of such a crime. But it's hardly

considered a crime when a nobleman is involved with a ladybird. No charges have been brought, but if these weren't cases of rape, one has to wonder why doxies, who know how to avoid increasing, should find themselves in a family way. Naturally, Barrington won't suffer for his probable crimes. No one even cares about them except for the resulting children who will likely end up in prison for stealing food and other necessities of life. And at least one of the ladies in question died in childbirth. Presumably *she* cared about Lord Barrington's actions."

Liza wrapped her arms around his and laid her head on his shoulder. He was hot and warm and good. Such a good man who was being so cruel. "No more, please, I beg you."

Jack stroked her head and held her tight, wanting to make it easy for her. But hearing this was as necessary to her cure as a dose of bitter medicine.

"You should also know that Barrington has infuriated his father, the marquess, by gambling away his entire allowance and then some. The man you are about to marry is thoroughly addicted to cards and gambles money away as soon as it hits his palm. It's been said that the Marquess of Perringford has entirely cut him off, and that Barrington will never get another farthing from his family. Barrington's title did not come with an estate and so he has no income. Add to that the likely crime of arson, and you begin to get a fair idea of what sort of mate he will be."

"Why are you telling me this?" she asked in a small voice.

"Because you need to know what sort of man he is before you plunge headlong into marriage with him. There is no telling what someone who possesses neither money nor character will do."

She said nothing, just tried to soothe her soul in the warmth of his embrace.

"Liza," he said at last, "I'm telling you this because I want you to know you do not need to make love to me now. Wait until you are free. Let me bring him down. I will offer for you. Let us do this right. I want to be honorable, for your sake. That's what you deserved from the start. I don't want to have to beg for your forgiveness again."

Tears flooded her eyes and she pressed her cheek to his, feeling like she had in her dream, *I'm here, Jack. I've been here all along.* No, she could not wait. Their plans might fail. She would not risk losing Jack without completing what they had started eight years before. She would not let this moment of passion, and this rare opportunity to consummate it, pass.

"Don't say no, Jack, I need you," she whispered. "Please. I long for you so hard it hurts. There is a pain in my chest, and I know it's my heart. Soothe me. Take away this ache inside me."

His expression went blank, then he rose to the challenge, in every sense. She could feel his hard shaft straining powerfully against her thigh. What a peculiar, almost frightening sensation. What was this strange, unwieldy and hot force that was sweeping them far, far away from reason? A dark fire lit his eyes and he took up where he had left off. He reached up, his fingers brushing her shoulder, and tugged down on her collar even further, until a nipple popped free. He pulled the material out so the entire full, plump breast was bared.

"So lovely," he said hoarsely. The nipple was erect and he nipped it gently with his teeth, then laved it erotically until it burned sweetly and a shot of desire zapped down to her thighs.

"Oh, Jack, that is so sweet. Oh, my darling, I did not know a man could be so tender. Please don't stop." Every second was a tantalizing new moment and she feared it would end too soon. She didn't know precisely what she wanted to happen. All she knew was that she hungered for something greater.

He buried his lips against her neck and nipped passionately while his hand determinedly clawed at the lacy hem of her gown. He flipped the material upward until he found passage, then gripped her calf. An electrical charge ripped through her body, and she stiffened and quivered from head to toe.

His hand inched up until he found the smooth, cool flesh of her silky thighs. His fingers began to tremble, for he wanted to touch all of her, and he had to go slowly. He had to ease her tight virgin's lair before he could enter.

He kissed her again. Their lips fused, and he continued onward with his quest. He gently placed his palm around the curve of her hot, moist womanhood. She trembled like a leaf. Her breasts rose and fell in quick spasms. He nudged her thighs apart by spreading his fingers.

His breath was shallow. Perspiration beaded on his brow. "Liza, I need you. God, you're wet."

She blinked from her stuporous ecstasy to send a worried looking wafting his way. "Is that bad?"

He chuckled tenderly. "No, my darling girl, that is good. Very good. Do not worry. You will be splendid. You always are."

His middle finger probed the soft, moist folds of her sex and she took in a hissing breath, clutching his arms. When he found the tiny opening he craved, he slid inward, stopping only when his hand could go no farther.

"Oh, Jack!" she said on a heaving whisper, her eyes wide. She caught tiny breaths of astonishment in her heaving lungs, and let them out in uneven gusts of pleasurable shock. She looked up at him with the most touching look of wonder and gratitude and uncontrolled sexual responsiveness he'd ever seen. He drew his wet finger out, and then thrust it in, long and slow, reaching deeper, then hastened the motion. She shut her eyes and began to groan as she built to her beautiful, innocent climax. She would burst soon.

"Jack, what is happening to me?" she cried out in a strangled voice. "I feel . . . I feel . . . oh!"

Suddenly she came in wonderful, wild waves that were honey-slow at first, then built to an explosive burst of searing ecstasy. Wave after wave of excruciating pleasure throbbed and gripped her, lifting her high into a world she'd never known. She cried out uncontrollably, and he smiled.

"Yes, my darling, that's it. I want you to come and come again."

When she sank in a heap in his arms, wallowing in the luxurious aftermath, he withdrew his hand, then fumbled with his trousers, unbuttoning them with trembling fingers. His hard, thick staff sprang free.

"I must have you now," he said severely.

He lifted her up and wiped his arm across the table, sending the dried flower arrangement and metal vase clattering to the floor. He lowered her onto the table and yanked her forward until her hips were at the edge. He forced her thighs to part even wider and leaned over her, his weeping rod pressing against her entry. She spread her legs wider, aching for him. He tugged down on her collar, careful not to rip her gown, and scooped both breasts in his hands, gently squeezing.

"I may hurt you, Liza."

"I don't care," she rasped. "Fill me, Jack."

He leaned down and suckled each breast, savoring the slightly salty taste of perspiration on her velvet skin, then stood up and looked at the blossoming flower of her pink sex that pulsed in need of him. He touched the rigid bead above, rotating with his thumb.

Liza jerked in response, and stared at him incredulously. *Again*? her wide eyes asked in the silence. *I can do this again?*

"Jack?" she asked in a little voice.

"Don't fight it, Liza. I want you to come again. Do it. Let it happen. There is no end to the pleasure you deserve."

He circled in ever quickening strokes until she exploded. "Oh, heavens!" she cried. "Jack? Jack! Oh, God, Jack!"

As her back lifted off the table with the force of her shuttering climax, he pushed his trousers to his knees, then gripped her hips and poised the tip of his shaft at her tight opening. He entered just an inch.

"Oh, oh, yes," she whispered, clawing at his muscular forearms. "Please."

Tightening his buttocks, he thrust cleanly into her. He held still, sweat dripping onto her ribs from his brow. Her body eased, then tightened around him. He sucked in a shivering breath as he tried to rein in control. "Are you . . . are you hurting?"

She shook her head. "No. What will happen next?"

"This." He drew himself out long and slow until the tip of his ample cock pressed at the portal. Then he reentered in a long, slow journey to the darkness of her being. He was thick and hard and craving release.

"I'm going to draw myself out and thrust myself in," he said, "over and over until I pierce your very soul."

She instinctively wrapped her legs around his waist as the journey back and forth quickened. Heat burrowed into her, and the pounding he gave her was sheer pleasure. He went faster and faster, harder and harder, until they both grunted and groaned and cried out in delirious celebration. This was the slow building to his release that he could, if he chose, draw out for hours. But he didn't want to hurt her, and he didn't want to be so controlled. Not with her. He wanted to give as purely as he had taken from her. He wanted her to see his wild, dark sorrow, and feel his fierce joy.

He was sweating, heaving into her in a hypnotic rhythm. But suddenly he stopped and pulled out, his hard staff standing at attention. He scooped her up and carried her to the bed. He lowered her and spread her legs wide with his knees. Then he lowered himself on top of her. He poised his shaft between her thighs, then stroked it up and down the valley of her sex. He massaged the silken head up, down, and then into her, then out. Up, down, in and out. She was panting now, ready to explode again.

"Now you can have all of me, Liza," he whispered, and hiked up her hips. He pounded into her with quick thrusts. The sound of slapping skin could be heard over short pants for air. He stared at her dazedly, grimacing as he came closer and closer to his own thundering climax. From a distant place, he heard her cry out again with a strangled release, then he let himself go.

He rammed his shaft deep inside her, spilling his seed, not thinking or caring about the risk they were taking, knowing only that he wanted her to have all of him.

Fourteen

Liza would never be the same. She knew that the moment she rose from the sweat-soaked bed in the cottage. It was further confirmed when she and Jack kissed and giggled and staggered like drunkards as they dressed each other and combed each other's hair with their hands, trying to restore some semblance of propriety. She'd never known such ease and freedom with another. It was as if he were her best friend. She felt absolutely no self-consciousness.

Now if only Aunt Patty were half blind as well as half deaf, she wouldn't see the evidence of lovemaking—swollen lips, flushed cheeks, groggy eyes, and that telltale smile of utter contentment.

Fortunately, Harding and Patricia Brumble had not even missed the couple. They'd dug into the feast the cook had prepared and had drunk a bottle and a half of wine. By the time Liza and Jack returned to the graveyard, the older pair were guffawing like school chums, telling jokes and gossiping to their hearts' content.

When they returned to the house, Liza went immediately to her bedroom and ordered a cool bath, claiming the long walk had overheated her. She was reluctant to wash the scent of Jack off her skin, for there was no telling when, if ever, she would hold him so intimately again.

While she felt free and wholly at one with herself and her lover, she had the first inklings of horrible discontent. For no matter how well suited she and Jack were as lovers, their passion could not erase the problem she'd been grappling with all along. Lord Barrington was blackmailing her. He had discovered a horrible secret about her family. And Liza was the only one who could keep him from revealing it.

She prayed Jack could help her out of this situation. He had to find enough evidence to condemn Lord Barrington of arson. And he had to do it before her engagement was announced; otherwise, she would irrevocably be connected to the wastrel viscount in the minds of good society, even if the engagement were later broken. Especially if it were broken.

There was another reason Liza wanted a quick resolution of her dilemma. Jack Fairchild was too clever by half. Given enough time, he would figure out precisely what sort of infamy Lord Barrington had unearthed. And then Jack couldn't offer for her even if he wanted to. A future and honorable baron couldn't in good conscience saddle his descendants with such scandal. And if there was one thing she knew beyond doubt about Jack Fairchild, he was a man of honor.

She wished she could speak to someone about her problems. Perhaps it was time to write Mrs. Halloway again.

. . .

After freshening up in his living quarters, Jack hurtled down the stairs to his chambers spouting orders like the *rat-a-tat-tat* of a militia shooting rounds of ammunition.

"Harding, I need you to find out which properties Mr. Cranshaw owns in town. Find out what building projects are under way, if any. Giles, I need you to find out who purchased Jacob Davis's property when he went bankrupt. Search in documents and discreetly ask questions in town."

The men looked up with curious stares. Jack crossed his arms and began to pace between their desks.

"Giles, I also need you to find out what inquiries Lord Barrington may have made into any of the local land in the last eight months or so."

"That information would be in Mr. Pedigrew's files, sir. He handled all legal matters in town. I know he met on a few occasions with the viscount shortly before he retired."

"Good!" Jack grinned and slapped his hands together, rubbing them to create friction. "I want to see any notes, documents, or briefs you might find on the subject."

"Consider it done, sir."

"Mr. Fairchild," Harding cut in, "may I ask what you are trying to find out?"

Jack leveled him with a sober look. "No, you may not. Sorry, old boy. This one is confidential. Just do as I ask and you will be well rewarded if you strike gold. I want to solve the mystery of the fire that destroyed Jacob Davis. It was clearly a case of arson. Someone is to blame. And I want to find out who, and I don't care what his disposition in life is. Do I make myself clear?"

Harding frowned and his lips curled in an uneasy grimace. "Perfectly."

Suddenly, the door opened and a footman entered bearing the Cranshaws' checkered green-and-white livery.

"A letter from Cranshaw Park, if you please, sir," he said in a dry, thin voice.

"Put it here, my good man." Jack motioned to the desk.

The footman placed the letter down in front of Harding and returned his bored gaze to Jack. "Is that good, sir?"

"Yes. Henry will take it to Waverly tomorrow."

Harding picked up the missive and recognized the handwriting at once. "Oh, dear."

The footman had started for the door, but turned back at this. "Is there a problem, sir?"

Harding tossed a significant glance to Jack. "This letter is from Miss Cranshaw."

The footman smiled patiently. "No, sir. It is from her abigail. The maid gave it to me herself."

Harding frowned, but nodded as if in full accordance with this view. "I see. My mistake." Harding darted another telling look at his employer. "Thank you. I'll make sure it gets into the proper hands."

The befuddled footman paused a moment, then turned to go. When the door shut behind him, Jack swiftly leaned forward and snatched the letter from his secretary's hand.

"I'll take that," he said nonchalantly. He slipped it into his pocket, then disappeared into his own chamber.

Giles and Harding stared after him, then looked at one another with saucer eyes.

"This does not bode well, Mr. Honeycut. Something very significant has happened. I haven't seen Mr. Fairchild this determined on a secret course since he had an affair with the countess of—" Harding bit his tongue. "That is to say, I am very concerned."

Giles twiddled his thumbs. "We all know who's going to read this letter in the end, don't we?"

"Yes," Harding said beleagueredly.

"Why not, I say?" Giles said, heading for the door. "Mr. Fairchild is a good man. He only wants to help Miss Cranshaw. That's good enough reason to open a letter."

Harding smiled wanly. "I hope you're right. But I do wonder if Miss Cranshaw would agree with you. If I were her, I'd be incensed to learn my letters had been part of a secret plot."

"What she doesn't know won't hurt her, Mr. Harding. And she'll never find out."

"Unless, of course, Mrs. Halloway finally *does* write to her."

"You can intercept the letter."

Harding went very still. "Good Lord, Mr. Honeycut, what if Mrs. Halloway returns to Middledale for a visit?"

"Oh, well, then you do have a problem."

"*I* have a problem. You mean *we* have a problem. You're part of this firm now, need I remind you?"

When Giles grinned proudly, Harding shrugged and waved him off. "Go to your investigations, Mr. Honeycut. Since you're related to everyone in this town by one degree or another, you should meet with some success. Why should I care a fig what Miss Cranshaw finds out? Let Mrs. Holloway return. She'll expose Mr. Fairchild's meddling and Miss Cranshaw will be rid of him once and for all. And then he can finally devote himself to work. The days until Lord Abbington comes for his pound of flesh are flying as swiftly as swallows."

Fifteen

Jack had trouble sleeping that night. He rose around one in the morning, trying not to disturb Harding. He threw on a quilted silk robe and stumbled his way into his parlor. He had no valet or bed servant to wait on him. But his housekeeper's nephew slept on the floor in the kitchen. He woke at the sound of Jack's shuffling feet and lit beeswax candles to light the room, then went yawning back to his pallet on the floor.

Jack resigned himself to a solitary brandy, but it wasn't long before he had company. Harding appeared in the doorway, tugging his robe around his fat belly, scratching the back of his short neck.

Jack looked up with relief. He'd never before felt so lonely as he had since making love to Liza. It was as if his arms were now achingly empty, whereas before he'd never noticed any lacking.

"Good to see you, Harding."

"Having trouble sleeping, sir?" He sank his round frame into a square armchair.

"So it would seem." Jack stretched out his long, muscular legs and waved a hand toward the decanter. "Pour yourself something to drink. I could use the company."

Jack watched him go through the motions of ambling to the sideboard, unstopping a decanter of brandy, and splashing liquor into a glass, feeling almost absurdly grateful for his secretary's company. He simply wasn't himself tonight.

Something in him had changed, and he had the uneasy feeling it had happened the moment he'd made love to Liza. Somehow during the course of their sweet, succulent lovemaking she had deftly opened him up like a surgeon and plucked out his heart. It was now hers to do with as she pleased. What made it so much more frightening was the fact that she didn't even want it. She'd simply longed for an awakening. She was still too intent on her duties to her family to even think of lifelong happiness. And she was just independent enough to think she could make love without love or marriage.

Bloody hell! What a position that put him in. Lord knows he didn't want love. But, dear God, it had finally occurred to him that he might need it. He was prepared to offer for her. It was a matter of honor. He wasn't sure, however, he was prepared for a marriage in which he was utterly besotted with his wife.

"What is troubling you, sir?" Harding deposited himself back in his chair and put his lips to the rim of his glass, sipping, then sighing contentedly.

"It has suddenly occurred to me, Harding, that I have yet to wake up in a woman's arms."

The secretary sniffed the liquor, swirled it in the bottom of the glass. "I don't quite get your meaning."

"I mean that I have made love to many women, but I

never cared enough about them to fall asleep with them."

"Pardon my practicality, sir, but that may be owing to the fact that waking up with someone is usually a privilege reserved for those who marry. Even if you wanted to loll around in the arms of your lovers until noon, you couldn't do it without a husband knowing about it."

Jack chuckled with a note of self-loathing and rubbed the jabbing pain that pricked his eyes. "What a waste my life has been. And here I am lamenting such a petty thing when other people are facing such very real problems."

"Like who?"

Jack lounged back and steepled his fingers, resting his elbows on the arms of his chair. "Jacob Davis, for one."

"You mean the chandler?"

"Yes. It would seem that Lord Barrington is responsible for a crime that has ruined a good Middledale family, the Davises. I did not want to possess this intelligence, but now that I do, I can't ignore it. I trust you will be utterly discreet."

"Of course. Lord Barrington! Isn't that Miss Cranshaw's intended?"

"The very one."

"Are you certain he is to blame?"

"Certain enough to know such a crime cannot go unpunished."

"Leave that to the sheriff, I say."

"No. I don't yet have the evidence. That's what Giles is working on. Moreover, I can't accuse Barrington without hurting Liza's reputation."

"Liza? You're using her Christian name now, eh?"

Jack felt a blush creep up his neck. Harding knew him too well. He'd doubtless already guessed just how far Jack's relationship with Liza had gone. Normally, Harding's assumptions meant nothing. But with Liza it was different. There was nothing ordinary about her.

He cleared his throat and took a sip of brandy. Then he regaled Harding with Davis's sad tale. Harding's frown deepened with every detail. When Jack ended the story, the secretary dropped his chin in his hand and sighed.

"Sounds bloody awful. So this is the matter you have us investigating."

"Yes. It puts me in a quandary. If Barrington knows I am investigating his crime, he will make sure that Cranshaw ceases to use my services. He may even try to hasten my journey to debtor's prison."

Harding sat up. "How could he?"

"He has his sources of gossip in London. If he wants to know to whom I owe my debts, he'll find out quick enough."

"Why can't Miss Cranshaw tell her father the truth about this bloody cur?"

"She doesn't want her parents to know." Jack was suddenly overwhelmed with the premonition that Liza had no idea just how deep a game she was playing. He tried to rub the worry lines from his forehead. "I don't think she realizes just how much danger she's in."

Harding scowled at him. "You think Lord Barrington is that much of a rotter?"

Jack skewered him with a jaded look. "I know he is. I've seen men like him before. Remember when the earl of Haverstoke killed his valet and was never brought to justice? Remember the mysterious death of the marchioness of Beaverly? The aristocracy get away with murder all the time, Harding. Not that he wants her dead now. He needs to get her money first. But what happens then? What is worse, if I can't find proof quickly, her engagement to Lord Barrington will be announced and her reputation will never be the same, even if she's lucky enough to end her engagement. She will always be tainted by her association with him."

"Surely her father knows that Barrington isn't quite the thing."

Jack shook his head. "Our dear Mr. Cranshaw is blinded by his desire for a title in the family. He's a simple man with an unusual ability to make money who knows little of the intricacies of the upper crust. He thinks a title ensures character."

"If only you could convince Miss Cranshaw to end the engagement on her own."

"It's the only way, Harding. But Miss Cranshaw holds the trump card in this game, and she keeps her hand very close to her chest. There is a reason she is not exercising better judgment. A reason that she has shared with only one person. Mrs. Halloway."

He pulled the letter that had arrived earlier that day out of the pocket of his robe.

Harding noticed it at once. "I am astonished you haven't opened that yet."

Jack regarded it in the flickering candlelight, turning it back and forth, studying the imperfections of the paper, the grace of the handwriting. "You realize, of course, that there is a good chance this letter will end up in a mud puddle like the last one."

"Indeed," Harding agreed, pausing to sip. "You will simply have to pay the postage when it's returned."

"Moreover, this just might hold a necessary clue in my search for evidence against Lord Barrington."

"It very likely does. Then there is only one thing to do, don't you think?"

Jack's eyes met Harding's. Without another word, he broke the seal and read the letter.

My Dear Mrs. Halloway,

I write with exceedingly good news. I have finally found a knight in shining armor to rescue me, using the greatest weapon in the land—the law. He is a solicitor, a kindhearted man who cannot help but do good, even when it isn't in his own best interests. Isn't that the very definition of a gentleman, even a hero? He has agreed to look into the matter of the fire. You know which one I'm referring to. I think I should be fairly discreet, in case this missive falls into the wrong hands. But let me simply say that if anyone can save me from Lord B.'s blackmail, it will be Mr. Fairchild. Mr. John Calhoun Fairchild is his name. This dear man, who has become a close friend in such a short time, is Lord Tutley's grandson. I think you know me well enough to believe me when I say the title he is due to inherit means nothing to me. It is his kind support and expertise which I cherish most. He has great faith in the law, and his devotion to such a noble ideal has given me hope. I can only hope that in some small way I can make his efforts on my behalf worthwhile. Perhaps with his help, this whole matter in Fielding can be made history. Perhaps then I can spare Desiree and myself as well. I want to reassure you, though, that I am still determined to marry his lordship if I cannot find a legal way to salvage the situation. I pray you will write soon. I long to hear from you.

Very Truly Yours,
L. C.

Without displaying any of the whirling emotions he felt, Jack pinched the folds of the letter and recreased them, then slid it back in his pocket. He steepled his fingers and shut his eyes. *Damnation!* he thought. She was still determined to marry that ass even after making love to Jack. It was infuriating. Did she have no sense of duty to herself at all?

Liza loved him. Jack knew it in his gut. She couldn't have made love the way she had if she didn't. Why wouldn't she admit it to herself? Why wouldn't she come to her senses? And why in hell did he care so bloody much? He hated this. He hated it!

"Well?" Harding was at the edge of his seat. "What did she say?"

He blinked. "She thinks I'm a prince among men."

"Well, she's bloody well right about that. Was that all?"

"No." Jack stroked his chin. His nails scratched over coarse whiskers. "I was right. She's being blackmailed by Barrington."

"Gads! That's despicable."

Jack shut his eyes a long moment. Harding's empathy stoked his fury. But Jack could not go off half-cocked. That would do her no good. "She also mentioned Fielding."

"That's the address on the letter."

"It apparently has something to do with a scandal Miss Cranshaw is trying to keep quiet. She also mentioned this Desiree again, in the same context, I gather."

The men sipped brandy by the light of the candles and listened to the clock ticking.

"I am sorry, Jack, that I was rude to her," Harding said after some reflection. "She really is lovely. How infuriating to think a nobleman would stoop to blackmailing

such a fair creature. Doubtless he thinks he can get away
with it because she's from the merchant class. What could
you possibly do to convince Miss Cranshaw to end her
engagement?"

"If she's being blackmailed, there may be nothing I can
do that's greater than the consequences she so fears."

"You could always seduce her."

I've tried that was Jack's silent answer. *It wasn't
enough.* A dull pain throbbed in his chest, settling between his ribs. He felt like a failure. He'd thought their
lovemaking would have meant more to her.

He looked out the window. The moon was full tonight,
a smoky orange. Perfect for a midnight assignation. He
wanted to make love with her again. The need for her
twisted his groin in knots. There was nothing he'd rather
do than seduce Liza again and again. But she was too
damned stubborn to let lovemaking shake her from her
course.

He gave his old friend a dour smile. "Harding, I'm
surprised to hear you, of all people, suggest that I seduce
a woman."

"Well, it always worked in the past. Then again, she's
a maiden. You'd have to marry her."

Marriage. Lord! The very word cut up his peace. But
that was precisely what all Jack's actions were leading
to—marriage. He'd said as much in the cottage. He could
not destroy Liza's chances with Barrington without giving
her every expectation of an offer from Jack himself. It
was, after all, his fault that she was engaged to Barrington
in the first place. Lud, could he really want to lock himself
into the shackles of matrimony and risk being loathed by
the woman he now cherished more than any other in the

world? Wasn't that really what frightened him the most?
The prospect of being hated by a wife he adored?

He felt suddenly ill. The familiar pounding started in
his head and he leaned it against his chair. He wiped a
hand over his face. "No, there has to be another way to
dissuade her. My usual bag of tricks is failing me, old
friend."

He slipped his hands in the pockets of his robe and idly
fingered Liza's letter. Then an idea struck. "By Jove, I
think I may have a plan. She said she still hoped to receive
a letter from Mrs. Halloway. She apparently listens to
everything Mrs. Halloway says."

Harding looked over the rim of his glass and caught
Jack's eye. Mischief kindled between them. "I think I
know what you have in mind, you devilish rogue!"

Jack gave him a self-satisfied smirk. "You flatter me
unnecessarily with such epithets, my good man. Now
fetch a quill and paper. By the by, I want you to go immediately on a secret mission to Fielding to see what you
can find out about Mrs. Halloway and this mysterious Desiree. Meanwhile, if I can circumvent some pain and suffering on Liza's behalf, I have to do it, using every
weapon a man has in his arsenal. This letter may be what
she's been needing all along."

Harding downed his brandy in one final gulp and retrieved the necessary writing utensils.

He went to a desk near the window and trimmed the
quill. "Mind you, sir, this is most deceitful."

"I am well aware of that," Jack observed without emotion.

"If she finds out you've deceived her, you'll be stricken
from her company."

"Yes, but so will Lord Barrington be. I will mourn the

loss of her affections, Harding, but will rejoice in her freedom from misery. Now let us begin."

"You dictate, sir, and I'll scribe the letter for you."

Jack rubbed his wrinkled brow. "Lord, this will never work. She will wonder at your handwriting."

"Fear not, dear sir, I have a solution. Now dictate, if you please."

Jack cleared his throat and clasped his hands behind his back.

"My dear Miss Cranshaw," he began, coughing to clear his throat. "Imagine my shock and sorrow when I received your letter. I did not read it immediately because I was on my deathbed. However, I have made a miraculous recovery and am now writing to you my best advice. You must break off your association with Lord Barrington immediately, no matter what the cost. I was wrong to advise you otherwise. He is a bloody bastard and deserves to die, damn him to hell. If he puts one finger upon your fair, beautiful skin, I will come to Middledale and plant a facer from which he'll never recover. I'll beat him into a pulp. I'll—"

Jack stopped when he realized that Harding had long ago ceased to pen his words and was presently looking at him as if he'd quite gone off his rocker.

"Very well," Jack growled. "I've strayed off on a tangent. If you think you can do better, then have at it."

"Indeed I can, sir," Harding replied equably. He dipped the pen in the ink pot and began to scratch across the surface of the fine paper.

"My dearest, *gentlest* Miss Cranshaw," Harding began in a superior tone. "Words cannot express my deepest concern and affection for you. I—"

"Yes, yes, that's good. Very good." Jack leaned over Harding's chair, breathing down his neck. "Go on."

"Forgive the penmanship, my dear Liza, but my abigail is writing this missive for me."

"Excellent!" Jack declared, slapping his hands together and pacing with a sense of excitement.

"I've been ill and am not up to the task," Harding continued, speaking to himself. "Do not fear for me, dear girl, for I am on the mend. But it was my illness that kept me from responding sooner. My abigail will be discreet, of course. I was most distressed to hear the intimate details of your predicament, and I can only say—"

"No, no, no!" Jack interrupted. "That's too formal. You must get to the point."

"She is a matron, sir," Harding argued, quill poised above the page, eyebrows raised as he gazed up at his employer. "Mrs. Halloway is doubtless a lady of sensibility. Trust me on this. I have read more correspondence than you."

Jack grunted in protest, then waved him on. "Very well, but tell her to break it off immediately and then get to the part in which Mrs. Halloway recommends a nice country solicitor. And do not forget to say something about following her own desires."

"Indeed, sir," Harding said with ennui, as if forging letters were an everyday affair. "Indeed. When I am through with this missive, Miss Cranshaw will be all but yours."

Sixteen

"Will that be all, Miss Cranshaw?" asked Liza's abigail.

"Yes, Susan, thank you."

The red-haired, freckle-faced girl looked over her mistress's shoulder in the mirror, flicking the perimeters of Liza's hair lightly like a sculptor admiring her artwork.

Ringlets of hair spilled from the bandeau swathed at a cant around Liza's forehead. A diamond-and-pearl necklace glittered among the porcelain curves and valleys of her neck. Her faintly lined eyes glittered exotically like gleaming sapphires seen through a purple stained-glass window.

"You look lovely, miss," Susan said. She frowned and bit her lower lip, lifting and dropping her shoulders as if it were a mystery.

Liza looked at her reflection in the mirror as she dabbed lavender water behind her ears. "What is it? Is something wrong?"

"No, miss." The lady's maid gazed at her almost adoringly. "It's just that I've never seen you so . . . so alive. It's almost as if . . . you were in love."

Two pink circles formed on Liza's cheeks. She looked down at her cosmetics table nonchalantly. "Shouldn't all young women who are about to marry look a little besotted?"

"Yes, of course, miss." She shook her head and laughed at herself. "Forgive me. You simply are so beautiful tonight."

An image of Jack flashed in Liza's mind, with his sardonic half-smile, and those penetrating eyes of his that had seen the prettiest faces of London, and she wondered if he, too, would find her pretty.

"Thank you, Susan. You are too kind."

"Best to hurry, miss. The party will be starting soon. The servants are in an uproar."

Liza smiled sympathetically and put on her pearl drop earrings. "I feel for them. My father doesn't understand what work an impromptu party takes. Imagine throwing a dance with only a day's notice."

Liza had been surprised when her father announced the evening festivities. Then she'd thrilled inside, for she knew that Jack Fairchild would be a guest. She couldn't wait to see him again, to look in his eyes and see the intimacy that was hers alone. An image of his sleek, hard muscles undulating against her came to mind, and she bit her lip, stifling an automatic groan of desire. She had to keep her memories firmly in place, or she would surely swoon.

Suddenly the door flew open and her younger sister hurried in. "There you are! Liza, I was expecting you downstairs. I simply must talk to you."

"You may go now, Susan." Liza regarded her sister's reflection in the mirror. Celia sat down a few feet behind her on the edge of the bed, leaning contemplatively against one of the end posts.

"You look beautiful tonight, darling," Liza said, smiling at Celia. She wore a simple yellow gown and her blond hair was curled and pinned up in a charming nest of tumbling coils. A strand of pearls capped the coif, and her cheeks shone pink in the candlelight.

"I may be fair, but you are positively glowing," Celia replied, a frown gathering on her delicate forehead. "Don't tell me you've finally fallen in love with Lord Barrington."

Liza smirked. "Really, Celia, did you take too much sun today?"

Celia's hands flew to her mouth. "Oh, good heavens! It's Mr. Fairchild, isn't it?"

"Upon my word, everyone has me falling in love tonight."

"That's it!" Celia crowed triumphantly. "You went on a picnic with him. And he was with you the night I courted disaster. And the kiss! How could I have forgotten that kiss by the shooting range?"

"Celia, I know you're a romantic at heart, but do not make too much of one indiscreet kiss. Now, what is it you want, dearest?"

Liza pivoted on her seat and gave her sister her full attention, hoping it would distract her from the truth.

Celia's excitement vanished and her shoulders stooped a little. She distractedly flicked at a piece of lint on her silk gown. "I . . . I came to say that I am willing to marry the earl of Bedwald."

"What? Don't be absurd!"

"No, I am. I am willing to marry him if it means you can stop this nonsense about marrying Lord Barrington."

"Oh, Celia, my dear sister!" Liza jumped up and went to the bed, sitting and taking her hands. "I would never make such a trade with you. I won't hear of it."

"I can't let you marry Barrington. I won't be responsible for your unhappiness."

Liza smiled and tucked a tendril of hair behind her delicate ear. "We Cranshaw girls certainly carry more than our fair share of responsibility, don't we? No, Celia, marrying the earl is out of the question. And if it's any consolation, I'm trying to find a way out of this mess. I have someone else's help now, so you needn't carry this burden on your lovely shoulders. Understand?"

Celia looked up with relief. "Very well, Liza. This person who is helping you . . . is it Mr. Fairchild?"

"Yes, it is."

"May I help him help you? If there is some way, I should very much like to try."

Liza blinked with an idea. "Perhaps you can. Do you remember anything at all about the fire that destroyed the chandler shop in town?"

"The Davises' shop?"

"Yes. I'm convinced it was deliberately set. Do you remember anything about that tragedy that seems unusual in retrospect?"

Celia thought a moment. "Two months before the fire Lord Barrington first came to Cranshaw Park, I remember that."

"Yes, that's true. But was there anything specifically about Annabelle or Mrs. Davis that comes to mind?"

Celia looked up with a slow-dawning realization. "Upon my word, I do remember something. I remember seeing a young lady getting out of Lord Barrington's carriage in Silver Wood just south of the village. I thought at the time it was Annabelle. But then, that made no sense and I dismissed the notion from my mind. Why would a chandler's daughter be in a viscount's carriage? But now I'm thinking it was Annabelle. Is that possible?"

"Perhaps she was carrying a message from the viscount to her father. I have reason to believe that Lord Barrington made threats to Jacob Davis before the fire."

Celia squeezed her hand. "Oh, Liza, you don't think his lordship was involved?"

Liza didn't want to distress Celia any further, so she pinned her shoulders back and put on a brave smile. "I certainly hope not. Now, not a word of this to anyone, do you hear?"

"I'm so glad to know Mr. Fairchild is looking after you. He's a gentleman of the first stare, isn't he? And a good man, too."

Remembered passion infused Liza's face with heat. "Yes."

Celia needled her with a girlish smile. "And I'm right, aren't I? You are in love with him."

Liza shook her head, but she couldn't deny it with words. "Oh, Celia, I never thought to feel this way."

"Feel what way, my dear?" said their mother from the doorway.

Liza froze and clutched her sister's hand. "Not a word to anyone!" she whispered; then she called out, "What is it, Mama? Do you need to borrow some earrings?"

"No, my dear, I have my own." Rosalind Cranshaw swept into the room in her usual loving manner. Her graying brown hair was pulled back in a chignon, and rubies dangled from her ears. Her deep sapphire-colored eyes tilted upward in a lovely oval shape. She wore a silver gown that fell like a waterfall from her still proud bosom. Liza always thought her to be the most beautiful woman in any room, even though she'd grown plump and was always in a loving tizzy, having forgotten this detail or that. Tonight, however, she looked uncharacteristically sober.

"What is it, Mama?" Liza asked. "Are you worried about the guest list? I'm told this is a small affair. Sir Walter Dewey is the only guest Papa will worry about impressing."

"And he's merely a baronet from Waverly," Celia added in a bored drone, gently mocking her father's tendency to compare the titles and importance of his acquaintances.

"Do not make fun of your father, dear," Rosalind gently reproved. "Now, do be a good girl and leave us alone. I want to talk to your sister in private."

Liza's heart fluttered. Had her mother also guessed her feelings for Jack? Had Liza been mooning too obviously? Had her skin been chafed too raw by Jack's whiskers? She wanted to crawl into the woodwork and disappear.

"Liza, my dear, come sit with me by the window." Rosalind tugged her hand, and they sat side by side on a burgundy sofa.

"What is it, Mama?"

"I am concerned about you."

Liza smiled brashly. "Don't be. I am in perfect health."

"You seem . . . distressed. Are you worried about your impending engagement?"

Liza had not yet pulled on her gloves. She looked down at her hands and twisted a pearl ring around her middle finger as she measured her response. So her mother was finally noticing that all was not well in paradise.

"No, I have simply been distracted by preparations for the engagement announcement. I am sorry if I seem . . . unhappy. That is not the case."

Rosalind folded her hands and sighed forlornly. "I don't believe you. I don't think you love Lord Barrington at all."

Liza's heart stopped a full beat. She turned to face her fully. "Mother, why are you doing this now when it is nearly too late?"

"I would have questioned you sooner, but I thought you wanted him. Your father was so delighted to have a nobleman court you. And you were the one who said you wanted to accept his offer."

"And I do," Liza said mechanically. "Why must you question me now?"

Rosalind sighed, and her ruby drop earrings swung to and fro from her ears. "I just believe the best marriages are love matches. Don't think your father wants a title so much that he would be willing to sacrifice your happiness."

"I know he wouldn't." Liza adored her father and loved making him proud. But she would never sacrifice herself to someone like Barrington just to please him. Her mother would simply die if she knew the real reason for Liza's actions. "Mama, love matches are not the fashion in high society, which is where Papa wants me to be. Surely you know that."

"I know, I know," Rosalind said in resignation. "I've just noticed the way you look at Mr. Fairchild. And the notion came to mind that I've never seen you look at Lord Barrington with the same obvious admiration."

"Mr. Fairchild is handsome and exciting. But he's a

rake. He will never marry. Please do not misinterpret my regard for him. I hold him in the highest esteem that one can hold a man of such worldliness. He is in no way competing for my affections with the viscount." He had in fact already won her heart hands down, Liza did not add.

"Very well, dear." Rosalind smiled wistfully. "I'll trust you to be your own best advocate, as you always are. Just follow your heart, dear, and it will always lead you on the best path. Since you are resolved to marry Lord Barrington, I see no reason why his request cannot be agreed upon. I will tell your father at once."

Liza looked up sharply. "What request?"

"Why, his lordship wants to have the engagement party earlier than we had planned. Didn't he tell you? This weekend. Of course, I told him that with such short notice we couldn't possibly prepare as we had hoped to, but he impressed upon me the advantage of having a smaller, more intimate affair. He says he is so in love with you he cannot wait any longer."

"But . . . but I am not ready to announce our engagement. It is too soon! Tell him it can't be done."

Rosalind pursed her lips, looking quizzically at her daughter. "If you are resolved to marry him, I see no reason to delay, my dear. The settlement has nearly been agreed upon. The only thing left to do is sign the papers and announce it to the world."

"Why can't he wait?"

"Why should he? In truth, my darling, there is no good reason to delay. If you are serious about marrying the viscount, you should move forward with your plans or put an end to them at once. You don't want to acquire a reputation as a jilt. Nothing would be worse."

Liza went to her dressing table, reaching for her perfume to hide her distress. In her haste, she knocked over the bottle and half the contents gurgled out before she could snatched it upright. Lavender filled the air. "Oh, heavens, look what I've done!"

"I'll send Susan in," Rosalind said, walking to the door. She turned back. "What shall I tell your father, dearest? Proceed with the wedding plans?"

Blood whooshed in Liza's ears. Her heart leapt desperately against her throat. She could back out now. Her mother was all but begging her to. But then, her mother did not know the price they would pay for Liza's change of heart. The price her mother, above all, would pay.

"Very well," Liza said in a choked voice. "This weekend is acceptable."

Rosalind left with a melancholy sigh, and Liza longed to run after her and tell her the truth. But she couldn't. Nor could she follow her mother's naive advice to follow her heart. Where would Liza's heart lead her if she followed? Straight into the arms of Jack Fairchild. And then where would her mother be?

Seventeen

ack could hear the music floating out the windows of the ballroom at Cranshaw Park when he exited his carriage that night. The plucky, sweet strain of a lively violin surged on the breeze that lifted the back of his hair. Music meant dancing, and a dance would give Jack a chance to be close to Liza. He trotted eagerly up the stairs, the letter burning a hole in his pocket.

Liza, Liza, Liza, he thought, her image filling him so completely that his knees nearly buckled on the top marble step. He paused a moment to collect himself, to try to force from his mind the memory of her silky thighs and her screams of pleasure. He cleared his throat and straightened his crisp cravat. Good Lord, he was acting like a besotted schoolboy, he thought as he continued to the front door.

Nothing had given him more satisfaction than giving her that release. Eight years of pent-up passion had been waiting for that moment. And to think what pleasure he

could give her if they had a chance to really get to know
each other as lovers. But would they have that chance?
Not if he couldn't find enough evidence against Barrington. And not if Lord Abbington discovered where Jack
was and decided to come calling. Jack had to convince
Liza to call off the engagement regardless of the outcome
of the investigation, and to do so quickly. Time was their
enemy, and so each moment had to count.

Determined to alter the course of fate, Jack followed
the butler into the ballroom. The intimate soiree was just
getting under way. There were two dozen people in at-
tendance—neighbors, as well as Arthur and Theo Paley,
the Cranshaws, and the family of an old baronet from
Waverly who looked like a sheepdog with shaggy gray
hair and drooping bags beneath his eyes. He was standing
by a life-size Grecian statue, guffawing heartily at Bartholomew Cranshaw's witticisms.

Jack stopped in the doorway a moment to get his bear-
ings and to find his prize. He spotted her dancing at the
far end of the long room, and suddenly the world was
right again. Barrington was a safe distance away, chatting
with a spectacled young man near a large painting of King
Henry VIII. The festivities had just begun.

The ballroom was awash in golden candlelight and a
refreshing breeze flowed through the open terrace doors,
cooling the napes of the women in their low-cut gowns.
The requisite opening minuet was under way. The dancers
made a pretty picture, like dolls come to life in a golden
haze of comfort and charming conversations.

"Good evening, coz," said Arthur, gaily approaching
arm-in-arm with his wife.

"Good evening, Arthur," Jack said warmly. "Theo, you
look lovely."

"Thank you. But not nearly as lovely as Miss Cranshaw. I daresay she shines everyone else down."

They gazed out at the graceful dancers. By far the most radiant among them was Liza.

"She is a lovely lady, to be sure," Jack said with studied indifference. "I have something for her, in fact. If you will excuse me, I'll give it to her straightaway."

"Of course," Theo said, her plump cheeks rounding in a teasing smile. "But only if you promise to dance with me later."

"Agreed," Jack said charmingly, and kissed her hand. He sketched a bow and started to make his way to the far end of the ballroom when a loud voice from behind nearly made him jump out of his skin.

"Fairchild, good to see you," said Bartholomew Cranshaw. Liza's amiable father slapped him on the back. "Impressive little party, eh?"

"Indeed, sir," Jack said, looking down at the jovial man. "It is an honor to be here."

"The honor is mine, Fairchild. The Dewey family came in from Waverly and it seemed a good time, along with your arrival, for some merriment. I am most impressed with your eagerness to work, my boy." He wagged a finger in the air, and his apple-red cheeks rounded with a smile. "You see, I understand the ways of the nobility. You will inherit that title whether your grandfather likes it or not. Money can always be made by a clever lad, and that's my bailiwick, making money."

"I envy you, sir."

"Yes, but one day you will have something I can never have—a title. And here you are, willing to work like a commoner! It's remarkable. I admire that, Fairchild, I do. Too much frivolity in so-called polite society, I say. I hope to make you rich, my lad. Now, if you're serious about working, I have a case for you. I'll send the papers over to you in the morning. It's quite complicated, and I'll pay you well."

"That would be capital, sir. Thank you."

Nagged by guilt, Jack shifted his weight from one foot to the other. If Bartholomew Cranshaw knew how far he'd gone to disrupt his daughter's wedding plans, he'd throw Jack out on his ear, not give him business. Normally, Jack wouldn't care. But this was Liza's father. *Liza, Liza, Liza.* Her name was a drumroll in his head. A mantra. A siren's song.

When a footman appeared at their side with a tray of champagne, Cranshaw took a glass and raised it in the air. Jack took one in turn.

"Let us toast to a long and fruitful association."

"Hear, hear," Jack agreed. He touched the air with his glass, and through the champagne's tawny bubbles he saw Liza approaching. In the pale, beige filter she was a blur of blue material and white diamonds and jet hair. She was a stunning bouquet of silk and lace, creamy skin, and a mesmerizing smile.

"Ah, here comes my daughter. Be a rum one, won't you, Fairchild, and dance with Liza? I don't want Barrington to give away their spring wedding by dancing too much with her. I'd like the announcement to be a surprise, though everyone knows they're smelling like April."

"I'd be delighted." Jack waited for her to turn that smile on him, and when she did, fireworks went off in his heart. He grinned as intimately as he dared. "Good evening, Miss Cranshaw."

"Good evening, Mr. Fairchild."

Her eyes, which looked periwinkle in the golden candlelight, flashed briefly with intimacy. Warm flames burned in their cool depths, sparking that fiery connection between them, turning his blood molten. His legs went taut, and he grew hard. Bloody hell, but he wanted to take her here in the middle of the party.

She turned to her father and smiled sweetly. "Greetings, Papa."

"Greetings, my darling." Cranshaw's face turned as soft as pudding. He grinned lovingly and clucked over his daughter, kissing each cheek. "You outshine the candles, my dear. What did I do to deserve you? You and Celia and your mother? Would you dance with Mr. Fairchild, my dear?"

"I'd be delighted. Shall we join the others?" she asked with a provocative smile.

"Lead the way." He offered his arm, and the touch of her glove on his arm sizzled and branded him, even through his coat. He wanted more. He wanted flesh on flesh. A little bit of her would never again be enough. Stilling his thoughts, he gave her a perfunctory smile as they took their place among the half dozen couples at the far end of the room. Jack surveyed the crowd. There was Celia and a young man whose shaggy blond hair marked him as the baronet's son, and others he did not recognize, but Lord Barrington had disappeared. Relaxing, Jack prayed for a country jig. He listened closely as the fiddler tuned his instrument. When the musician's bow danced on the strings with a few practice strokes, the twangy sounds of a swift tune took shape.

"Oh, a country dance!" Liza said, laughing delightedly.

"Fancy that," Jack said laconically, though his broad grin betrayed his own excitement. "I pray, Miss Cranshaw, you don't let me crush your delicate feet." Then he added in a seductive whisper, "And if I stumble, I hope I may fall into your arms."

"You're entirely too bold, sir," she sniffed, but her eyes twinkled. When she coyly placed her hand in his, a hot jolt trembled up his arm. She placed the other hand on his shoulder, and it was all he could do to keep from pulling her close and devouring her lips in a deep, hungry kiss. The fiddler began the song in earnest and the other couples began to jig around in a broad circle. Jack and Liza followed suit and their hearts soon pumped from the loping steps.

An invisible strand held them tight as their gazes locked, eyes laughing, spirits soaring. As invigorating and merry as the dance was, though, half of Jack's mind was still calculating. He could not forget the sword of doom that hung between them.

"I have a letter for you," he said, bending his head to her ear as they took a half twirl.

The smile fled from her eyes. "Did you find out something?"

As the figure of the dance separated them, he scanned the room and found that Barrington had returned. He was leaning against a white pillar, looking none too pleased to see them dancing.

"Who sent the letter?" Liza asked when they came together again, lifting her chin to be heard above the loud music.

"We must talk privately. I can say no more."

When she circled around in the dance, she realized why. The viscount was watching carefully for untoward intimacy. How she hated him! She turned to Jack. "Meet me after the next dance. On the terrace, behind the ivy trellis."

Liza knew that was the only place they could hope to find even a moment of privacy. Like Jack, she kept one eye on Lord Barrington during the rest of the dance. He'd ruined their illusion of freedom. To her surprise, though, Barrington slipped away before the dance was over. She assumed he went to smoke in her father's study. He was fond of drinking and smoking, and he'd already had more than his fill of champagne. She could tell by the bleary look in his eyes, and she prepared herself for a good berating. He was always surly when he drank.

The music ended too soon. Jack and Liza stopped where their last step had taken them—behind an enormous white Roman pillar.

"It's over," he said, chuckling as he caught his breath. He touched the back of a hand to his perspiring forehead. "I'm getting old, Miss Cranshaw. I can't keep up with you."

"No, Mr. Fairchild, you simply don't dance enough. I should go," she whispered, her eyes caressing his face.

Her mind told her to let go, to step back, but her heart would not let her. She tightened her grip on his hand and shoulder. His luscious mouth was so close, so dusky and smooth and inviting. His brown eyes beheld her with such intense focus it was as if the world outside his arms simply didn't exist. It was hard to care about what Lord Barrington thought, when she was in Jack's arms.

Jack was hers. When they had made love, they'd claimed each other. This was where they belonged. Close. Hearts pounding as one. The others started jostling past them as they exchanged partners, and Liza realized that at any moment their unwillingness to dance with others would raise alarms. Jack might be her world, but it wouldn't matter in a few short days when her formal engagement virtually made her the viscount's property.

"The terrace," she reminded him, and dropped a curtsey. She walked briskly away before another could snag her for a dance. Feigning pleasure with anyone else was more than she could handle in her shaky state. She went to chat with Aunt Patty, waiting a dance out as she had instructed Jack. Patty sat on a settee near the entrance. She was a sweet-smiling and friendly little dumpling in white lace and pink rouge.

"What a lovely party," Aunt Patty said, pressing Liza's hand and regarding her niece with sparkling eyes. "Where is that wonderful Mr. Harding? Didn't Mr. Fairchild bring him?"

"Papa didn't invite Mr. Harding," Liza distractedly replied while she listened to the music, waiting for the end of the song.

"What a pity. He so amused me. I certainly hope your father didn't omit him because he's merely a secretary. Surely Bartholomew isn't assuming airs. He himself is only a merchant, after all."

"A very rich one, though, Aunt Patty."

"Why, you know Uncle David was a rat catcher when I first met him, God rest his dear soul. And a loving husband he was. I was fortunate to find him. Your mother and I were nearly starving back then."

"Don't say that too loudly, Auntie. Father doesn't like to discuss the past when the viscount is here."

"I do so hope to see that dear Clayton Harding again."

"I will be sure to invite him next time, Auntie."

At long last, the song ended. When the last note died, Liza rose lithely and made her way to the terrace. Thankfully, it was empty. She found Jack at the far end, leaning his hands against the hip-high stone fencing, with one leg jutting out behind him as he leaned over and regarded the herb garden below. He cut a stunning figure in his snug black trousers and well-cut coat. As she approached, she inhaled pungent marjoram and the thick smell of roses that grew up trellises in pots around the terrace. She wanted to hide behind a sprig of roses and kiss him passionately, but they had to plot and plan and use their heads, which were nearly too sodden with feelings to be of any use at all.

"Jack," she said, stopping by his side.

He turned with a start and a delighted smile. "Liza. I missed you. I can hardly bare to be apart from you for even one song."

His sincere frown touched her, and she felt a wave of sad longing. "I cannot possibly explain the array of emotions I have been feeling since . . . since . . ." She turned crimson, then pierced him with a resigned smile. "Oh, Jack, I have never been so deliriously happy and wretchedly miserable in my life."

"Why?" He stepped closer and surreptitiously gripped her hand, squeezing firmly. "I don't want you hurt or worried."

"I know. And I don't want to hurt you. So I will speak frankly, for I want you to know this was not my doing."

She heard laughter at the door and saw Celia breezing by with the baronet's son. Liza motioned Jack to follow. "Let's step behind here where we won't be seen. No telling when his lordship will return."

She tugged his hand until they were safely shielded by a tall and wide trellis of roses. She wanted to tell him the bad news, but she could say nothing until she'd held him one more time. His warm arms wrapped around her and she offered up her lips, so hungry for his she could die.

"Kiss me, oh, my dear Jack, kiss me."

He obliged, and she did swoon. Her knees buckled and he caught her weight. She stood again and ran her fingers up the back of his neck, through his hair. He kissed her, and kissed her again, each time consuming her lips with tantalizing precision. Finally, she pushed him away. She had to tell him. It was the only decent thing to do.

"Jack, I've betrayed you."

He went still. "How?"

"The engagement party has been scheduled for this weekend. I . . . I agreed to the change." She cast her eyes down, then looked up guiltily through a lush row of dark lashes. "I'm sorry. I thought we would have more time."

"We must have more time. Why did you let them do this?"

The air between them snapped. She searched his eyes for the intimacy she so craved. "Please do not be angry. I couldn't help it. Mama threw down a gauntlet. Either end the settlement negotiations or declare my intentions. I could not tell her the truth."

Jack felt as if a giant blade had been thrust in his heart. He could hardly breathe. "I see."

"I want to call it off, Jack, you know that. But I can't without ruining my family."

"For God's sake, Liza," he urged her sotto voce, "tell your mother the truth. Tell her what you won't tell me— the reason Lord Barrington is blackmailing you. End this madness now!"

"No! Then Mama would be obliged to save me, even if it meant ruining the family forever."

"Damn!" He raked a hand through his hair. He forced

himself to take a deep breath. "Do you know what this means? After this weekend, you will all but become Barrington's personal property. He will never let you picnic with me. You will never have a chance to visit Davis or help me investigate the fire."

"But we have the rest of the week to search for clues."

He shook his head despairingly. "It's not enough time."

"I spoke with Celia, and she says she saw Annabelle Davis getting out of the viscount's carriage just days before the fire was set."

Jack looked up sharply. "Davis's daughter? What the devil do you suppose she had in mind being in his carriage?"

"Perhaps he was hand-delivering another threat."

"If so, Annabelle didn't tell her father. I'll look into it." Jack groaned. "Oh, Liza, this isn't going to work. We will never resolve the riddle of the fire in a few days. And we need proof of a crime to cower that bastard viscount. Even if I could find the evidence we needed to end the engagement, after it has been announced your name will be so blackened with scandal you would never recover. Celia would never find a proper match. Barrington is worried that he's about to lose you. That's why he's pressing you to commit. He knows something is wrong. If you can hold out longer, Liza, we can use his fear to our advantage. You've got to find a way to put off the engagement."

"How?" she cried. "Even my mother is growing suspicious. You're asking me to perform a miracle."

"Am I?" he asked pointedly. "Or am I merely asking you to show a little courage?"

She tipped up her chin, skewering him with a furious gaze. "You have no idea what you are talking about. How can you know the measure of my courage until you know my predicament?"

"How can I know if you won't tell me? I can't help you if you won't confide in me!"

Liza went cold inside. Holding back from him was unnatural. If only she could tell him the truth! The irony was that she might have been able to if they hadn't made love. But they had, and now she was thoroughly in love with Jack Fairchild. She wanted to accept his offer of marriage, perfunctory though it was. That could never happen, though, if she revealed her family's dark history. For Jack was very much a member of the aristocracy, even though he liked to pretend otherwise. He was the future Lord Tutley. And a lord would never marry a girl like her if he knew the truth about her past.

"I can't, Jack," she said coldly. "You're simply going to have to accept my judgment in this matter."

Clenching his jaw, he jammed his hands in his pockets, then pulled out a letter from one of them. "Oh, I almost forgot. Here is a missive from Mrs. Halloway."

"Mrs. Halloway?" Liza's eyes widened. "Oh, what a relief!"

He handed over the letter and watched morosely as she ripped open the seal. Clearly this forgery had been a waste of time. He doubted anything in this world short of the Second Coming of Christ might induce Liza to alter her plans. She scanned the missive by the light of a torch.

Jack studied her reaction closely.

She underwent a rainbow of emotions as she read. At first she frowned, doubtless at the unfamiliar handwriting, then she blinked with acceptance, but frowned again and grew pale.

"Ahem. I say, you look a bit dismayed. Bad news?"

She looked up, bewildered, then down again, rereading it quickly. She folded the letter back up, then licked her lower lip.

"No, there is nothing wrong." Her voice was thin and unconvincing. There was a bruised look in her eyes. "I feel as if there is a conspiracy. It seems Mrs. Halloway has had a change of heart. She has been so moved by my letters that she has entirely reversed her former stance. I cannot . . . I cannot account for such a change. It shocks me, truly. I do not know whether I can accept it."

Jack nodded and raised his brows thoughtfully. "I see. Well, Mrs. Halloway must be a wise woman. Perhaps she has her reasons. She knows that plans for marriage sometimes crumble in the eleventh hour."

"Yes, but she's advising me to court disaster, and she knows it. Why would she want me to risk social ruin?" Liza began to pace, making a fist with her free hand. "How could she reverse herself now when it was, in part, her approval of my plans that encouraged me to stay the course . . . the very course that has now left me so desperate?"

"Perhaps," he offered, "she knows what other sorts of ruin await a woman who marries without love."

"No!" She whirled on him. "No, she is not at all sentimental. She is a practical woman." Liza tilted her head, skewering him with a suspicious glare. "How did you know that marriage was the subject which she had addressed?"

Jack cleared his throat and held out open hands in an innocent gesture. "I can only conjecture. You seemed so eager to open it, even at a moment like this, I simply assumed you expected it to address the subject of your engagement."

She did not avert or relax her discerning glare. Jack's chest tightened. He tugged at his cravat, which had too much starch for comfort. He should never have written that letter. He was too close to her now to craft neutral prose. She was no longer bound by polite restraint and was more than ready to challenge.

"Don't look at me that way, Liza, I am simply the messenger."

"I see that I am alone in my determination to protect my family," she said wearily.

"No." He reached out and took one of her hands, giving it a supportive squeeze. "I do not want to see the Cranshaws' good name besmirched. I am only begging you for more time. If you care for me at all, if our time in the cottage meant anything to you, find a way."

She gave him a pained smile. "I will try, Jack." She rushed into his arms, and he held her close, his heart cracking open and aching. She seemed like his lost half, and the only time he felt whole was when he held her. He never wanted to let her go.

"My poor girl," he whispered into her hair. "You can get through this."

She pulled away and smiled wistfully. "I do believe, sir, you have more faith in me than I do. By the by, Aunt Patty was asking after Mr. Harding. I think we might have unintentionally started something scandalous when we left them alone all afternoon." She smiled at her own joke. "I must go back. Wait a few moments so it does not appear as if we were together."

He smiled wryly. "As I recall, we've done this before, on a balcony eight years ago. I think we should be experts by now."

She nodded and slipped out of his arms, disappearing

around the trellis. The sudden emptiness of his arms left
him feeling bereft. He listened distractedly to the sounds
of her departure—the swish of her silk gown brushing
against her striding legs, her shoes clicking on the tile,
then growing faint, the pulsing sound of crickets, and then
relative silence. When it seemed enough time had passed,
he rounded the trellis, only to slam hard into reality.

"Lord Barrington," Jack said, dread choking off the air
in his lungs. Lord, what had the man heard? Had he been
lurking in earshot? If not, why hadn't Jack heard the viscount's boots on the tile as he exited the ballroom and
approached the trellis?

"There you are," Lord Barrington said. His words were
slightly slurred. Jack noticed the red flush of alcohol in
his cheeks. "I've been looking for you, Fairchild."

"What is it?"

"Something I shan't discuss here in public." He met
Jack halfway and they took their stands a foot apart, eye
level, like male dogs with raised fur. "I need to talk to
you privately."

Jack squinted in the darkness. "About what?"

"I'll tell you when we're alone. Let us say in two hours
at your chambers?"

Jack nodded. "Very well."

Barrington drilled him with his cold gray eyes, then
turned tail, leaving Jack with the distinct impression that
the viscount suspected his intended was now fair game.

Eighteen

Jack's carriage pulled up in front of 2 Hanley Street an hour and a half later. To his relief, Giles was in his usual place on the sofa, reading a law book by candlelight.

"Up with you, man," Jack ordered crisply, kicking the door shut behind him and going straight to rifle through the papers on Giles's desk. "For once I'm glad to find you loitering."

"Loitering?" Giles said with mock indignation. "I'll have you know, sir, I'm devouring one of your law books."

"Where are the papers you collected regarding Lord Barrington? Put them away."

"What, sir?" Giles sat up promptly and snapped his book shut. "Has something happened?"

"I'm glad you never made it home tonight, and even happier to find no barmaid in your arms."

"A barmaid, sir?" Giles frowned, sitting up. "You'd

have me go from Miss Celia to a barmaid?"

"Still your tongue, you impertinent wretch. Lord Barrington will be arriving soon. Light more candles, put
away your papers, and try to look presentable, will you?"
Jack glanced his way. "Oh, you do look presentable.
Downright dandyish, in fact. I keep forgetting you're a
new man. I can only hope you'll make a good second if
Lord Barrington calls me out."

"Oh, fiddle, sir, that will never happen. He's not honorable enough to withstand the scandal."

"Make sure he sees you and then make yourself scarce,
but not too scarce. I want him to know I'm not alone. If
there's trouble, I may need you."

"What's up, sir? He doesn't know you are looking into
his affairs, does he?"

"I pray not, though that may be his motive. I trust
you've been discreet."

Giles nodded readily. "I may be lazy, sir, but I am
trustworthy. Why do you suppose Mr. Pedigrew kept me
on?"

"I thought it was your uncanny ability to be related to
everyone in Middledale." Jack gave him a quick, digging
grin.

"Well, Pedigrew is my cousin once removed. Did I tell
you that?"

"Good God, no, though I suppose I'm not surprised."

"But that is not why he hired me. I do have some skills,
you know. I'm glad I'm here for you tonight." He glanced
critically around the room. "Mr. Harding left this place a
mess, if I do say so myself."

Jack resisted the urge to roll his eyes. Disarray followed
Giles like a shadow, and Harding had been showing exceptional patience with the young man. However, if Giles

was now able to see chaos in his midst, it meant there was hope for him yet.

"Do your best. Greet Lord Barrington and send him back to my office."

A half hour later, Giles appeared in Jack's chamber. He was pale and his eyes hammered an unspoken warning. "Mr. Fairchild, Lord Barrington is here to see you."

A crash sounded behind the clerk, and Giles winced.

"Oh, bloody hell!" Barrington cursed. "Sorry, old boy, I hope that vase wasn't expensive. Oh, hell, I'll pay for it."

Giles stepped aside and the viscount loomed in the doorway, weaving back and forth. His upper lip was covered in perspiration, and his breathing was slow and labored. He was foxed! Jack suppressed a smile. He could usually get the upper hand with a drunkard.

"I'm here," the viscount announced, weaving slightly.

"So I see, sir." Jack stood as if nothing were wrong.

Barrington pulled out a jade snuffbox, dropped it, and bent to retrieve it, then put all his concentration on taking a pinch. Sniffing, he glanced around. "The place looks better than when old Pedigrew was around. I'm glad you're here instead, Fairchild. Pedigrew was too bloody honest for his own good."

"And you think I am not?" Jack poured two glasses of port.

"I have my reasons to think you can be compromised." He went to a chair and dropped himself into it. The chair jutted backward, scraping the floorboards.

The intense dislike Jack felt for the viscount turned in that moment to hatred. How dare he accuse Jack of compromise?

"You speak as if you've heard something that would

impugn my honor, my lord." Jack handed him a glass and sipped from his own.

"Indeed." He laughed loudly. "Indeed, I have."

"What have you heard?"

"That you're in dun territory and face ruination if you don't pay a three-thousand-pound debt immediately."

Jack clenched his teeth. This had to be common knowledge by now at the clubs in London. It shouldn't madden him that this scoundrel knew about it.

"That angers you?" the drunk man was sober enough to observe. "You see, Fairchild, you can try to take what's mine, but in the end I will find out all I need to protect my interests. I've"—he paused to belch—"I've been asking friends about you. I learned, much to my surprise, that it is just a matter of time before your creditors hunt you down. All they need to do is find you. You weren't running away from London, perchance?"

Jack's jaw tightened. "No. I fully intend to repay my debt. I simply need a chance to earn the money. Does Cranshaw know this?"

"No. Not yet. I will keep this intelligence to myself to use as I please. Crushing debt always makes a man vulnerable to compromise."

The viscount leveled bloodshot eyes at him. He then tossed his port down his throat and shut his eyes against the collective effect of a night of hard drinking. Sweat beaded on his forehead, and the veins in his cheeks thickened with blood. It occurred to Jack that here was one first-rate carouser.

"You'll never be able to pay such a debt as an ordinary solicitor," Barrington continued, blinking his unfocused eyes. "Not even if Cranshaw gives you a share of the Henslow deal. Fortunately, you're working for me. And I can help you get that kind of money as quickly as you need it . . . for a price, of course."

Jack sat back in his chair and steepled his fingers. "What is it you want from me?"

The viscount kicked his heels up onto a small, oval table. "I want you to remember your place and to give Miss Cranshaw a wide berth. If I so much as smell a whiff of you near her, I will crush you. I will bring you down so far and so fast you will never again be able to rise from the gutter. You'll be in debtor's prison so fast that the sponging house will be a blurred memory."

Jack calmly went to the viscount's side and filled his glass nearly to the brim. "Is that all?"

"No. I want you to handle a difficult matter. It will require utter secrecy. I want you to find out who my intended is meeting in secret."

Jack didn't so much as blink. Any flicker of the eyes, any blush of color, any twitch of the mouth would imply guilt. Was this a joke? Did Barrington already know Liza was having an affair with him?

"You have reason to believe Miss Cranshaw is meeting someone furtively?"

"I know she is," he replied coldly, stroking his chin. "It has been going on for some time. I simply need to know who it is. Do you know who, Fairchild?"

Jack sipped his port and sat casually. "I scarcely know Miss Cranshaw. What makes you think I can find out?"

"You are new here in town. People do not yet know your ways of business. You can investigate without raising queries among Liza's acquaintances. And you'll be discreet because you are my solicitor."

Jack sipped his sticky, potent port, then licked his lower

lip. "I was given to understand that I work for Cranshaw himself."

"You can think that if you like, but you'll soon see who holds the reins in Cranshaw's affairs. It will all be settled by this weekend. Upon my word, Fairchild, you could use a woman yourself. I have a nice little doxy in a small village not far from here I'm growing bored with. She's only twelve, if you like them young. A gentleman with your history should sheath his sword somewhere before it ends up in the wrong place, eh?"

Jack smiled wanly. "No, thank you."

"Oh, yes, you prefer married women. Wouldn't try that here, old boy, the town is too small. But that's your problem, not mine. Mine is a cold, rich little fish. But I mean to teach her what pleases me, and well before our wedding. That way she'll have no choice but to show up at the altar, right, Fairchild?"

He laughed again, a low, cynical sound, then tossed back the entire contents of his glass.

"You'll soon learn that I leave nothing to chance. I have a plan for everything. In fact, I may act sooner than planned. I just might visit Liza tonight." He smiled tauntingly at Jack. "Does the thought of that bother you?"

Jack feigned a lazy yawn. "Your personal affairs are no business of mine, my lord. Have another glass of port before you go."

He didn't wait for acquiescence, but filled his visitor's glass to the brim. Lord Barrington was drunk, but not drunk enough. Jack had to make sure the brute lost consciousness before he could return to Cranshaw Park and harm Liza.

"Here's to your health, sir," Jack said with a charming smile, and his grin deepened when Barrington downed his drink with one swill. By tomorrow Viscount Barrington would have a splitting headache he wouldn't soon forget. And, he prayed, Liza Cranshaw would end this madness while she could.

Nineteen

The next afternoon, when Giles returned from an errand, he found his employer prone on the couch, eating an apple. Jack had whittled it down nearly to the core. He frowned at what remained, nipping away the small white remainders with his teeth, chewing contemplatively with each bite.

"I say, Mr. Fairchild," Giles said lightheartedly, dropping a stack of papers on the front desk, "you've taken my spot. If next I find you in the tavern, you'll be taken to task. If not by me, then by Mr. Harding."

"Watch your manners, you insolent wretch," Jack said without emotion, still studying the core of his apple. "Did you find out anything important?"

"Yes and no."

The clerk ran a hand through his tawny curls and sat down in a chair with as much preoccupation as his employer. No longer a walking rumpled heap, his dashing new clothes made his lanky movements seem graceful.

"I found out that Lord Barrington staggered out of here last night and found himself this morning in a flea-ridden bed in the Red Boar Inn. When he arrived here last night, already foxed, he sent his carriage down the street out of sight, apparently to keep his visit quiet. When he left here, after being so skillfully plied with more liquor by you, he couldn't remember where it was. So he walked or crawled down to the inn, where he promptly passed out."

"Good." Jack stared at his apple core and grinned with the first moment of satisfaction he'd had all day. He'd been ill-at-ease all morning. He'd expected a note from Liza saying she'd come to her senses. When she'd left on the terrace last night, it seemed she was prepared to reconsider. Thus far he'd received no word from her.

The ache in his heart warned him that he was being selfish. He simply wanted her for himself. But logic argued otherwise. Liza was in danger. Barrington was so determined to claim her that he would rape her if necessary to ensure a wedding.

"Where's Harding?" Giles inquired.

"He went to the tailor to have his new waistcoat fitted."

"He's barking up the wrong tree."

"Some men care about their dress, young ruffian," Jack snapped irritably.

The clerk tugged on his sleek waistcoat. "Yes, I understand, sir. I've been utterly reformed in that regard. However, I'll avow that new clothes won't get Mr. Harding any attention from the ladies."

"All the more reason to have a good waistcoat. A lonely man has to have some comfort, doesn't he? Have some compassion, young man, for those unfortunate enough to be older than you."

"I do, sir. But Harding's problem has nothing to do with clothes. He needs confidence."

"Oh, la!" Jack returned. "When you're done giving unsolicited advice, why don't you tell me what in the bloody hell you've found out about the fire?"

"I visited old Mr. Pedigrew at Waverly. His brother-in-law, you know, is a lord with a great estate not far from there.

"Yes, I know," Jack remarked dryly, turning the apple core to make sure he'd done it justice. "Why do you suppose my grandfather engaged him as his attorney?"

"Pedigrew did indeed have some papers on Lord Barrington."

Jack went still, then sat up abruptly, tossing the spent core in the trash. "What? Why didn't you say so?"

"I just did."

"Go on," he ordered, dusting his hands.

"It seems," Giles said, grinning from ear to ear, "his lordship asked Mr. Pedigrew if there was any legal way to rid the Davis property of Mr. Davis."

Jack and Giles shared a significant look.

"What was the date?"

"This second query into the disposition of the property was made shortly after the first. The day before the fire."

"That's splendid."

Giles sank into his chair. "Unfortunately, the day of the fire Mr. Pedigrew met with Lord Barrington in London. So he couldn't possibly have set the fire himself."

"That means nothing," Jack argued. "Barrington could have sent his man of affairs to do the deed. What was his name? Roger. Upon my word, I'd expect no other course of action. Roger was doubtless an ape hired for that very purpose. Man of affairs indeed."

Giles shrugged. "Perhaps, but speculation won't prove your case, sir."

Jack sighed. "Of course not."

"There is one other matter."

"Hmm?"

"I looked closely at the notes and found a paragraph scratched out. The writing was my own, notes I had made for Mr. Pedigrew. I don't know who scratched it out, and I don't remember what I wrote. But I could recognize one word, a name: Beauchamp."

"Beauchamp?"

"Yes, that's the butcher who works across the street from Davis's property."

Jack sat back against the couch and twiddled his fingers. "This Beauchamp would be a good person to talk to, no doubt. He might have seen something the night of the fire."

"I'd have heard about it if he had some speculation on the fire."

"Would you have?" Jack tipped his chin up, looking down at Giles like a stuffy barrister puffed up in his white wig.

"Yes, I hear everything in this town."

"That is only if someone is talking, Giles. Did it ever occur to you that Mr. Beauchamp might have a reason to keep his tongue? Perhaps he was threatened."

"No, that never occurred to me."

Jack wagged a finger at him. "And when it does, dear boy, *then* you'll be ready to become a solicitor."

The door flew open and Jack's secretary entered with a radiant smile. "Good day, sir! Good day. And what a fine day it is."

"Turn around, Harding," Jack said, twirling a finger in

the air. "Let me see your new waistcoat and coat."

"Oh, what nonsense, sir," Harding replied, waving him off with a blush, but he turned around nevertheless. "You can see it is just a regular sort of coat."

"On the contrary. You are the pinkest of the pinks!"

Harding's color deepened. He stopped and smoothed his gray lapels. "It is rather nice, isn't it? You were more than generous, Mr. Fairchild. You shouldn't have really."

"I should have and you know it."

"Do you think that Mrs. Brumble would find this an agreeable shade of gray?"

"Mrs. Brumble, eh?" Giles said needlingly with a teasing look in his eye.

"I'm quite sure she'll be charmed," Jack avowed. "Miss Cranshaw says her aunt has been asking after you. Perhaps you should pay her a visit."

Harding's head snapped his way. "Mrs. Brumble was asking after me? Did Miss Cranshaw say that? I mean, those exact words?"

"More or less. I suspect a visit from you would be most welcome at Cranshaw Park."

Harding exhaled a sigh of wonder and his face lit like the sun. "Oh, splendid!"

Giles and Jack exchanged amused glances.

"Cranshaw Park!" Harding looked down at the letter poised in his hand. "Oh, sir, that reminds me, I was greeted outside by Mr. Cranshaw's footman. He brought this note."

"Good God! Why didn't you say so?" Jack fairly lunged at his secretary, snatching it from his hands. He broke the seal and scanned it quickly.

"What is it, Mr. Fairchild?" Giles asked, straightening.

"You look as if you've seen one of your ancestors at midnight in a graveyard."

Jack blinked slowly and crumpled the note, grinding it into a little ball. "I've been invited to Cranshaw Park this weekend. To celebrate the engagement of Liza Cranshaw and Lord Barrington."

"That's an honor," Giles remarked.

"Bloody hell," Jack cursed. "It's a raving insult."

He threw the invitation onto the floor and barked out orders. "Send word round to my cousin, Harding. Tell him I won't be there this afternoon as we had planned. I have other business to attend."

"Where are you going?" the secretary inquired, exchanging a worried look with Giles.

"To see Miss Cranshaw."

"Whatever for?"

"I'm going to ask her to marry me. And she bloody well had better say yes!"

Twenty

It was a well-known fact that suppositions would be made about a reasonably attractive, unmarried man if he came to call at the home of a reasonably attractive or, failing that, rich, unmarried woman. Therefore, considering that Liza was both, Jack called on Mrs. Brumble instead. Now that he'd raised Barrington's suspicions, he had to be especially careful about appearances. Besides, he suspected he had an ally in Mrs. Brumble, and his instincts proved satisfyingly accurate.

"Good day, Mr. Fairchild," she said when the butler showed her into the drawing room. The doors closed behind her, leaving them alone in the large, pale yellow chamber. The sweet woman, wearing a pretty muslin dress and a white lacy cap, crossed the room with measured steps. "So good to see you again, my dear boy."

"Likewise, ma'am," Jack said loudly.

She stopped in front of him and proffered her gloved hand, which he kissed with special care.

"My dear lady, what a pleasure to see you again." When he righted himself, her eyes were beaming mischief at him.

"Look here, dear boy, no sense cutting shams with me. I know why you're here. I think if we walk on the south lawn, Liza will see you at full advantage. If we then wander into the garden, it shan't be long before she decides the marigolds need deadheading. Is that an acceptable plan?"

Jack's sculpted cheeks broke with a dimpled grin. "My dear Mrs. Brumble," he said loudly in reply, "am I that transparent?"

"Utterly. And you don't have to shout. I'm not as hard of hearing as you might suppose. I turn my deaf ear when it pleases others, but I'm really quite capable of understanding anything spoken in a normal tone of voice if I turn my head just so. When you are hard of hearing, others assume you've lost your wits as well. As a result you hear the most wonderful conversations."

She smiled charmingly and Jack laughed out loud. "Good heavens, Mrs. Brumble, you are a woman after my own heart. Perhaps I should be courting you instead."

"I daresay you couldn't keep up with me." She grinned with enormous satisfaction, her cheeks wrinkling. "And I am a little old for you, though not for your charming secretary. He looks like a man who could use the companionship of a nice widow."

"Agreed, ma'am."

Her eyes twinkled with satisfaction. "I am glad you think so. It saves me from having a difficult conversation with you. Do be a dear and tell Mr. Harding that I will be at Burford's Coffee House tomorrow at four. If he should, by chance, be there . . ."

"I quite understand, ma'am. I'll see it done."

Her powdered and rouged cheek dimpled with satisfaction. "Then shall we proceed?"

Just as Mrs. Brumble had predicted, it wasn't long before their stroll through the garden attracted the attention of Liza. She walked nonchalantly toward them with a basket of flowers. Jack's first reaction was undisguised joy. A second later a wave of hurt and anger washed over him. He felt as if he'd drunk acid. He'd never before known what it felt like to wait on a woman's whims. Oh, bloody hell. He was beginning to think debtor's prison was preferable to this uncertainty.

"Why, Mr. Fairchild," she called out, "fancy meeting you here."

"Liza! What a surprise." Mrs. Brumble squeezed Jack's arm and they shared a conspiratorial look. "It worked."

"You clever girl," Jack whispered.

"I'm surprised she didn't come sooner," Aunt Patty whispered in reply. When Liza met up with them, Mrs. Brumble turned from them and shooed them like flies. "Run along now, children. I'll take a seat here beneath the elm. If you continue through the arcade it will take you directly into the maze, where you'll be safe from view. I'll make sure no one follows. Your secret is safe with me."

She sat carefully in the shade and lifted her quizzing glass as if she were merely studying butterflies. Jack offered Liza his arm. "Shall we?"

When she slipped her hand into the nook of his arm, it felt like a key fitting into a lock. Still, his raw heart beat unsteadily. There was so much to say. So much to do. And no more places to hide or run.

"This way, Mr. Fairchild," she said. She led him through the vine-covered arcade in silence, the chirping birds crying out in poignant relief. Sun blazed intermittently through the canopy of dark green triangular leaves, glinting through with heat and light, lulling them into temporary tranquility. He wished he could take her to some sort of no-man's-land, or a deserted island, where they could stroll arm in arm forever.

The long, arched pathway opened into a box maze of eight-foot-high hedges. Liza knew the convoluted way and soon they found themselves in the center of a splendid topiary garden. A half dozen large bushes had been carved into the likenesses of a hare, a squat troll, a dragon, a dove, and other creatures.

Jack and Liza stopped in the middle of the peculiar living sculptures. He'd meant to start with a lecture, to rage against the insult of being invited to the party he'd expected her to delay. But he quickly learned that when one allows feelings into the act of making love, there is no controlling the emotions that follow. When one submits to the sort of innocence that Liza had offered up like a vestal virgin at the sacrificial altar, one could not go away with a hard heart. One would very likely drown in a sea of love.

He looked down at her shining black hair, pinned up in pretty curls, and felt like weeping.

"What have you done to me?" he rasped, pulling her into his arms. He cupped her cheek and searched deep in her eyes for an answer. "What have you done with my heart?"

Tears came into her eyes and spilled from the corners.

"You have it in your hands," he said hoarsely. "You took it from me in your cottage."

"Did I?"

"What will you do with it?"

She cupped his cheeks with her hands and pulled his head down until their lips touched. It was a tender kiss, full of feeling. She had never felt closer to him, never felt so equal and so confident.

He pulled back suddenly. "You have to marry me."

She took in a long breath, and let it out slowly. "Jack, we've been through this repeatedly."

"This time I'm not asking. I'm telling you, Liza, you will marry me. You can pretend you don't care, but I know better. I will take you for my wife. I had a most disturbing interview with the viscount last night. So I know what is best for you, and you must do what I say."

"What?" Her jaw dropped. Eight years ago he might have commanded her at his will, but she'd grown up since then. "Since when do you make my decisions for me?"

"We'll go to Gretna Green before your engagement is announced." He started to pace. "Lord Barrington can call me out if he wants, but all he'll get for his trouble is a bullet in the heart. I don't care if I have to spend the rest of my life in prison."

"Jack, this is absurd."

"The matter is settled. In fact, I'll tell your father right now."

"No!"

He started to leave, but stopped suddenly and rubbed his forehead.

"What is it, Jack?"

"Nothing," he answered with a grimace of pain. "I will not accept no for an answer. I . . ."

His voice faded and he gripped his forehead with both hands, weaving unsteadily.

"What is it? Jack, are you well? Is something wrong?"

He could scarcely hear her for the sudden pounding that had overtaken him. Damn it to hell, he would do this if it killed him. She needed him now. Marriage was the least he could do for her.

"Nothing is wrong." He tossed back his head and tried to even his wrinkled forehead. "I feel perfectly well. Now, will you be my wife and end this charade, or do I have to carry you to Gretna Green myself?"

His skin grew clammy, and the blood drained from his face. Hot air filled his lungs, and he knew in a moment he would keel over.

"Jack, you look awful. Sit down. Over here on the bench."

He felt her tugging his arm, and he obeyed, grateful for a chance to sit before he embarrassed himself by falling. He sank onto the stone bench and dropped his head into his hands.

"What is wrong?" she crooned, stroking his damp, cold temples as she knelt before him. Then she tipped up his chin with the crook of her finger and burrowed her eyes into his, hers narrowing with sudden insight. "It's marriage, isn't it? The very thought of it makes you ill. You can't even talk about it seriously without the risk of fainting. Jack, oh, my poor darling, I am so sorry for you. It's about your parents, isn't it?"

He nodded and leaned into her when she embraced him. He laid his head on her shoulder and allowed her to stroke his hair as he breathed deep to quell the dizziness.

"My poor darling, we must cure you."

He snorted a laugh. "You aren't the first woman who's wanted to cure me."

She caught his mirth and kissed the corner of his mouth

sweetly. "No, but I'm the first one who will succeed."

"How?"

She crossed her arms and sank back on her heels, regarding him with a slight tilt to her head. "I'll warrant you've never spent more than an hour or two with any of your paramours."

"Two hours on a good night."

"What you need, sir, is companionship. You need to spend enough time with a woman to know you can do so without calamity striking. I don't think you quite trust yourself."

"My family doesn't exactly have a good track record when it comes to love of any sort."

"Even if I agreed to break off with Lord Barrington and accept your offer, what good would that do? You'd simply fall into a fit on the altar. No, whether or not we were meant to be, you must overcome this phobia."

He raised his head. Sweat had beaded above his upper lip, but at least he could breathe again, and the pounding had receded. "How? How do you propose I do that?"

Her eyes lit with excitement. "I know exactly how it can be done."

He adored her pragmatism. Was that all he'd needed all this time, a sensible woman? He grinned in open admiration. "Tell me, my love, and I'll do whatever you say."

"Lord Barrington has unexpectedly gone away for three days. Let us spend that time together. Let us imagine we are man and wife."

He pulled a face. "Then we would never make love and never speak to each other."

"Stop being cynical! We're in the country, not among the *haut ton*. It's perfectly acceptable here for husbands and wives to love one another. Every time you feel ill, or feel like running away, tell me and I'll stroke your head and soothe you until you associate marriage with good things. Do you think you can manage that?"

He gave her a weak smile. "Do you think that will work? I really do want to m-m-m—"

"Don't say it." She held her forefinger to his lips. "Can you pretend to court me now, Mr. Fairchild, and simply enjoy the time left to us?"

He nodded, resolving then and there to enjoy her company while he could, for she was right. He was in no condition to follow through on his offer of marriage. It was time to learn the pleasures a woman offered outside the boudoir.

Twenty-one

n the coming days, Liza and Jacked slipped away
whenever they could. They were always in the company of others, of course, but never with anyone so
watchful that they couldn't sneak a knowing glance, an
intimate smile, or a short stroll that allowed for a whispered conversation.

Aunt Patty and Celia were willing conspirators, always
turning a blind eye at critical moments, and, in Patty's
case, even turning a deaf ear. Even Liza's mother seemed
to be in on the conspiracy. She never asked Liza where
she was after long, unchaperoned absences, and whenever
Jack came to the house, she always flitted around like a
butterfly in spring, smiling and welcoming and then disappearing into a different wing of the house.

With each passing moment spent in Liza's presence,
Jack's very outlook on life began to change. After sharing
a great deal of laughter and confidences, he began to think
of her as the best friend he'd ever had. No longer was she

a woman to be wooed and pleased. She was simply his constant companion and his lover.

They whispered in closed carriages, and were equally content to be silent together, communicating only through entwined fingers. They laughed at private jokes and played cards until late at night with Celia and Aunt Patty, learning to be partners even in that field of battle. Amidst so much happiness, it was difficult for Jack to be gloomy about anything, though the viscount's return was just days away, and Jack's imprisonment loomed in a matter of weeks. Even his lingering sorrow and bitterness seemed to lessen simply for having shared with the remarkable Miss Liza Cranshaw his thoughts and feelings about his parents' deaths.

He almost began to feel as if he were part of the Cranshaw family, and he considered asking Bartholomew if he could borrow the three thousand he owed to Lord Abbington. It would probably tickle Cranshaw to no end to bail the future Lord Tutley out from impending disaster. But Jack's pride would have none of it, and with good reason. How could he help Liza if he were so indebted to her father that he dared not offend him by challenging Lord Barrington's proposal?

Truth was, Jack had no answers and no predictions for the future. All that was left for him was the present, and he was enjoying it thoroughly.

On their third day together, he and Liza traveled with her aunt and mother to Waverly to visit Sir Walter Dewey's family at Fulthrop Grange. They sat in the Cranshaws' carriage side by side, facing the older women.

As Rosalind and Patty chatted amiably, Jack clutched his walking stick, determined to keep his hands to himself. Now and then they shared a secret smile. He inhaled her unique woman's scent and longed to touch the hollow at the base of her neck, taste and kiss it. She was so close, yet so far. This was their last day together before Barrington's return. Would they find time alone? Could he have one last kiss? Or more?

He wanted to simply hold her, but that was too much to ask in polite society, and he thought about Harding's comment that waking up with a woman was a privilege reserved for marriage. If only Jack had been wise enough to offer for Liza eight years ago, he would not be in misery today.

"Do you plan to take a wife, Mr. Fairchild?" Rosalind said unexpectedly before they reached the grange, as if reading his thoughts. The gabled roof of the quaint building appeared in the distance, rising above a mist that had settled along the way. "I hope you do not think me too bold in asking, but the baronet has two daughters of marriageable age."

Jack looked to Liza and she turned her doleful eyes his way. So much was said without words. It was just as he imagined a good marriage to be. A silent communion. He turned his attention back to Liza's mother.

"I never thought I would care to marry, ma'am," he said, "but I've recently had a change of heart. I would treasure the companionship of a good woman. In fact, I should very much like to marry."

He turned back to Liza with a slow, triumphant grin. He'd actually said it without so much as breaking out in a cold sweat.

When they arrived at the grange, Sir Walter and his wife, Lady Dewey, greeted them on the drive. Jack was spared the tedium of being introduced to the baronet's marriageable daughters, as they had taken a trip to a cousin's estate. The laughing Lady Dewey, who put on only the slightest of airs, nevertheless praised her daughters' good qualities all throughout tea.

After refreshments were taken, Jack and Liza followed the others to the field behind the house to view Sir Walter's new stallion. Mist lurked around their feet as they walked along the stone wall that bordered the pasture. Jack and Liza slowed their pace in silent conspiracy, putting distance between themselves and the others.

When they were finally alone, separated from the others by a wall of fog, he grabbed her shoulder and turned her quickly, stealing a slow, sensual kiss.

"I think you've cured me, Miss Cranshaw."

"All it took," she replied evenly, "was a bit of pleasure."

"More than that, I think. You should acknowledge your own contribution to the cause."

"You simply learned that you were sacrificing your own happiness as a sort of punishment for your parents' mistakes. We cannot make up for the past, nor sacrifice the future for it. You will make someone such a splendid husband, Jack."

"It should be you."

She shivered at his certainty. A tiny door opened in her mind, letting a brief flash of light into the morbid darkness. Was it possible for them to be together after all? Had his acceptance of his own desire for marriage changed everything? She had forgiven him, but could she finally also trust him to be there for her?

Sir Walter's laughter rose out of the fog. They would be missed by the others soon.

"When we return," she whispered, moving on, "go to

Birch Road in your carriage and meet me where I fell. Do you remember where that was?"

"Of course."

"It's time I told you why I agreed to Barrington's terms."

Liza could scarcely wait until the visit to Fulthrop Grange was over. When they returned to Cranshaw Park, Jack made his farewells and rode off in his own carriage. Liza waited a discreet amount of time, then strolled through the garden and hurried through the woods to their appointed meeting place.

She walked briskly through the mists to the rise in Birch Road and waited patiently by the side of the road until she heard the rumbling approach of carriage wheels. She heard the crunch of gravel before she saw Jack's handsome carriage cut through the silver fog.

Knowing the risk she was about to take, her pulse pounded in her throat and she felt lightheaded. She could not tell him everything. But even a fraction of the truth would be enough for any ordinary gentleman to have disgust for her. She would risk it only because Jack was no ordinary man.

The coach eased to a stop, and the door opened. He acted as his own footman, lowering the step and exiting, offering her his hand. His coachman waited patiently, eyes forward. Had Jack prepared him for this scandalous little rendezvous? Doubtless, Jack's employees had long ago been trained to look away at all the right moments.

She climbed in and sat on the plush seat, eager for him to join her. He sat beside her, shut the door, banged on the roof, and the coach lurched forward. The momentum threw her into his arms. She'd come to talk, but suddenly she was ensnared in his mesmerizing sensuality.

He pulled her close and splayed a warm hand over her cheek. His lips found hers and he feasted with bone-melting intensity. He kissed her as if the world would end tomorrow, and for her it would. She reached up and clutched his neck, tugging hard, wanting all of him. She nearly burned his lips with friction as she kissed and nibbled and groaned and kissed again.

"You are like a beautiful china doll, except you're definitely not cool to the touch," he said huskily, stroking the creamy skin at the base of her neck. She sprawled languorously across his lap, lolling in his arms, gazing at his sharp and handsome profile.

"Do you know what I have on underneath this gown, Mr. Fairchild?" She tempted him with her heavy-lidded eyes.

He grinned and shook his head. "A chastity belt, Miss Cranshaw?"

"Too late for that," she murmured with a sultry laugh. "You'll have to find out for yourself."

He slowly slid his hand up her leg, around the swell of her calf, over the garters that held her stockings in place. And then he felt hot, silky skin and his knuckles brushed against the nest of hair that hid her secret place of pleasure. She sucked in a quivering breath.

"Now you know," she said, biting her lower lip as he caressed her intimately and felt liquid heat.

"I love this about you, Liza," he said urgently. "I love your sexuality, my darling girl. Like you, it's bold and honest."

She gazed at him from beneath her thick lashes with sultry eyes. "Touch me, Jack."

He probed her moist crevice and smiled when she

arched her back and spread her legs further. "Yes, Jack, that's what I want. That's what I've been wanting for the last three days."

"So much for companionship," he murmured sardonically.

When he slid two fingers deep inside her, she groaned and shut her eyes. He deftly maneuvered, touching a place so deep and foreign it unleashed a primal hunger that demanded satisfaction.

"Make love to me," she rasped.

"Here?" he asked tauntingly.

"Yes." Her voice quivered each time he thrust and parried inside her.

He sighed his acquiescence, wanting so very badly to give her every conceivable pleasure known to man. Still touching her, he unfastened his trousers with his other hand. Then he sat back against the seat and lifted her up, moving her so that she knelt over him, straddling his legs.

She felt the cool air between her hot thighs as he positioned her just so. He slid his warm palms up and down her derriere, squeezing and massaging as his mouth sought her breasts through her gown. He nipped at her hardened nipples, then freed his hard member, guiding it to her opening. As he pulled her down, the head delved into her tightness and her body parted for him. She sank down and took all the hard length of him there was to take.

"Oh, Jack, you're impossibly perfect."

It felt so good, so right to be thus impaled. This was real. This was all that mattered. Loving Jack. Letting him fill her with his honest desire.

"Liza, I cannot seem to get enough of you," he said hoarsely as he squeezed her buttocks.

She rose up slowly, pulling away from the pleasure, then sank down hard again, feeling the stab of him in that deep place.

"I feel the same way," she replied, looking intently in his eyes. There was no mood, no thought, no fear that separated them. The carriage moved forward slowly, rumbling softly beneath them.

He lifted her hips and then pulled her down hard again.

"Oh, Jack, I want you forever. Forever. Forever." She spoke in the rhythm of their bodies, then fell silent as she concentrated on the pleasure. He pulled her down harder, faster, and met her thrust for thrust. He reached down, fumbling through the folds of her gown, and massaged the secret place between her legs. Soon she arched with spasms of ecstasy, one wave after another. Hearing her stifled, flailing cries of passion, he arched, thrusting hard as he growled with painful pleasure, lifting her hips high in the air as he came into her depths. When the last pulse ripped through him, he collapsed onto the carriage seat, sweating, breathless, feeling utterly satisfied. And still the carriage rode on, driving a convoluted path of country roads, as Jack had instructed the driver to do.

In cozy silence, he leaned up and kissed her tenderly, tongues tangled in a soul-deep dance. Then he pulled back and grinned wickedly. "Want to do that again?"

She gave him a half smile. "Are you serious?"

"I suppose we can't drive around forever," he said at last, chuckling deeply. "And you did want to discuss something of great importance, as I recall."

She rose off of him, collapsing next to Jack, and they straightened their garments. Finally catching their breath, they sat shoulder to shoulder, hand in hand, as Liza collected her thoughts.

"Jack," she began.

"Yes, darling lover?"

"If I don't marry Lord Barrington, he will tell the world about Desiree. That is the only reason I gave in to his demands." Liza tried to swallow, but her mouth had gone dry. "Desiree is a . . . a distant relative. She was once an infamous French courtesan, and before that, here in England, I believe she was something far less romantic in nature, a barque of frailty, a trollop even."

She glanced up wincingly, expecting to see the beginning of his withdrawal, but he merely regarded her with patience and kindness.

Encouraged, she continued, "Desiree was even more beautiful than my mother and Aunt Patty. But whereas my mother strives to be proper, Desiree cared nothing for the family's reputation. She lived openly as the mistress of an earl and bore a child out of wedlock. I'm quite sure my father knows nothing about her or the child. I didn't know myself until the viscount told me. That is what Barrington is threatening to expose. I did not want to tell you for I knew that it would mean you could not accept me with such a past. You will, after all, one day be Lord Tutley."

He frowned, and touched her chin, forcing her to look directly into his loving eyes. "Do you know me so little? Liza, I do not care. And neither will Society if she's a distant relation. You cannot be blamed for the actions of someone you never even knew. Every family has skeletons in the closet."

Liza shook her head quickly. "You don't understand. My mother has spent a great deal of time, money, and effort pretending that she came from a well-educated, genteel, and very proper upper gentry family. You heard her boasting in the portrait gallery. If this comes out, everyone will know what a liar she has been. Her whole life will be seen as an indiscreet lie."

"But a distant relative—"

"My mother rarely even talks about Aunt Patty's late husband because he was so poor."

"If Barrington mentions Desiree to anyone, simply deny her existence. I've never heard anyone in the *Ton* speak of this Desiree. So she's not that infamous."

Liza shook her head impatiently. "Barrington says he has proof that Desiree is related to my mother, though the precise nature of that proof remains a mystery. Perhaps he has nothing, but I dare not call his bluff. He has the power not only to ruin my mother's reputation, but to destroy Celia's chances of making a good match. My family would be ruined."

"Liza—"

She turned to him. "Jack, you know I do not care a whit about myself."

"Perhaps you should."

"But I do have to think about Celia. And I simply cannot let my father find out about Desiree from the viscount."

"Then tell him yourself."

Liza bit her lower lip and her eyes glistened. "No. I love him too much to hurt him. The secret must remain precisely that. I very much fear if he realized the extent of my mother's deception, he would stop loving her. And me."

"Not you, surely." When she didn't respond, he asked earnestly, "What can I do to help you?"

She squeezed his hand. "What you've been doing all

along. Be my friend. Understand. Accept my weaknesses. And keep my secrets."

Jack nodded, but his mind was already scheming. He finally had something to go on. He had enough, at least, to bluff his way through some sort of confrontation with Barrington. He would work out the details tonight, for tomorrow the engagement would be announced.

Thank God he'd taken the time to get to know Liza and gain her trust. At last, he was beginning to feel confident that this marriage would not take place.

Twenty-two

The next day Liza gardened in the late afternoon just hours before her engagement party, feeling very like Nero must have, fiddling as Rome burned. She couldn't seem to get her hands deep enough in the earth. The sun blazed down on her back, on her simple gown, and the hotter she became, the more she tried to dig down into the cool blackness of Mother Earth. It was the only thing that seemed real anymore. Other than Jack. He had sent her a note earlier in the day. "Meet me in the garden before supper. I have a plan." What could he possibly have in mind?

She'd felt enormous relief yesterday after telling Jack about Desiree. Of course, she had not told him everything. Not even Jack Fairchild could handle the entire truth. But at least he now knew the nature of her problem. She should have enlightened him long before now. It hadn't been fair of her to ask him to help solve a problem he couldn't even begin to understand.

Ill-advisedly, Liza dawdled in the garden, hoping Jack would come early. No one would suspect she was waiting for an assignation if she worked in the flower beds. No one would imagine that she would dare to meet someone in such humble attire. Her hands, covered not in kid gloves but in dirt, and her gown, not the finest silk or kerseymere but a mud-stained muslin, would be her disguise. Soon her mother would frantically search for her in the house, but for now she had her reprieve. No one would accuse her of waiting for a man she desperately loved.

No one, that is, except for the viscount.

"Liza," he said sharply.

At the unexpected sound of his voice, she gave a start and sank back on her heels, shading her eyes so she could better see him in the sun. "Lord Barrington, what are you doing here?"

His eyes were the color of a dead, gray animal, and his pale lips were grimly set. He stood rigid in the shadow of the full sun.

"Liza, what are you doing in the garden at this hour?"

"Pruning the flowers," she answered simply, reaching for another soft plant. He hated her gardening as much as her charity work. Everything demeaned her, it seemed, in his eyes. At least they were at the far end of the garden, near the pavilion that led to the deer park. This way the household servants wouldn't hear him berating her.

"In three hours our important guests will be arriving for our formal engagement dinner. Why are you sullying your hands now like a slattern?"

Her frowned deepened. He'd never called her such a disrespectful name before.

"You should be readying yourself in your chamber.

You will be the wife of a viscount, damn you. Haven't you yet learned to appreciate the significance of that, you merchant's brat?"

Her hair stood on end and her spine stiffened. "I don't *feel* like readying myself." She cast him a hard blue gaze and returned to her work. "I will be prepared when the guests arrive. Trust me, your lordship. Though I know that is so hard for you to do."

"And you just gave me one more reason to distrust you, didn't you?"

The comment was so triumphant that she looked up, this time in earnest. "What is it? What have you really come to talk about?"

He came around so that she could see him without squinting into the sun. He held out a piece of paper. She recognized it immediately. She tried not to gasp.

"Read it," he snarled when she hesitated.

She took the paper and read the words she had read earlier that day. *Meet me in the garden before dinner. I have a plan.* How could she have been so careless with Jack's note? How had Barrington gotten ahold of it? She'd locked it in the escritoire. She folded the note and offered it back to him with forced ennui.

"Is that from one of your doxies, Lord Barrington, asking for an assignation? Why show it to me?"

He grabbed her arm and jerked her to a stand, then slapped her hard on the cheek.

Her head flung back and she winced, but she refused to cry out. The impression of his palm stung on her cheek, but she would not rub it. "I hate you. Have I told you that?"

"You didn't have to," he snarled, tightening his grip on her arm. "And it doesn't matter. After tonight the world will know beyond question that we are engaged and you will have no recourse. So don't think I will be put off by some indiscreet assignation on your part. And don't think I will give any man a chance to cuckold me. My heir will bear my name and my features, do you understand? You have no choice in this matter."

"Did I ever?" she spat back, wrenching her arm free.

"Of course. You simply knew the consequences of refusing my offer."

She rubbed her arm where he'd twisted her flesh. "How did you get that note?"

"My man of affairs picked the lock on the drawer of the desk. The drawer you slammed on my fingers. I was still curious about what it was you didn't want me to see."

"That is not the note I was writing when you imposed yourself on my privacy."

"No, the note is from Jack Fairchild. I recognize his handwriting. Don't forget he's working for me now."

"I could still refuse you. Even after tonight. Do you realize that?"

"And face ruin in every sense of the word? You won't do it, Liza. You don't have the spine. You're just a little merchant's girl. You have no address. You're of the least possible consequence. In any event, after tonight it won't matter what you do or think."

He wasn't looking at her; he was gazing through her. As if she didn't really exist and were merely a receptacle for his schemes and machinations.

"Come with me." He started toward the pavilion, yanking her along beside him.

She tried to dig in her heels, but only ended up skittering along awkwardly behind him. She turned to see if anyone was looking from the distance, then glanced at his doughy profile. "What are you doing?"

"What I should have done long ago." He took the pavilion stairs two at a time, and she stumbled trying to keep up.

A roof overhead protected the tiled pavilion and table and chairs from rain, and walls on two sides hid the view to the house. Shaded from the sun, it was cooler here. A breeze seeped through her simple gown and chilled her nipples.

"What do you want from me?" she asked when he stopped in the middle of the tile floor and let go of her arm.

"I want what's mine," he coldly replied. He took off his coat and threw it over the back of a chair, then began to unfasten his shirt. "Take off your clothes."

She didn't answer for a moment, certain she'd misheard. Then she laughed in disbelief. "What?"

"You heard correctly, Liza. Don't continue with your prim pretense. Take off your bloody clothes or I'll have to do it for you."

He pulled off his shirt, exposing his white, hairless chest. Liza couldn't have been more stunned if he'd taken a gun and shot someone before her eyes.

"My lord!" she cried, taking a step back. "What in God's name are you doing?"

He smirked. "I should think that much was obvious. I'm securing my right to your dowry. Once I ruin the goods, no one else will want them. You're mine, Liza, to do with as I please. And you'll do well to learn that now. Once I have my heir, I don't care a fig who you tup."

"Bloody hell! You have this all planned out," she said incredulously.

His mirthless smile widened. "Of course. I told you I leave nothing to chance." He calmly draped his shirt and coat over a chair.

"I understand my duty, sir. And I will do as I must to protect my family. I will be your wife in every legal sense, even though the very thought sickens me. But I *will not* submit to you one moment before absolutely necessary. Do you understand?"

"Perfectly."

When she whirled past him, he snatched her arm. Then he yanked the collar of her gown below her breasts, exposing them to the shocking air. She gasped in outrage while her traitorous nipples hardened in the breeze.

"Ah, I see my attention has aroused you."

She swung an arm to smack him, but he grabbed it as well. He looked down and his gaze slathered lasciviously over her pear-shaped, lily-white globes.

"Lovely, my dear. Quite. Luscious, in fact." He yanked her close by the waist and grabbed a breast roughly with his free hand, palming it mechanically. "Feel good, dearest?"

Reeling with disgust, remembering Jack's stories about the viscount's doxies, she jerked free and backed away in earnest. He followed her step for step.

"Where are you going, dearest? I've just started."

"I hate you, Barrington," she hissed as she pulled her gown back up over her breasts. She felt dirty and humiliated. Her cheeks flamed with heat. "God, I hate you. If you—"

She stopped when her back hit the wall and he slammed into her, smashing his chest against her breasts, breathing in her face.

"You need a lesson or two in the art of lovemaking,

my dear," he murmured. "You're supposed to run *to* not *from* your beloved."

He stepped back to unfasten his trousers. "This won't take long. I simply want to destroy your maidenhead and deposit my seed."

She shook her head in furious denial. "What a degenerate you are, sirrah."

He smirked. "Yes, I am." He reached down and grabbed her between the legs through her gown. Liza gasped and slapped him hard on the cheek. The sound cracked in the silent pavilion. The force of the blow twisted his head to the side and it stayed there a moment. He pressed a hand to his cheek, and she cringed, waiting for a return blow, but he surprised her by smiling with a look she'd never seen before—carnal hunger.

"Well, well, you might have some sport in you after all, my dear. What a pleasant surprise! I should have brought my whips."

The wind carried the cloying scent of his clove-scented sweet waters to her nose and she nearly gagged. She could not let his skin touch hers again. She lunged sideways, but he grabbed her arm and pulled her into a rough embrace. He kissed her cruelly, forcing her lips apart and then forcing in his slithery tongue. He raped her mouth with it, and in desperation she grabbed two fistfuls of his hair, yanking his head away.

"Ow! Let go, you slut!"

He grabbed her wrists, but she refused to release her hold despite the painful pressure on her wrists. Unable to free himself, he looked at her with livid hatred. "You little bitch, let go!"

"My father will kill you for this," she spat at him.

"He'll thank me for it. It's the only way he'll get his

noble grandson. And it's the only way I'll get the money I need to pay my debts in the gaming hells. Don't you realize how expendable a woman is in the grand scheme of life?"

He leaned his head down and bit her forearm. Liza screamed in pain and let go of his hair. That's when the blow came. He backhanded her hard, knocking her to the ground. She scraped her cheek on a loose tile and sagged to the ground. God, it couldn't end this way. She had to get away.

When he saw her inching back on the ground like a wounded fox, he bent and grabbed a wrist, yanking her up.

"Come along, my dear. I'm ready now. How did you know that I like to play rough?"

He pinned her to the wall with an arm across her chest while he fumbled to unfasten his trousers with the other. Liza shut her eyes and pictured Jack Fairchild in her mind's eye. He had given her confidence. He had made her at ease with her own sensibilities. He wouldn't accept defeat. There had to be a way out of this. Then it came to her. If she acted like a doxy, he would let down his guard.

"Wait!" she nearly shouted, grabbing his wrists to still his motions. "Don't do it that way, my lord. Let us make this pleasurable."

He stopped and stared at her suspiciously. "You don't know how to pleasure a man."

"I've read about these things," she said, smiling coyly. "Let me try. I'm sorry for being so prudish. Perhaps I will enjoy lovemaking, if you give me a chance."

She gently pushed his hands aside and began to tug at his trousers, unbuttoning his drawers. Trying not to grimace, she knelt down and began to pull down on his garments.

"There are many ways to pleasure a man, my lord, besides fornication."

When his erection bobbed before her, she stifled a gag and continued to pull his trousers down to his ankles. Having accomplished her task, she rose and forced herself to stroke his cheek.

"My lord?" she murmured seductively.

"Yes?" He was literally panting now. It didn't take much.

"I have one thing to say before I proceed."

"Yes?"

"Farewell." With that, she shoved him hard. He toppled over like a toy soldier, but not before his hands flew out in the air, tangling in her hair.

Liza cried out in pain as he pulled her, staggering back to catch his balance. But he couldn't. Not with his ankles bound in his own trousers. He fell backward, and her hair slipped out of his hand. She steadied herself, then began to run.

"Bloody hell!" he cursed as he writhed on the ground, trying to rise.

She did not stay to hear the worst of his epithets. She ran as if her life depended on it. She flew as fast as her feet would take her, hiking up her gown so her legs would be free to make great strides. She zigzagged through paths she knew he would never remember or find his way through until she reached the pond, stopping only a few times to catch her breath.

He never called for her, and she realized with triumphant satisfaction that he couldn't. Not without giving away his attempted crime. Doubtless, he would return to the house and pretend nothing ever happened.

She kept going until she reached her haven. Her little abandoned cottage. She was sure Jack would come after her. Jack, dear Jack. He had warned her that this might happen. He had told her of the danger Barrington posed. She hadn't listened. She'd been too intent on sacrificing herself for her family. But that would change. This afternoon had changed everything.

Twenty-three

J ack strode up the hill to the Cranshaw residence well before the allotted time for dinner. Without horse or carriage, he would draw no notice, and the walk was close enough for comfort. The oak trees at the top of the hill rustled in a pleasant breeze. He stopped at the end of the drive, studying the ostentatious house with a sense of irony. He had come to Middledale to settle into the life of a modest country squire, but he'd immediately involved himself with the daughter of a rich merchant. In spite of his own desperate circumstances, he didn't want a farthing from Liza Cranshaw. She had given him something much greater.

He did not pause long for reflection, for he had much to do in the next few hours. First, he had to tell Liza the details of his plan. After a sleepless night, he'd come to the conclusion that he had to engage the viscount in a private conversation. It would be a verbal card game in which neither knew what sort of hand the other possessed.

The only way to stop Barrington from ruining the Cran-shaws' reputation was to convince him that Jack had enough evidence of arson to ruin his standing in Society. And without divulging that supposed evidence, which was negligible, Jack needed to find out what, if anything, Barrington possessed that could connect the elusive Desiree to the Cranshaws.

Perhaps Barrington was merely bluffing. If he had nothing more than a rumor in his cavalry, the battle would be over. Liza could end the engagement. The party would be canceled. Barrington would not dare to sue her for breach of promise. But until Harding returned from Fielding with some new revelation about the Desiree scandal, Jack would have to assume the worst. The viscount just might have some document or memento that would blow the family apart.

Jack entered the estate through a side entrance into the garden. Avoiding notice, he worked his way toward the maze. He was quite sure he would find Liza waiting for him there because of the privacy it afforded. But when he reached the topiary garden at the center of the maze, he was astonished to find Celia.

"Mr. Fairchild!" she said, rushing forward. "I'm so glad you came."

"How did you . . . how did you know I'd come here?"

"Aunt Patty said she thought you might try to meet Liza here before the party. Oh, Mr. Fairchild, I'm so worried about her."

"What is it, Miss Celia? What has happened?"

"Liza has disappeared. I was hoping she had gone to town to meet you."

"No, I haven't seen her. What makes you think she's run away?"

"She's been gone for hours. The party will start soon. One of the gardeners said he heard someone cry out from the pavilion hours ago, a woman's voice. I saw Liza earlier in the garden. Oh, Mr. Fairchild, I'm so afraid that horrible viscount has done something to her."

Jack's entire body went rigid with fury. "That bastard!"

"She might have run off to her little cottage. Do you know where it is?"

"Yes. I'll go at once. Tell no one where I'm going, Miss Celia."

"Upon my word, you have my utmost secrecy. Please hurry, Mr. Fairchild. Bring her back safely, won't you?"

"I swear upon the graves of my parents that I'll bring her back safely or I'll see Barrington dead."

By the time he reached the cottage, the sun was low in the sky. A breeze began to blow, but it was not enough to cool Jack's burning temples. He was out of breath and perspiring, as much from fury as from his arduous run. When at last he saw the quaint and decrepit stone cottage, he stopped and bent over his knees to catch his wind. He walked the last few paces, the vision of Liza growing stronger with every step. He couldn't wait to take her in his arms. What had that bloody bastard done to her?

He pushed open the door and inhaled the familiar scent of a burning beeswax candle and dried thyme. He didn't see her at first and panicked.

"Liza?"

"Here." She'd been slumped down in a high-backed chair and jumped to her feet. She sailed the distance between them and flung herself into his open arms. "Oh, Jack, I knew you'd come."

He squeezed her tight, his heart full of love.

"My darling, what has he done to you?" He drew back and with shaking hands cupped her face and marveled at her beauty. Her hair was disheveled, her gown dirtied and oddly loose. She had no cosmetics on her face, no jewelry, no flattering cap or dazzling plumage on her head, and yet, she was the most beautiful woman he had ever seen. Then she nestled her cheek in one of his hands and he saw precisely what had happened. She was bruised. The cretin had struck her in the face.

"Damnation!" he roared. "What did Barrington do to you?"

She blinked, startled by the depth of his rage. "I'm well, Jack." She touched her cheek, only now beginning to feel the lingering pain. "Do not fear for me."

"Did he strike you?" He firmly placed his hands on her shoulders. "Did he, Liza? He did, didn't he?"

She squeezed her eyes tight and nodded rapidly. "Yes."

"I'll kill him!" Jack shouted and he stepped away from her, slamming a fist in his palm. "I'll kill him. I swear it!" He headed blindly for the door, fumbling for the latch.

"No, Jack! Don't go."

"I will not let this stand, Liza. I won't rest until my hands are around his worthless throat. The damned blue-blooded bastard thinks he can get away with it because you're a commoner! Hell, what's wrong with this latch?"

He finally managed to fling open the door and bolted forward. Liza ran after him. He didn't know what he was doing. He was so furious he was even walking in the wrong direction, batting at the branches of apple trees that got in his way as if they were foot soldiers protecting the king he would kill on the field of battle. She reached out as he strode with long legs through the orchard. "Jack, come back!"

She caught up with him and threw herself at him. She missed and fell to the ground, grabbing his legs just in time. Jack tripped and fell forward, landing amidst the ripe fruit that had fallen. The scent of apples filled his face, as did the smell of dirt. He felt her crawl up his body, pulling herself along as she lay on top of his back.

"Jack, my darling, Jack," she whispered, combing his hair away from his ear. "You do not have to kill him. It's over. I'm going to end it tonight."

He held his breath, unsure if he'd heard correctly. Then he breathed deep the loamy earth, as the tension melted from his taut muscles.

"Yes, my love, I'm going back to the house and telling my parents I cannot marry Barrington."

Jack rolled over in the grass and stared at her in the orange glow of the setting sun. "What?"

"This can't go on. I must follow my own advice. I cannot sacrifice the future to the past. I do not know what I will say, but I will make it clear I cannot marry the viscount. I simply wanted to tell you before I did it, in case . . . in case the worst happens."

Jack sat up. "I will come with you."

"No. I do not want my father to blame you, for I'm not certain how he will take the news."

"If you're going to do this alone, Liza, then you have to bluff your way through this. You must pretend to know all about the fire. You must confront him as I had planned to. Tell Barrington you have enough evidence of arson to bring him down, and then demand that he tell you what evidence he has to ruin your family. If he admits he has nothing, then you needn't tell your father about Desiree. Simply tell your parents you had a change of heart and you refuse to marry the viscount."

"You expect Lord Barrington to answer honestly simply because I ask?"

"No. I expect him to tell you because he's afraid you'll report his crime to the authorities."

"Why would he believe me?"

"Tell him you've been speaking to the Davises."

"Then he will try to find them and harm them."

"I'll take the entire family and put them in hiding away from Cranshaw Park."

"Do you think it will work?"

"It has to. You want to save your family, don't you? And you now know you can't go through with the engagement."

"Then I don't have to tell my parents anything about the blackmailing?"

"Not if you play your cards right. Come on, Liza. You're a brave girl. You play a mean hand of whist. You can bluff your way through this, can't you, old girl?"

She threw herself into his arms. "Oh, Jack, I love you."

He froze, then squeezed her tight, letting the love heat his cold heart at last.

Twenty-four

When she returned to the house, servants were running to and fro, shouts rose from the stables, and horses came and went. Hounds bawled and a half dozen torches jostled like fireflies in the distance. There was so much chaos that no one noticed Liza. If the search party was looking for her, why hadn't the hounds picked up her scent?

As she cautiously approached the back of the house, she could see that the ballroom was dark. Her parents had canceled the party. But the west parlor was lit up like a blazing torch. Her mother would be there, pacing the floor, worried out of her mind. Liza hurried into the house and entered the parlor without changing.

She found her mother, Aunt Patty, and Celia gathered around a tray of tea. When the footman opened the door for Liza, the women looked up and gasped in unison.

"Liza!" Celia cried out, jumping to her feet and rushing into her sister's arms. "Thank heavens you're back."

"Liza, my darling," Rosalind crooned, coming around the tea table and hugging both her daughters. "I am so relieved. Oh, dear, you're a sight. At least you got away."

"Got away?" Liza asked, spinning with confusion. Did they already know the viscount had tried to rape her?

Soon Aunt Patty was there as well, clucking over her. "And to think that Mr. Davis would do such a thing."

Liza gripped her mother's arm. "Mama, what is this all about? What do you mean, Aunt Patty?"

"Viscount Barrington explained it all," Celia said. "At first I thought he might have hurt you, but then he said that Jacob Davis had kidnapped you. That's why you screamed at the pavilion."

"What!" Liza looked incredulously from one to the other.

"Your father and Lord Barrington are searching the woods for Mr. Davis," her mother explained. "Your father is vowing to see him into the gaol before the night is through. He's already sent word to the sheriff."

"Lord Barrington says Davis is armed and should be shot on sight if anyone finds him," Celia added.

"No!" Liza said, shaking her head violently. "It's not true. Mr. Davis has done nothing to harm me. I must help him at once."

Liza extricated herself from the gentle embraces and started for the door.

"Where are you going?" her mother called out.

"To save Jacob Davis before it's too late." She paused in the doorway and caught her mother's eye. "Mama, I think you should know that I'm not going to marry Lord Barrington after all. But do not tell his lordship. And do not tell Papa just yet. Let it be our secret awhile longer. I'll explain everything when I can."

All three women gaped, speechless, then each uttered a sound of relief, and smiles broke out everywhere. Liza grinned at them all, adoring her family as she never had before. Then she went to the library and dashed off a note to Jack. If anyone could save the Davises, it was the remarkable Jack Fairchild. He would come up with some way to rescue the situation. He always did.

Twenty-five

After receiving word from Liza, Jack left 2 Hanley Street and returned to Cranshaw Park in his carriage. Together, he and Liza returned to Birch Road, then traveled the rest of the way on foot. Fortunately, the Davises' hideaway could not be reached on horseback, and that gave them the advantage over the search party.

Narrowly escaping detection, Liza walked home after bustling the Davises into Jack's carriage. He returned to his rooms and let Giles take over from there. The clerk fed the hungry and frightened family, but no one slept. There was too much at stake.

Shortly before dawn, Jack was ready to depart. They crammed themselves into the carriage and headed to the one place Jack thought he'd never willingly return. Tutley Castle.

It rained all the way, which made the roads rougher than usual. The carriage pitched and groaned on the rutted thoroughfare, and the thudding of rain on the roof made conversation difficult. It was just as well. The distraught members of the Davis family were weary and worn and in no mood for talk. Jacob wore his usual angry demeanor, but his wife was frail, thin, and haunted-looking. Their pretty daughter had the resilient air of youth, but Jack imagined her soft green eyes had once kindled more brightly, and that her disheveled auburn hair had once bounced with vitality.

Tutley Castle always looked nobler in inclement weather. Mist rose and swallowed the green grounds and the first level of the castle, leaving nothing but the upper reaches to rise out of the gray soup. The enormous stone castle would outlive them all by centuries. That fact always managed to put Jack's travails in perspective. By the time he reached the massive front door, he felt more confident about the prospect of helping the Davises. Jack was glad to be greeted by dear old Kirby.

"Master Jack, what a surprise."

"Yes, to me as well, Kirby. I want to speak with Grandfather."

"Very good, sir, very good."

"You sound clogged, Kirby. Are you ill?"

"I've just taken a slight chill, sir. Thank you for noticing."

"Yes, it's as if autumn has suddenly sprung upon us. I have some friends in the carriage. Would you take care of them? They need some nourishment and a warm place to wait while I visit the old man."

The butler squinted through the steady gray rain and focused on Jacob Davis. Jack held his breath. The dirty and unkempt chandler wasn't the usual type of visitor with whom the butler had to contend.

"Do it as a favor to me, Kirby, won't you?"

Kirby frowned curiously at Jack, breathing through his mouth, and wiped at his snuffly nose with a kerchief, then smiled. "Very good, sir. If I take them round to the back entrance Lord Tutley will never know."

"Good man, Kirby. You always were."

"Shall I show you to Lord Tutley's chamber, sir?"

"Yes. The time of reckoning has come."

The journey down the long corridor to Lord Tutley's private quarters felt like the longest walk of Jack's life. He never thought he would come begging on bended knee, but he would do it for the Davis family. For Liza.

When at last Kirby opened the double doors to Tutley's bedchamber, Jack cringed at the smell of old age. He paused in the doorway, suddenly awash in a sea of regrets. Might he have forgiven the old man sooner? Might he have tried harder to understand his grandfather's motivations?

He moved on to the foot of the bed. Kirby excused himself and left Jack alone. The old man was sleeping.

While Jack stood and waited for him to stir, listening to the unpleasant rattling of his grandfather's lungs, time seemed to stop. To recede, in fact. How suddenly and poignantly clear were his memories! His mother laughing in her staccato, almost uncontrollable way with his grandfather. Jack saw her beautiful fingers flying over the keys of the pianoforte, and felt her kissing his forehead between songs, and smelled the rose water that permeated her soft bosom. He remembered, too, his grandfather, having bought material for her on a trip to the Continent, showing it to her, beaming, waiting for a hug of gratitude. Then praising her when a dress was made and she paraded in front of him. She always hugged Jack especially warmly when Lord Tutley was happy.

God, that had been so long ago he'd almost forgotten. He'd almost forgotten how he had basked as well in the light reflected from his domineering grandfather. Then the baron had been a vibrant character, a man whose ruddy, hungry nature made the castle team with activity—hunting parties, balls, dinner parties, card games until dawn. When Richard Hastwood was in a room the candles always seemed to gutter, as if he consumed all the air with his strapping body and relentless energy.

Jack's mother had adored him. Naturally, she had done his bidding, even marrying the man he'd chosen for her. But after her marriage to Henry Fairchild had rescued the ailing estate, Grandpapa had grown disenchanted with his choice for a son-in-law. He didn't think Henry was worthy of his daughter. And since he was such a charismatic figure, used to bending people to his will, he'd expected Jane Fairchild to grow disenchanted with her husband as well. When she refused to separate from her ill-chosen mate, Lord Tutley had punished her by withdrawing his considerable affection. Ironically, this had propelled his stubborn daughter more firmly into her husband's domain.

So what had made her choose the husband she disliked over the father she adored? Perhaps an attempt to establish her own free will. Or perhaps she was trying to force her father to bend to her will by withdrawing her affections. If that had been her plan, it hadn't worked. In the end, both she and Jack had been summarily excluded from his will and stricken from the castle.

What a damned pity, Jack thought, staring at the old man. He could use a daughter to comfort him now. He looked so frail. His eyelids sagged like those of a droopy dog, his skin was corpse white, and his once strong fingers were now reduced to swollen joints and paper-thin skin. But weakness of the body did not necessarily indicate a similar fragility of the mind or the soul. Jack had no doubt that his grandfather would not let Jane Fairchild into this castle today, even if her ghost rose from the grave and knocked on the door. Sadness whistled in Jack's bones, settled in his empty gut. Tutley would rather die lonely than ever admit he'd made a mistake. Just as Jack would rather rot in debtor's prison than admit he needed the old man's financial help.

Jack didn't want to be that way. After making love with Liza and enjoying the fullness of her companionship, he'd learned how true two people could be, how utterly in step with one another. Experiencing such warm brilliance of feeling, he now realized that hatred, vengeance, vindictiveness, and pride were utterly useless emotions. And he reluctantly admitted to himself that he no longer had it in him to hate the old man.

Hatred had served a purpose, though. It had kept Jack from feeling the full brunt of his grandfather's rejection. But the old man couldn't hurt him now. Not when he had Liza by his side. Theirs was a unique world of two in which there was no room for scalding hurt or burning pride.

"Grandpapa," he said at last, though he knew, perhaps *because* he knew, the old man couldn't hear him. He rounded the bed and sat on the edge. He leaned close to his ear and whispered, "I am sorry that you are so ill. The world will be a lesser place when you're gone. You lived life to the fullest, sir. I always admired that about you. I understand that a man so full of passions could not temper them easily. And only now, remembering the past, do I realize that my mother hurt you. You loved her so much that the only way to endure her seeming betrayal was to turn her out. You know, old man, I always thought you did it because you blamed her for her unhappy marriage. But now I think, Grandpapa, that you blamed yourself. You wanted to make it up to her, and when she refused your plan, you were infuriated."

A clock ticked on the mantel. Jack looked at it accusingly. What was time in a moment like this, when everything seemed suspended? When he wished he could reverse time and live it all again with this new understanding.

He didn't know this man lying before him. This man who was once so strapping and tall, now frail and unable to rise. The old bugger had let time get the best of him. Didn't he know he was supposed to live forever?

"I shall miss you, Grandfather." Having said his piece, Jack turned to go, but stopped on his toes when he heard a low croaking voice.

"The bloody hell you will."

The corners of Jack's mouth curled upward. He turned slowly. "So, old man, you're not dead."

"Disappointed?" The word was full of venom, but it bore no sting. "What do you want?"

Jack sauntered forward and leaned casually on the bedpost, crossing his arms. "I'm glad to see you still retain your good humor, sir."

"What do you want from me? You wouldn't have a nice word to say about me unless you wanted something. I know you too well, you worthless jackanapes."

Jack drew his brows together. "In fact, sir, I do want something from you."

He expected a snapping refusal, but the old man's eyes

merely stewed and simmered with a glint of curiosity.

"I have in my care an unfortunate family from Middle-dale. You may remember them, the Davis family. Jacob Davis was the town chandler. He was burned out of his home and business by a nefarious viscount. Now Davis is being hunted down like an animal for a crime he didn't commit. I need a place to keep the family until I can sort out this mess and make sure he doesn't land in debtor's prison again."

The baron's lips widened in a humorless smile. "Unlike you, young man, I don't waste time with people who should have taken better care of their finances."

"Sir, this is a matter of arson. You can't blame Davis because someone far richer decided to burn him out of his home and destroy his business."

"If you had been the grandson I expected you to be, you wouldn't have to tangle yourself in this petty busi-ness. You'd be at Court dealing with politics."

His grandfather began to cough, a wracking that sent shivers down Jack's spine. He took a step forward, but then stopped. His grandfather was too proud to accept comfort from him. Jack nevertheless poured him a glass of water from a bedside pitcher and lifted his head so he could drink. The old man's milky blue eyes became star-tlingly clear. He looked at Jack as if he'd never truly seen him before, then his face softened and he sipped, sinking back in weary relief. It was time to go, but Jack couldn't leave before taking one last stab at reaching through the crusty old bastard's thick skin.

"Grandpapa," he said, putting the glass back on the table. "If I do not help the Davis family disprove this accusation against them, a very lovely and extraordinary young lady will be forced to marry a man she loathes.

You wouldn't want that to happen, now would you? I am begging you. I am humbling myself before you, sir. Please give them a place to stay."

Richard Hastwood shut his eyes. "I will be dead soon, John. But you are already dead to me. You can dance on my grave if you want, but until then leave me in peace."

Jack let out a short sigh. It was a pity, but no longer a tragedy. He silently wished his grandfather well, then turned to take care of the people depending on him.

Without so much as a farewell, Jack walked out of the room. The return journey down the hall went more quickly, for his mind was busy planning an alternative route. He went to the stable and told the coachman to pull around to the kitchen, where the Davises were fortifying themselves.

Giles greeted him at the door with obvious relief. "There you are, Mr. Fairchild."

"Did they eat, Giles?"

"Yes, sir. A fine repast." The clerk led him into the kitchen, where smells of beef broth and hearty ale abounded.

Jack surveyed the warm kitchen and nodded gratefully to Cook, a big box of a woman with a gentle smile. The Davises were gathered around a chopping block, looking anxiously at him for word of their fate.

"What is the verdict, sir?" Jacob asked at last.

Jack scratched the back of his neck. "Well, Jacob, I am afraid the news is not good. Lord Tutley has declined to offer you hospitality."

"Lord, that's poorly done," Giles muttered.

Jack put a consoling hand on his shoulder. "Fear not, Giles. I will not rest until there is a roof over everyone's head tonight. Let's load up in the carriage."

No one moved. The wind had gone out of their sails. How low could a family go, Jack wondered. And on their behalf, he allowed himself to flush with fury at his grandfather's refusal. With a little prodding from Giles, everyone resumed their place in the crowded carriage and the coachman cracked his whip. They had just wheeled around the front drive when a footman came running down the steps, waving at them. Jack rapped on the roof of the carriage and the coachman reined in his four-in-hand. Kirby came shuffling down in the rain, coughing and sniffling.

"Master Jack! Wait! Good news."

"What is it, Kirby?" Jack thrust his head out the window.

"Lord Tutley says you may use High Hill Abbey for as long as you need it."

Jack squeezed his eyes shut. Emotion clogged his throat. *High Hill.* It was too sweet, too perfect. He recovered his composure and reached a hand out the window. Kirby took it and both squeezed hard. "So the old man has a heart after all, eh, Kirby?"

"Indeed, sir. I've always known it. It's the rest of the world he must convince."

"Thank him for me, will you?"

"Oh, no, sir," Kirby said with a laugh, waving him off and stepping back. "I won't mention you at all. He might change his mind if he remembers who asked him for the courtesy."

Jack gave him a smiling salute and off the carriage went to High Hill, the home Lord Tutley had given Jack's parents as a wedding gift.

.   .   .

The ride to High Hill was not far. The abbey lay firmly in the inner sanctum of the estate. Though it was high enough to be seen from afar, the convoluted pathway that led there discouraged accidental visitors. One of Jack's ancestors had purchased the abbey during the Reformation and transformed it into a home. With moss-covered stone archways casting long shadows in the cloisters, and an occasional stained-glass window, it still retained its contemplative qualities and was a tranquil abode.

Tutley's gardeners still tended to the greenery and flowers that beautified the peaceful cloisters, and several fruit orchards planted by the monks of old still thrived on the hillside. The rambling stone building was nestled in woods so dense that the pre-Reformation inhabitants might just as well have been tree-worshiping druids rather than monks.

Jack and his parents had lived there until the falling out. It had gone unused since then, except by an occasional important guest. Jack was surprised to see how well his grandfather had maintained the abbey. It was pleasant to be back here again. He led the Davises to their rooms in the wing that had once housed monks' cells, and then rejoined Giles at the stables.

Giles was patting the flanks of one of the sweaty geldings that had carried them safely here. The scents of tangy manure and sweet hay were strong in the courtyard. Jack breathed it in, and realized he'd nearly been holding his breath since they left Middledale.

"Shall I ride back and tell Miss Cranshaw where you are?" Giles inquired. "I could change the horses at the castle."

"No, I can't spare you now." Jack put his hands in his pockets and looked out thoughtfully at the treetops that stretched like a green carpet down the hillside. "Miss Cranshaw will know when her father and Lord Barrington return empty-handed that I succeeded in stowing away the Davises. Harding is in Fielding. You and I need to conclude our investigation."

"I've spoken to Beauchamp, sir." Giles eyed him with a glimmer of pride.

Jack cast a radiant smile. "Well done, lad!"

"You didn't think I would ignore such an important lead, did you?"

Jack clapped him heartily on the back. "Good man! What did Beauchamp say?"

"He remembers the night of the fire. He saw Lord Barrington's man of affairs running away from the fire. He's certain of it."

Jack nodded with satisfaction. "Good. But he may not be so certain if he's threatened into silence by the viscount."

"He was afraid to say anything before, but he wants to help Davis now that the chandler is determined to stand up for himself."

"Barrington won't back down on the word of a butcher. I still need undeniable proof, Giles. Either that or a miracle from Harding. I hope he comes back from Fielding soon. Meanwhile, I want to speak privately with Annabelle Davis. My gut tells me she may hold a small but critical piece to this puzzle."

Giles frowned. "Annabelle? How could she possibly help you?"

"She may know more about the viscount's misdealings than she cares to admit."

Twenty-six

Harding had arrived in Fielding three days earlier. It had taken him a full day on the mail coach from Waverly to reach the quaint little town in Somerset. He arrived just as the umber sun spilled dark sunlight on the hillsides that rose and fell around the village in a patchwork of green and brown. The town itself sat in the shadow of Huntly House, which was nestled into a nearby hillside. The stunning Elizabethan great house was the seat of the earl of Osborn.

With a determined air Harding exited the carriage next to a whitewashed inn whose name was displayed on a worn, hand-painted wooden sign that read REARING HORSE INN.

Harding appreciated the cleanliness of the cobblestone street, but this was no leisurely pleasure visit. He had to find information quickly. This was the only inn in town, and that would make his information gathering simple. He'd always found that innkeepers knew everything worth knowing.

Harding tugged smartly on his new coat and headed into the establishment. He engaged a room for the night and then ducked under a low door into a cozy, smoky public room filled with farmers and laborers. Though as finely dressed as he would ever be, Harding chose this room over the parlor, where the genteel dined. Common folk would be more inclined to gossip, he hoped. The innkeeper, a man who introduced himself as Mr. Teele, joined him at a rough-hewn table with a pint of ale.

"If ye need anything at all, sir, just let me know." Mr. Teele straddled a bench, nodded his bulbous red nose, and winked at Harding. "Ye're a right fine gentleman, I can tell. Go on into the parlor, sir, and I'll serve ye there. Ye'd have the place to yerself."

"No, no, my good man," the secretary replied. "I was hoping to strike up a conversation with someone who might lead me to where I want to go."

"Oh, I was born and raised here, sir. What is it ye want to find?"

Harding sipped his bitter, warm ale and exhaled with satisfaction. "I can't say precisely. I am looking for someone who hails from these parts. Her name is Desiree."

The chatter and laughter and the click of dice and the shouted orders for more ale continued to mingle merrily in the room, but it was the wary silence from Mr. Teele that followed his declaration that Harding noticed the most. The innkeeper rubbed his chafed lower lip with a calloused thumb and his eyes winked wistfully.

"Desiree. I haven't heard her name in years. What do ye want to know fer?"

Harding swirled the ale in his mug and pressed his tongue against the inside of his cheek. "That's a very good question, Mr. Teele. I work for a solicitor who has . . .

er . . . some family business to conclude for one of his clients. Does Desiree live nearby? Perhaps I could call on her now."

The innkeeper eyed him suspiciously, then he laughed good-naturedly. "I don't think she'll make herself available to ye, sir, if ye don't mind me saying so."

Harding tipped up his chin at the insult, then remembered that Desiree had some sort of salacious reputation. Harding blushed furiously. "I'm not looking for . . . I don't want . . . look here, this is strictly business, mind you."

The innkeeper threw his head back and laughed. "Don't get yer cravat all starched up now, sir. No offense meant. The best person for ye to speak to is Lord Osborn."

"Lord Osborn." Jack had said Desiree was the mistress of a nobleman. "I see. That's her . . ."

"I think ye take my meaning." The innkeeper let out a guttural laugh.

"I'm not sure I'm prepared to speak to his lordship."

"He's an earl, but a fine gentleman who takes the time of day to speak to anyone. A first-rate gent, he is. Go to Huntly House first thing in the morning, sir, and ye can ask his majordomo for an appointment."

"But I don't have a letter of introduction."

Mr. Teele winked conspiratorially. "Just mention Desiree and that will be introduction enough, I avow."

The next day Harding hired a hackney coach to take him to the great house on the hillside, all the while worrying how he would wring out an audience with an earl on such short notice. But if there was a way, he'd find it.

Soon the clip-clopping horses carried him over the cobblestone drive that wended through the meticulous grounds of the enormous Elizabethan mansion. It wasn't until the coachman came to a stop at the two flights of stone stairs that led to the giant front door that Harding began to perspire in earnest. What the bloody hell was he doing here? Did he actually think he was going to introduce himself to an earl and then ask him intimate details about his mistress? The notion was absurd. But he had to do this, for Miss Cranshaw's sake. Lord knows she deserved saving. What a lovely lady she was. She'd make someone a perfect wife. Just as her dear aunt would. Harding stopped on the second stair, his foot grinding into the worn stone, struck with a realization. Why couldn't he marry Mrs. Brumble? And why couldn't Jack marry Liza? Of course, Jack couldn't do much of anything as long as he was in debt, but if he could reconcile with his grandfather, all would be well. Heavens, why hadn't Harding thought of it sooner? He had hoped Mr. Fairchild would become a celibate country lawyer, but that idea was far-fetched. Marriage was the perfect way to kill a man's sexual appetite! And marriage was just what Jack Fairchild needed.

With a renewed sense of purpose, Harding ran up the rest of the stairs, took a moment to catch his short breath, then knocked on the door. It opened at the hands of two fancifully dressed footmen, and he was greeted in short order by the majordomo, a prudish and unhappy-looking man whose displeasure was etched plainly on his thin, gaunt cheeks.

"May I help you, sir?" he said, his lips pursing in obvious condescension.

Harding smiled bravely and tugged self-consciously on his coat, which suddenly seemed inadequate. "I should very much like to see his lordship. I come on . . . personal business."

"I see. Perhaps you'd care to leave a card, sir. The earl is unavailable."

"Ah." Harding bit his lower lip, then added, "That's disappointing. You see, it's about Desiree."

The majordomo's lips remained pursed, and the hawk-like frown appeared to be permanently fixed, but something almost imperceptible shifted in his demeanor. "Very well, sir. Come back tomorrow at one and the earl will see you."

The moment was a defining one in Harding's mind. The word Desiree was the key that had opened the lock to Pandora's box. Suddenly he felt significant. He leisurely agreed to the majordomo's terms and went away happy as a lark. Finally, Jack Fairchild would get somewhere.

Harding returned the next day at the appointed time and waited a quarter of an hour in an ornate carmine-colored drawing room before the majordomo returned and led him to the earl's billiard room. Huntly House had been built by the first Earl of Osborn to receive the enormous entourage of Queen Elizabeth I in the late 1500s. It was so ornate and large that by the time they reached their destination, Harding was completely agog and slightly winded.

He'd never seen so much marble, oak paneling, heavenly frescoes, ancient tapestries, and richly painted walls in his life. There was one enormous stateroom after another, and each one was newly dusted and richly appointed as if the earl were awaiting the visit of the present monarch. The walls were littered here and there with portraits of somber and genteel-looking folk with broad mouths, flat pink cheeks, and long noses. There were paintings of ancestors wearing enormous powdered wigs, monarchs wearing glittering crowns, bishops wearing dignified miters, and government ministers wearing the invisible cachet of power, all of whom had doubtless visited here over the last two hundred years. And now came Harding. He was nearly weak in the knees as well as winded by the time they reached the billiard room.

The chamber was a giant rectangle littered with amusing devices. Scattered over a rich red carpet were card tables, a secretaire for letter writing, and a spectacularly large billiards table at the end of the room. His lordship played there by himself. At the sight of him, Harding felt like shrinking into invisibility, but he reminded himself of the importance of his task and stopped just inside the doorway while the prim servant announced him.

"My lord," the majordomo said in a clear, bored tone, "Mr. Clayton Harding is here."

The earl was bending over the balls and didn't look up until he'd studied them thoroughly and then made his next shot. The click of one billiard ball striking the other resounded pleasantly in the silence that followed. The earl watched to see where they would come to rest. Satisfied, he rose to his full height and turned to regard Harding, leaning lightly on his cue.

He had a kind, aristocratic face, one that must have been terribly handsome in his youth. There were deep vertical lines grooved into his leathery cheeks, indicating a tendency toward broad smiles. His hair was a short mixture of gray and copper, and his face and hands were dusted with rusty freckles.

He had a manly, though meticulous, air about him, and was pleasantly dressed in a silk robe and trousers. He was not afraid of looking a man in the eye, and he did so with a powerful presence now. It was all Harding could do to keep from gulping.

The earl reached in his pocket and pulled out an amethyst and crystal snuffbox. "Welcome, Mr. Harding. Do you take snuff?" His voice was gruff and friendly.

"No, my lord." Harding took the opportunity to snatch a breath and relax as he came forward. "It is a gentlemanly fashion in which I do not indulge."

The earl considered this a moment, then nodded, dropping it back in his pocket without indulging himself. "Tea? I take it you do drink tea?"

"Of course, sir. I'd be most delighted."

The earl waved a hand at the puffy majordomo. "See to it, Hilary."

Osborn put aside his cue and motioned for Harding to join him at two matching armchairs by the fireplace. They sat and the earl stared at him for an uncomfortable moment before speaking.

"I must tell you, Mr. Harding, that no one has asked me about Desiree in a long time."

It was an opening gambit that Harding knew was designed to elicit information while divulging as little as possible in return. The earl's warm but sophisticated eyes watched him closely for his reaction.

When Harding played it coolly, the earl added, "What did you want to know about Desiree?"

Harding cleared his throat. "Well, sir, I come on the behest of my employer, Mr. John Calhoun Fairchild. He's a solicitor and the grandson of Lord Tutley."

"Hmmm." The earl grunted his approval. "Go on."

"I cannot say much, for in truth I know little, but Mr. Fairchild would like to know more about Desiree. In fact,

I should very much like to meet with the lady in question myself on his behalf."

"That's impossible." He rubbed his nose with a forefinger.

"I assure you, my lord, that I will be most discreet. I simply need to know . . ."

"Mr. Harding, Desiree has been dead for twenty-five years."

". . . if anything . . ." Harding was slow to register this intelligence, but petered to a stop when it penetrated. "Dead? Desiree is dead?"

The earl nodded and then looked out the window, where a soft rain was beginning to fall. In the laden silence that followed, an aging butler brought in a tea tray and set it on the low table at their feet. As he poured two cups, the sound of liquid filling china sputtered then quieted. He left without remark and the earl dragged his attention back into the room.

"I was so fond of her," he said sadly, taking his cup and sipping while Harding collected his own. "Why do you want to know about her now after all these years?"

Harding sat forward. "You see, my lord, Mr. Fairchild believes he's dealing with her relations."

The earl's features sharpened at this news. "What sort of relations?"

Harding shrugged apologetically. "I cannot tell you yet, sir, it is a most private matter. But I will tell you everything I can as soon as possible."

The earl's intelligent eyes stewed over this a moment, then he nodded.

"Very well, Mr. Harding, I will tell you everything I can. At this point in time I have nothing to lose and everything to gain. Desiree died twenty-five years ago; I believe it was during childbirth." His voice had thinned measurably. "I am embarrassed to say I do not really know. It is no secret that she was my mistress. Even my wife knew this and accepted it. I had set Desiree up at Sheffield Keep, one of my holdings a few miles from here.

"Though she was of humble birth, the daughter of an English costermonger, she became well known in Paris at a young age as a courtesan. It was her exceptional beauty that raised her from the ash heap like a phoenix. I fell in love with her during my tour and lured her to England when I was still romantic enough to do such impractical things. I would have married her, I was that madly in love, but my father pressured me into a more appropriate match. I still kept Desiree as my mistress, and still loved her.

"I believe that Desiree died giving birth to my child. A daughter. And I have reason to believe the girl is alive today. However, I cannot find her. Everything I know I learned from overhearing Desiree's housekeeper talking at Sheffield Keep. She quit when she realized I was wise to the child. She lives here in town, but she's no longer in service and refuses to speak with me about anything personal in nature."

Harding hung on his every word.

"I believe the housekeeper helped Desiree give birth to my child, and then placed the baby in a home after Desiree died."

Harding quickly calculated. This had all happened twenty-five years ago. That would make Lord Osborn's child a contemporary of Miss Cranshaw's. *Liza Cranshaw.*

Just as the large clock in the corner struck the half hour, a thunderous thought struck the secretary. The notion was so sudden and so profound that his limbs went numb and his face went pale.

"Sir, do you know your daughter's name?" The secretary drank like a man in a desert. The tea soothed his frayed nerves.

"No. I never saw my daughter. I simply heard Mrs. Halloway's whispered conversation about her after Desiree's death. I latched on to this news eagerly, for my wife had no children, then or after. If I were to find this child, I would be willing to legitimize her and leave her my fortune. She may not even know her true identity."

Harding nearly choked on his tea. "Excuse me, sir, did you say Mrs. Halloway?"

"Yes. That was the housekeeper. Do you know her?"

"I've heard of her. She's been writing to Desiree's relations."

The earl steadied his cultured gaze on the secretary. "Do you think one of those relations is my daughter, Mr. Harding?"

"I . . . I'm not certain, sir. It's possible," Harding hedged, while secretly he would lay odds on it. It all fit. Mrs. Halloway had placed Desiree's baby with the Cranshaw family. And that baby was Liza. Apparently Lord Barrington had discovered the secret, and Liza was trying to spare her adoptive parents the scandal. No wonder Miss Cranshaw had been confiding in Mrs. Halloway. The housekeeper was the only one whom she could trust with her secret—that she was illegitimate, a nobleman's by-blow.

Lord Osborn fell silent and sipped his tea thoughtfully, then turned his gentle, yet penetrating gaze on Harding again. "I accepted your call, Mr. Harding, because I thought that perhaps you had come about my daughter."

Harding placed his cup in his saucer and looked up with regret. "I am sorry, my lord. I do not bring such good tidings. And my business must be private, for my employer is a solicitor and must abide by strict confidentiality. All I can say is that the name of Desiree has been whispered in Middledale. Mr. Fairchild can tell you more when the whole mess is put to rest. However, if you have a portrait of Desiree, I'd like to see it. If I learn anything of your daughter, perhaps it will be through seeing a similarity to her mother?"

"Over there." He pointed to the far wall. Harding saw yet another stately portrait, yet this one was of a fetchingly beautiful woman. It was a small canvas, no more than a foot tall, and it was strangely placed, slightly off center, as if it had once hung as a pair with another painting.

"Come and see for yourself how beautiful she was," the earl said and guided Harding to the other side of the room.

The secretary looked up in amazement. The woman in the painting had snow-white skin and dark blue exotic eyes. Her hair was white as well. She wore a powdered wig, which was fashionable in those days. Her waist was tiny and accentuated by her corset and gown, and she looked wistfully and serenely at whomever dared to hold her stare.

"She truly is . . . er, was . . . magnificent," Harding said. And he did see a resemblance to Liza Cranshaw, though he would keep that tantalizing detail to himself for the time being.

"Yes. Desiree was the most beautiful woman I have ever known." The earl crossed his arms, as if realizing it again for the first time in a long while. Then he caught

Harding's attention shifting to the empty spot next to the picture, where there remained the faint outline of a square of exactly the same proportions. "That was where I had hung another portrait of Desiree. But it was stolen last year. They were both painted by the artist Thomas Lawrence. He's becoming quite famous. The pictures would bring in a generous price were they to be sold."

"One was stolen? What a pity."

The earl warmed to the empathy Harding displayed. "Indeed. Particularly because it was stolen by a viscount, of all people. A young man with so little conscience he reflects poorly on his peers. I took him in as a guest because I know his father, but the young scoundrel made off with this portrait. No doubt to pay off gambling debts or to lose himself in an opium den. He had that look about him. I've kept quiet about it out of respect for his father, the Marquess Perringford."

Harding began to tingle all over. All the pieces of the puzzle were hurtling into place at a dizzying speed. "Excuse me, sir, I do not mean to be impertinent, but was it, by any chance, Lord Barrington?"

Osborn looked down at him with a powerful frown. "Yes, by Jove. Look here, sir, I think it's time you told me your true purpose here."

Harding looked him square in the eye. "My lord, I would not be worthy of my position if I did not keep my employer's secrets. However, I can say I believe I may have some information about your daughter, and perhaps even about your painting. It is simply a guess on my part, but I can assure you that I will tell you anything that I know once Mr. Fairchild is done dealing with that scallywag of a lord. I may know the merchant family who took in your daughter and raised her as their own. And once I am sure of my suppositions, I promise to write. Is that fair enough, my lord?"

"I suppose it will have to be. Since I had given up hope of ever finding her, any help you can give me will be a boon." A slow smile blossomed on his firm lips. "Now let us finish our tea. You bring the best news I've had in years. I want to savor this moment as long as I can."

Twenty-seven

Harding spent the night at the Rearing Horse Inn and returned to Middledale the next day. The earl insisted on sending him home in a luxurious barouche so plush and richly appointed that Harding was glad pride had not necessitated a refusal. Of course, he never let pride get in the way of comfort. If only Mrs. Brumble were here to enjoy it as well. The seats were almost downy and he felt like a king riding alone with four horses carrying him to his destiny.

Harding thought long and hard about his interview with the earl. He'd been stunned by Osborn's revelations. Barrington's theft of the portrait clearly confirmed that this Desiree was the woman whom Miss Cranshaw had referred to in her letters. Barrington was apparently using the portrait to blackmail her into marriage. And Harding was all but certain that Miss Cranshaw had neglected to tell Jack the truth. She had to be Lord Osborn's daughter. Harding could scarcely wait to tell Mr. Fairchild.

Lord Osborn's carriage deposited Harding in Middle-dale at sundown. He was disappointed to discover that the solicitor and his articled clerk were gone. A brief note indicated they had gone to Tutley Castle under a dramatic turn of events. Harding would hire a horse tomorrow and meet them there, but it would be too dangerous to set out after dark with no outriders.

He spent a restless night at 2 Hanley Street and rose early to tend to some pressing business for Bartholomew Cranshaw. After all, Mr. Fairchild still had his debts to pay and a living to earn. It was midmorning by the time Harding gathered up his hat. He was just about to depart when there was a knock on the door. Irritated by the interruption, he momentarily considered ignoring it and slipping out the back, but his sense of responsibility would not allow it.

"Just a moment." Harding scooted to the door and opened it. It took a full five seconds to realize precisely who had come. When he did, his heart nearly stopped.

The first thing he noticed were her eyes. They were a deep, sapphire blue and a lilting, oval shape. Though heavier than before, her face was utterly feminine. She was very beautiful, though in a more matronly fashion than before. There was something else that didn't quite match her portrait. What was it? Ah, yes, her hair! She no longer wore a powdered wig; rather, she boasted her own natural brown color, streaked with gray, pulled up with combs into a chignon. If Harding had not visited Huntly House yesterday, he would not have known today that this woman was Desiree. Desiree, the French courtesan, standing in his very midst. She was like a ghost come to life. Apparently the earl had been misled. Desiree was very much alive.

Harding cleared his throat with effort. "Er ... good day, ma'am, or miss, or ..." He cleared his throat and blushed furiously. "Have we had the pleasure?"

She smiled warmly. "No. Is Mr. Fairchild in?"

"No, I am afraid not. I'm his secretary, Clayton Harding. Would you like to make an appointment to see Mr. Fairchild?"

"Yes, that would be very nice indeed, thank you."

"May I ask who is calling?"

"Of course. My name is Rosalind Cranshaw."

Twenty-eight

J ack and Giles spread out their papers on a desk inside the old abbot's quarters at High Hill as if preparing for a military campaign. They were trying to analyze precisely what evidence they did or did not have against Lord Barrington. As Giles sat at the desk and flipped through papers with a frown on his forehead, Jack scratched the back of his neck and paced with an uncomfortable combination of stubborn rage and helplessness that churned like bad porridge in his belly. Not even the historic dignity of this room could give him comfort.

The stone chamber had vaulted ceilings and dark beams that harkened back to bygone days when warriors and priests ruled the land. The world Jack lived in was a safer, easier place in which to live, but infinitely more complex. He had to conquer a nobleman without firing a single shot or raising a sword. Without money or a title or political connections, he had few weapons with which to fight this battle, only stubborn indignation, and the law.

"There has to be something more substantial," Jack muttered, running his hand around the back of his taut, muscular neck. He wore only a loose shirt and breeches, and yet he was burning up with frustration. A gentle breeze sailing through the open, mullioned windows did little to cool him.

"It all points to Barrington, sir," Giles replied. "Especially now that we have Beauchamp's account."

There was a knock on the door.

"That would be Annabelle Davis," Giles said, going to open it. "I asked her to come down after she had bathed and changed into the clothing Lord Tutley's housekeeper sent over."

Jack slipped on his waistcoat while Giles opened the door. Annabelle stood there with a look of trepidation. Her recently washed hair fell in loose, moist waves down her back. Freshly scrubbed, Jack realized for the first time just how lovely she was. Her green eyes were almost translucent and her skin glowed pink. But dark smudges beneath her eyes spoke of sleepless nights, and a tremor of fear in her smile touched Jack deeply.

"Miss Davis, do not be afraid," he said warmly, leading her in with a gentle touch to her elbow. "I simply want to talk to you in the hopes that you might be able to help your father out of his predicament. Would you be willing to speak with me?"

She hesitated, then nodded.

"Sit here at the table, Miss Davis, won't you, please?" Jack said kindly. He pulled out a chair for her, then he and Giles took seats as well.

"What is it you need from me?" Annabelle said in a sweet, rich voice that was stronger than Jack might have expected. Thus far they'd only exchanged cursory greetings. "I've told my father everything I know. I don't know who set the fire. I don't know why you expect me to know. It's as if you all believe it's my fault."

Jack was taken aback by her defensiveness. He would have to proceed gently. "Miss Davis, we believe nothing of the sort. This is a very complex matter. In a very strange and convoluted fashion, the crime against your family may be tied to an attempted crime against Miss Cranshaw."

Annabelle's gaze shot up at this. Jack was heartened to see concern for Liza melting her defenses. "Miss Cranshaw? Has she been hurt?"

Jack leaned back and crossed a leg over the other knee. "No, but she might very well have been hurt if she hadn't been prepared to defend herself. And that is what I'm asking you to do, my dear lady, defend yourself and your family. To that end, I'd like you to tell me everything you can about Viscount Barrington."

She jerked as if he'd just scalded her. Then she flew to her feet. "I told you, I've done everything I can. I know nothing that I haven't already told my father."

Her hands went protectively and unconsciously to her abdomen, and a cold realization washed over Jack. He turned to Giles and said quietly, "Leave us, won't you? Watch the door. I want to speak privately with Miss Davis. Make sure no one overhears us."

"Very good, sir," Giles said unquestioningly, then did as he'd been instructed.

Jack leaned forward, resting his arms on the table. "Miss Davis, won't you please sit? While I do not want to distress you, I must speak very frankly with you, for the good of Miss Cranshaw and your family."

A wild look of sorrow flitted over her face, then that

cool mask returned and she sank back in her chair with obvious reluctance. "How can I help you?"

"I believe that Lord Barrington is responsible for the fire that destroyed your father's shop."

She speared him with her enigmatic eyes. Then she shuddered with an emotion he couldn't identify. Remorse? Hatred?

"I also have reason to believe," Jack added carefully, "that he has taken great advantage of young women in the past."

Her face went blank, and she turned her gaze to him as the tears poured down her cheeks. "You know, then."

"I do not know anything, my dear Miss Davis, but I can well imagine."

"You are a solicitor?" she asked.

"Yes, and everything you say to me will be confidential. I swear to you, upon my honor."

She nodded, and her sweet little mouth that curved like an archer's bow began to tremble. "He forced me." Her tear-filled eyes darted back and forth as if the event were taking place in front of her now. "He took advantage of me. He offered me a ride in his carriage when I was walking in the woods. I am so ashamed that I accepted. But I thought he was a great lord doing a small kindness. It was snowing and I was so cold. He . . . he did it in the carriage on the way to my father's shop. A month later, I went to the same place, hoping to catch him. I stopped his carriage in the woods and told him that . . . that I was increasing. That was when the threats began. He told me if my family didn't leave Middledale, he would ruin my father. He said he was going to marry Miss Cranshaw and didn't want anything to get in the way of his good fortune. I tried to tell Papa that we should leave town, but I could not tell him why . . . and then the fire destroyed everything."

She took a sniffling breath and smoothed away her tears. Jack produced a kerchief and she silently took it, dabbing her eyes as she sniffed.

"Thank God I lost the child," she said. "My parents still do not know. I beg you, Mr. Fairchild, do not tell them."

"Of course not, my dear Miss Davis. Your secret is safe with me. I only ask your permission to speak about it with Lord Barrington."

"Oh, no! He'll kill my father if he finds out I've spoken to you."

"No," Jack reassured her. "I will use this intelligence to back him into a corner. I am a solicitor, Miss Davis. I know how to use the law to my advantage, and Lord Barrington knows it. In my hands, evidence of rape and arson will be enough to cow even a criminal nobleman. Will you trust me on this?"

She took in a slow, quivering breath, then nodded.

"I doubt very much it will be necessary, but would you be willing to accuse the viscount if that is what it takes to vindicate your father and free Miss Cranshaw from Lord Barrington's blackmailing scheme?"

She thought for some time, then nodded with resignation. "If I must, I will. I have no chance of marriage without a dowry in any event. What difference will it make if my reputation is ruined? All I ask is that you make him pay, Mr. Fairchild. Please make him pay."

"Oh, you can count on that, my dear Miss Davis." Jack grinned darkly. "I will make him pay with relish."

At last Jack had a crime with a witness who had plenty of reason to point the finger at Lord Barrington. Annabelle

Davis was no doxy to be dismissed out of hand. She had been a virtuous young woman whose hopes of finding a decent match had been utterly ruined. And Barrington knew her accusations would hold weight. That's why he'd tried to drive her family out of town. Jack finally had the trump card he'd been waiting for, and he could scarcely wait to play his hand.

"Incredible news, sir! Absolutely staggering!" Harding burst into the abbot's quarters an hour later just as Jack and Giles had finished a light meal of cheese and bread.

"Harding!" Jack strode across the room and gave him a bear hug. "God, you're a wondrous sight. What did you learn in Fielding? Come in, come in."

"The most incredible turn of events, sir. I—" Harding stopped short when he spotted Giles, then he winced with regret. "I'm ever so sorry, Mr. Honeycut, but this matter is most confidential in nature."

Giles nodded agreeably, but not before a flash of disappointment shone in his guileless eyes. "I understand."

"Fear not, Giles, I'll tell you everything I can," Jack said placatingly. "Let Harding tell me what he knows and I'll sift through it all and enlighten you later."

"Very good, sir." Giles stood and smiled. "I would expect no less of you than utter confidentiality."

Jack watched him go with a sense of satisfaction. He turned to Harding. "I believe, old boy, we have a solicitor in the making in that young man. Now, what is it you've discovered?"

"Sit down," Harding ordered him, pacing anxiously. "Over here on the sofa. I want to see you clearly when I tell you this."

Jack did as he was told, sinking down anxiously on the

sofa. "Lord, Harding, end the suspense, will you? What is it?"

"Are you prepared for this?"

"Yes, I believe so."

Harding stopped dead in his tracks, sank down next to Jack, and said, overenunciating, "Liza Cranshaw is the daughter of Desiree!"

Jack's face slowly congealed into a stunned scowl. *"What?"*

"Yes, Liza is the daughter of Lord Osborn and his mistress Desiree."

"Good God!"

"It's even more incredible than that, sir. Desiree is none other than *Rosalind Cranshaw!*"

Jack's jaw dropped. He squinted, picturing Liza's mother in his mind's eye. "The plump and harmless Rosalind Cranshaw was a courtesan? No! It can't be!"

"It's true, sir. I spoke with Lord Osborn himself. He's been looking for Liza all these years. He thinks Desiree is dead. He wants to make Liza the heir to his fortune."

Jack sank back in his chair, thunderstruck. "No wonder Liza went to such extremes to protect Desiree. She could not expose her own mother as a Cyprian." And Liza understandably was reluctant to admit to Jack that she was a nobleman's by-blow. Illegitimate. The poor darling. She'd kept such a heavy burden all to herself.

"I cannot fathom any more astounding revelations," Jack said, wiping a hand over his exhausted features. "I wondered why Liza had been so concerned about a distant relation, as she called Desiree. But, Lord, I cannot imagine Rosalind Cranshaw . . ."

He could not even say it aloud. He looked up at Harding with an odd expression. "You don't suppose Mrs. Brumble was also . . ."

"Sir!" Harding replied indignantly. "Of course Mrs. Brumble wasn't a courtesan."

Jack shrugged. "Of course not. Forgive me. But at this point it seems anything is possible!"

"I'm beginning to understand the picture now that the pieces are falling into place," Harding said, rubbing his hands together. "Lord Osborn made an offhand remark about Desiree's humble background. I gather that Mrs. Cranshaw and Mrs. Brumble were very poor as children. That would explain Mrs. Brumble's marriage to a lowly rat catcher. Mrs. Cranshaw faired better because of her extraordinary beauty. But her low-class status meant she could never be more than a mistress to any nobleman."

"I wonder, why did she cast off what some might consider an enviable position? There are worse things than being an earl's mistress," Jack mused, stroking his chin.

"I daresay she wanted to give Liza a better life. It would be better for Liza to be a rich merchant's daughter than a nobleman's side-slip."

"How do you suppose Barrington learned of all this?" Jack mused.

Harding crossed his arms over his barrel of a belly. "I'm guessing he met the Cranshaws in Middledale, and when he visited his father's old friend at Huntly House, he recognized Mrs. Cranshaw's likeness to the portraits. The jackanapes actually stole the painting, apparently to use it in his blackmailing scheme. Lord Osborn says the only reason he didn't make a fuss over the theft was out of respect for Perringford, Barrington's father."

"Do you suppose Osborn would accuse Barrington of theft if he thought it would benefit Liza?"

"I daresay he would. He was furious with Barrington. Called him a scoundrel. And he's very eager to reunite with Miss Cranshaw. I should think his lordship would do anything to help you, since you've been helping his daughter. Especially if it meant his daughter could disentangle herself from that ass."

"Splendid!" Jack shouted and jumped up. "The evidence of Barrington's crimes is starting to stack up."

If Lord Osborn was willing to accuse Barrington, Jack could spare Annabelle Davis a public spectacle. Jack was prepared to confront Lord Barrington immediately. He mounted up on a fast horse an hour later and had just started down the road to Cranshaw Park when he saw a coach approaching. His heart leapt when he recognized it as Cranshaw's. The chariot slowed and Liza thrust her head out the window as she had that first day in Middledale. Her cornucopia of black curls gleamed in the sunlight. She wore no hat this time, and the sun hit her full in the face, making her dazzling eyes gleam and bounce with life.

"Are you well, sir?" she said, gently mocking their first encounter. "Are you hurt?"

He grinned slowly, ravishingly. "If I say I am, will you linger to tend my wounds?"

"Yes," she answered, smiling broadly.

He dismounted, handing his reins to the coachman, and entered the barouche, sinking down beside her and taking her into his arms. They hugged tight, and he felt the familiar surge of heat and happiness.

"It didn't work, Jack," she said at last, drawing away to look at him. "I confronted Barrington, but I do not have your diplomatic skills. He did tell me he has a portrait of Desiree, but he did not believe that I had any proof of his crimes whatsoever. He's threatening to take the portrait to auction in London if I don't run off to Gretna Green with him immediately. The sale of that painting will stir up the scandal I was hoping to avoid."

Jack took both her hands in his. "Liza, my darling, I know all about the portrait."

Her brows pinched in surprise. "You do?"

He nodded, kissing her cheek. "Yes, and I know all about Desiree."

Panic flashed in her eyes.

"Do not worry, Liza. It means nothing to me. The scandal . . . none of it."

"But how—?"

"Harding went to Fielding and met with your father, Lord Osborn."

She blinked back tears and cast her eyes down. "Oh, Jack, I'm so sorry."

"I'm not," he said firmly, lifting her chin with a forefinger. "Do you hear me? My offer for you still stands. And I finally have the evidence against Barrington that I need. Now let us go back to Cranshaw Park together and end this debacle once and for all."

He was awarded with her full and complete embrace, and the warm hope that one day soon he would awaken thus entangled in her arms.

Twenty-nine

Jack never received the chance that he so craved to confront Lord Barrington. Before Jack and Liza arrived at Cranshaw Park, a bailiff from Waverly was waiting on Birch Road to arrest Jack for his debts. It was an ambush, and one that Liza was powerless to overcome. The burly bailiff appeared suddenly in the middle of the road.

In hindsight, Liza realized they should have kept driving. But Jack got out of the carriage, ordering her to remain inside. She watched in tense silence as the two men talked. Then Jack started back toward the carriage with a look of fury she'd never seen in him before. The bailiff followed with an angry shout, reached out and gripped his arm, and swung Jack around. Jack drew back his fist and punched the man in the face. He sprawled backward, but didn't fall. That's when Liza leapt out of the carriage.

"Jack! Hurry. Get inside!"

"Liza—" Jack returned, but was cut short when the

bailiff rushed back and walloped Jack on the side of his head with interlocked fists. He fell to his knees.

"Jack!" Liza screamed and ran to his side. "Are you hurt?"

"Come along, sir," the bailiff snarled. "To the sponging house you go."

Blood trickled from Jack's lip. Liza pulled a kerchief from her sleeve and tried to dab it.

"Back now, miss. He ain't hurt."

"Leave him alone!" she shouted. "You can't take him away like this."

"I've got an arrest warrant, miss."

"How did you know he'd be coming down this road?"

"Lord Barrington said as much. Now back up, miss, if you please."

The bailiff yanked Jack to his feet and dragged him into his gig. Liza reached up and clutched her lover's knee. "Jack, what can we do?"

"Go home now, darling. I will be well. Do not worry for me. Tell your parents what has happened. Tell them *everything.*"

Before he could say more, the bailiff clucked at his horse and away the gig went. Jack looked back at her until they rounded a bend in the road and disappeared.

Tears of fury burned Liza's eyes, but she would not cry. Instead, she returned to her carriage and prepared herself for vengeance. This was all Barrington's doing. He had doubtless gone out of his way to find Lord Abbington to apprise him of Jack's whereabouts. This was the last straw. Liza was finally prepared to bring Barrington down at any cost to herself or her family.

She ordered her coachman to hurry on to the house. She walked with angry determination directly into the par-

lor and found to her utter delight that her parents were
having tea with none other than the viscount himself. Now
she could corner him like the animal that he was.

He was dressed in his finest, sipping expensive tea and
eating lacy white crumpets. Her mother looked perturbed,
doubtless from having to keep secret, even from her own
husband, Liza's plans to end the engagement.

"Good afternoon, Mama, Papa," she said blithely, her
cheery tone giving away none of her distress. She swept
into the room and kissed both her parents' cheeks. They
sat side by side on the sofa. Barrington sat opposite them
in a chair.

"How good to see you, my lord," she said, approaching
him with a sugary smile and venomous eyes. When he
stood, she kissed the air near his cheek and saw a flash
of fear in his eyes. Oh, vengeance was sweet indeed.

Barrington's nostrils flared defensively. "Greetings,
Liza, my dear. Is there something amiss?"

She took the seat next to his and he lowered himself
back down warily. She pilloried him with bright, wild
eyes. "Did you know, my lord, the most interesting thing
happened to me on my way home. I'm sure you'll find it
most facinating."

"Oh?"

"Yes! A bailiff just arrested Mr. Fairchild and took him
off to a sponging house in Waverly."

"What?" her father said, lowering his cup to his saucer
with a clatter. "What the devil for?"

"For the three thousand pound debt his father owed to
Lord Abbington," Liza said. "Mama, would you be so
good as to pour me some tea?"

Rosalind looked at her worriedly, then distractedly

poured her tea and offered a cup. Liza sipped carefully and smiled again at the viscount.

"I'm quite certain Lord Barrington can tell us all about it. You were the one who investigated the matter, isn't that correct, my lord? When you went away for three days, you ferreted out all you needed to know about Mr. Fairchild. You found out he was deeply in debt, and then you informed Lord Abbington of Jack's whereabouts so that an arrest warrant could be delivered. Isn't that so?"

Barrington leaned back in his chair, his wan smile of greeting now long gone. "Yes."

"You were afraid that I was falling in love with Mr. Fairchild and that you, therefore, might not get your hands on my dowry."

Liza sensed her parents' growing dismay.

"Papa, did you know that Lord Barrington has been blackmailing me for the past six months?"

Bartholomew Cranshaw's apple cheeks billowed and flushed. "What?"

"Look here, Liza. Be careful what you say!" Barrington choked out, scrambling to the edge of his seat.

"The viscount found out about Desiree," Liza said, eyeing her mother with teary eyes. "I am so sorry, Mama. I did not want to tell you."

"Oh, Liza," her mother said, tears filling her own eyes.

"He said he would tell the world about Desiree if I did not marry him. The viscount is desperately in debt himself, you see. He was willing to do anything to ensure that he got his hands on my dowry. You see, Papa, Desiree is—"

"I know all about Desiree!" he cut in, turning his furious glare on the viscount.

Liza sat back as if she'd been slapped hard on the

cheek. "What? You knew about Desiree all along?"

"Of course," he replied, "what kind of fool do you think I am?"

Liza gave her mother a flabbergasted stare. Rosalind merely looked adoringly at her husband.

"I want you to leave at once, you scoundrel," Bartholomew thundered, rising and puffing up his chest in indignation. "How dare you take advantage of my daughter in this way?"

"Don't send him away just yet, Papa," Liza interjected. "I want you to know everything. He tried to rape me. He was also responsible for the fire that destroyed the Davises' home and shop. And he stole a portrait from . . ." She couldn't quite bring herself to mention the name of her real father. "He stole a portrait of Desiree. He is the most despicable man I have ever met. And I am ashamed that I allowed him to bully me into silence. I should have spoken to you about this long ago."

Lord Barrington had been sitting in a kind of frozen stupor. Suddenly he shot to his feet. "She's lying. She's lying, do you hear me? I've had enough insults for one day. Enough, do you hear?"

He bolted from the room. Her father started after him, but Liza reached out to pull him back.

"No, Papa, let him go. Mr. Fairchild explained it all to me before he was arrested. Mr. Honeycut is documenting Lord Barrington's crimes and will confront his lordship with the terms necessary to ensure his silence. Mr. Harding will pay the viscount a call forthwith, I'm told."

Liza's mother rose and crossed the room, running the last few steps in her desperate need to embrace her daughter. "Oh, Liza, my poor child. What have you gone through for me?"

Liza began to sob, clutching her mother's waist. "Oh, Mama, I love you so. I didn't want you hurt. I didn't want Papa to know about your past. I was afraid . . . he wouldn't love you. And that he wouldn't love me because I was Lord Osborn's child."

The women cried hard, shaking together as their tears flowed and they keened with regret. Bartholomew wept, too, covering his face with a hand. Liza heard him and threw her arms around his neck. "Papa, how could you love me all these years, knowing who I really was?"

"Liza," he choked out in a blustering voice, holding her close. "I adored you from the first moment I laid eyes on you. I was afraid you would leave if you knew who your real father was. I thought you wouldn't love me if you knew you were an earl's daughter."

Liza finally stopped crying and laughed incredulously. "How could you imagine such a thing? I would walk over burning coals for you."

She pulled away, wiping her tears, and they all sat on the sofa, recovering themselves, drinking more tea, sorting out all the misunderstandings.

"Your father . . . I mean Bartholomew," Rosalind clarified, "met me the night I left Lord Osborn, the night of your birth. Mrs. Halloway helped me slip away from Sheffield Keep unnoticed when the birthing began. Later she told Osborn that I'd run away and died in childbirth at a wayside inn. In truth, I did fall ill after you were born, and I was forced to stay at an inn for weeks until I recovered. Your father, Bartholomew, had stopped for a night. He fell in love with me, I think."

"At first sight!" Bartholomew added.

"He refused to leave the inn until I was better. Your father helped Mrs. Halloway take care of us and keep our secret. I was so moved by his kindness that I, too, fell in love with him. We were married soon after, and he moved to Middledale, where no one would know either of us, so that he could claim you as his own without raising questions. In all these years, I've never left Middledale for more than a day, always fearing someone might recognize me."

"Why did you leave the comfort of Sheffield Keep, Mama? Was Lord Osborn cruel?"

"No, he was a wonderful man. But I wanted you to grow up without shame. I wanted you to be a wife, not a mistress. And as long as you were the daughter of a Cyprian, your prospects were grim."

Liza sighed, loving her mother all the more for all she'd sacrificed for her children.

"We were very poor, Liza. Aunt Patty and I were nearly starving. I had to find a way to feed us."

"Mama," Liza said sympathetically, pressing her hand. "There is no need to explain."

"You are my daughter, Liza," her father said soberly. "In every way that matters, my dear. I wanted you to marry a nobleman because I thought that was your birthright. I am so sorry I was blind to the pain my ambition caused you."

"Don't blame yourself, Papa. Lord Barrington was a rotter through and through. It was just an unhappy coincidence that he came to Middledale to conduct business with you and soon after saw Lord Osborn's portraits of Mama. And none of this would have been resolved without dear Mr. Fairchild."

"Oh, my!" Rosalind exclaimed, squeezing her husband's hand. "Whatever shall we do to help poor Mr. Fairchild?"

"I'll go to London at once and settle the debt with this Lord Abbington, if I can find him there," Bartholomew replied. "It's a small price to pay for all Fairchild has done for you, Liza."

"Thank you, Papa. I quite agree."

"He'll only have a few days at the sponging house in Waverly to try to pay up before they send him off to prison. I won't be able to settle the matter on such short notice."

"I'll go with you to London, Papa. I want to visit him in prison. I want him to know how grateful I am."

"You can't go to a prison in London!" Rosalind cried.

"Of course you can't," her father agreed. "You and your mother can go to Waverly and explain everything to Fairchild while he's still there. Keep him company. Tell him not to worry. By the time the bailiff brings him to London, the matter will be resolved. I'll bring the dear boy home with me safe and sound in less than a month."

Two weeks after Bartholomew Cranshaw had left for London, Liza received a letter full of good news. Her father had cleared Jack's debt to Lord Abbington and by the time she'd received the missive, her father predicted, he and Jack would be on their way back to Middledale. An elated Liza had begun preparing a welcome home celebration.

The next week, however, she received a second letter that dashed her hopes of a quick reunion. Her father wrote to inform her that a second creditor had come out of the shadows, apparently encouraged by Lord Abbington's success in eking blood out of the Fairchild Tea Company. A Scottish lord was demanding fifteen thousand pounds, and Liza's father said it would take time to settle so large a sum.

Liza immediately decided to travel to London. She would not let another day pass without moving heaven and earth to reunite with Jack. Her mother protested heartily, but when Liza displayed her usual tenacity, Rosalind reluctantly agreed to make the journey with her daughter. That is, until Liza fainted. It happened for no apparent reason the day before they were to set out on their arduous trip.

Rosalind Cranshaw called the physician, who ordered immediate bed rest. Though Liza was anxious to see Jack, she had to admit that sleep was welcome. She'd had trouble sleeping ever since the day of Jack's arrest. But if sleep deprivation was her only disorder, why was she suddenly so nauseous as well?

"May I come and sit with you, my dear?" Aunt Patty said late in the afternoon after the doctor had departed.

Liza was propped up in bed in her white silk chemise, rereading her father's letter. "I am determined to leave tomorrow, Aunt Patty. I don't care what the doctor says."

"Leave your sorrow?"

"No! Leave tomorrow, I said. Oh, I'm sorry, Aunt Patty, I shouldn't be impatient, but do be a dear and give me your good ear. I don't feel like shouting today."

Her aunt went to the other side of the bed and sat on its edge. She took Liza's hand in hers and stroked it.

"Will you take a letter to Mr. Harding with you when you go, my dear?"

Liza looked up in shock. "Why, of course. Are you exchanging letters with Mr. Harding?"

Patty nodded, beaming. "Yes. He says spending his days at the Fleet with Mr. Fairchild has taught him a great deal about how fortunate we all are to have our health and our sanity. He doesn't want to waste another moment in idle amusements. He wants to marry me."

"Oh, Aunt Patty! That's splendid."

"Is that acceptable to you, my dear? You are, after all, gently bred."

Liza leaned forward and hugged her. "Don't be a goose, Aunt Patty. I'm a merchant's daughter and I don't expect to be assuming airs anytime soon. Of course I approve of Mr. Harding. I only hope I feel well enough to travel tomorrow or I won't be able to deliver your letter." She sank back onto her pillow, suddenly feeling flushed. "Do you think I'm dying? Wouldn't that be too ironic? I'm finally free to marry the man I love and then I die."

"You're not dying, my dear," Patty scoffed with a laugh. "You're increasing."

Liza slowly frowned at her, as if waking out of a dream. "*What?* Increasing!"

"Yes, you're going to have a child."

"What! How? How can that be?"

"Why, I suspect you made love to a man at some point in time."

"No!" Liza blushed crimson and covered her eyes with a hand. "That's not what I mean. I mean how . . . how could it have happened so quickly?"

"It only takes one time, my dear."

"I simply didn't think that . . . that this would . . . result."

"One rarely does think of these things in a moment of passion. I did think you were gone awfully long on your walk during the picnic by the churchyard."

Liza grinned and sank down, covering her head with her sheet. "Stop, Aunt Patty, you're embarrassing me."

"Don't worry, my dear. If I were thirty years younger, I would have done the same thing. So don't waste a moment regretting it. And your mother is the last person in the world who could criticize you."

Liza sat back up and thought about it seriously. "I don't mind, you know. I'm happy. After all, it's Jack's child. I suppose that's why I gave no thought to the consequences of our passion. In fact, I desperately want this baby."

"Then you mustn't go to London."

Liza frowned. "Why not?"

"The journey is always difficult and uncomfortable. If something goes wrong, you could lose the child. It happens often enough under the best of circumstances."

Tears welled in Liza's eyes. She wanted to see Jack so badly, but she knew she could never do anything to jeopardize his child. "Oh, Aunt Patty. You're right. But I miss him! Why hasn't he written?"

"Mr. Harding says Mr. Fairchild is glum and scarcely eating. I should imagine he's feeling somewhat humiliated."

"Then I must write to him every day."

"You have been, Liza!"

"Then twice a day."

"Speaking of letters, I have one for you here in my pocket. Mr. Honeycut brought this when he came to see Celia today. I walked with them through the garden."

"I certainly hope you will be more cautious with Celia than you were with me, Auntie," Liza said primly as she took the letter. "Look what happened to me!"

The older woman smiled with delight. "It couldn't have turned out better."

"Why, it's a letter from Mrs. Halloway!" Liza broke

the seal and pealed open the page, reading quickly, then frowning.

"What is it?" her aunt queried. "Bad news?"

"No, not exactly. It's simply that . . . she says she doesn't know why I haven't written. She complains it has been four months since she received any letters from me, and she apologizes for not having written herself."

Liza's hands dropped in her lap. She gave her aunt a stunned look. "But I did write to her. And she wrote back to me. She told me I should not marry Lord Barrington after all. I remember it distinctly. Jack brought the letter to—" She stopped and gasped. "It was Jack! Aunt Patty, will you kindly go to the escritoire in the library and bring me my letters. The key is in that box over there. Hurry. I must get to the bottom of this at once."

Liza waited impatiently while her aunt did as she was asked. She returned with a handful of letters. Liza sorted through them until she found the one that had ostensibly been written by Mrs. Halloway's abigail. Liza snatched it up.

"Here it is." She looked at the handwriting, mentally comparing it to the note Jack had sent her. The style didn't match at all. Disappointed but not thwarted, she gave her aunt a speculative look. "May I please see your letter from Mr. Harding? I promise not to digest the contents. I simply want to look at the penmanship."

Patty pulled the missive out from between her breasts. Liza's eyes widened and her ears reddened. "Aunt Patty, I had no idea you were such a romantic!"

"I could teach you a thing or two, I avow."

Liza ignored her aunt's superior and suggestive smirk and compared the letters, her eyes flitting back and forth between them. Then she smiled triumphantly. "That's it!

I knew it. Mrs. Halloway never received my letters. I've been duped!"

"By whom, my dear?"

"By the scoundrels you and I plan to marry!"

Thirty

After spending a few days in the sponging house in Waverly, Jack was transported to the notorious Fleet Prison. He immediately recognized the combined stench of despair and unwashed bodies on the commoners' side. Fortunately, he was led directly to the masters' side, the area designated for those who could pay for their own room and bed. He surveyed his small, gloomy surroundings, and when he spied a rat in the corner of the stale-smelling chamber, he hunkered down and prepared himself for a long, uncomfortable stay.

He would very likely be here until his grandfather died. Once Jack received the title, they couldn't keep him here any longer. But what of Liza? Could he survive apart from her until then? How ironic to think he'd once wondered if he could survive *with* her for more than two hours at a time.

Prepared for a long stay in prison, Jack was astonished when Bartholomew Cranshaw arrived a few days later and announced that he'd happily paid Jack's debt to Lord Abbington. But then glee had turned to despair when another creditor stepped forward demanding payment for an even greater debt.

Jack's faithful secretary had been visiting every day. Harding was staying at the rooms Cranshaw used whenever he was in Town. Together they were fervently conspiring to end this debacle. After a week or so, Jack grew used to his spartan accomodations and the view of the polluted air visible through his barred window. He had time to think about all that had come to pass, about how much he owed his grandfather, for without the impending title he would very likely rot here.

And of course he thought about Liza. Nearly every moment of every day he thought of her. There was so much he had to say, so much he wished he could confess. After sorting his thoughts and recognizing the pure, true depths of his love for her, he sat down to write her at long last.

My Dearest Liza,

Words cannot express how painful it is to be apart from you. And it would not be nearly as painful if I had only taken the time to adequately express myself in person. But perhaps it is easier to do so in writing. Words give a certain dignity to the human condition. And so, my darling Liza, I hope and pray these words will do justice to you and my feelings for you.

Did I ever tell you that I love you? Did the words ever fall from my lips, along with all those passionate kisses? Did I ever say that you are the only woman who has ever touched my heart? Oh, I have thought fondly of many fair ladies, you know it to

be true. But I have never held a woman whose absence from my arms literally made my heart ache.
Liza, when I am with you the world is simply right.
And when I am not with you, the world as I know
and love it ceases to exist.

I love you, my darling girl. I cannot live without
you. And yet I cannot die for the want of you, for
then I would leave you to your own miserable solitude. So you must wait for me, as I know you will.

I love you, Liza. I want to marry you. I want to
raise a family with you. I hope my miserable insol-
vency will not matter, for you know I would have
given up everything I possess to protect you, even
my pride.

I hope I have adequately expressed my intentions.
Before I close, however, I have a confession to
make. I forged a letter to you from Mrs. Halloway.
You may recall I gave it to you on the terrace. I
also read the letter you sent to Mrs. Halloway after
Henry returned it to my offices undelivered. You
must believe me, dearest, when I say I opened it
merely to find out how I could properly return the
missive. When I learned of your plight, I determined
then to rescue you. As it turns out, you rescued me
from a life of empty intimacy. Please forgive me,
darling Liza. I only meant well.

> *Very Truly Yours,*
> *Jack*

Harding did not arrive for his usual visit the next day.
Jack was disappointed, for he wanted his secretary to take
the letter safely away and see it posted as soon as possible.

He had just resigned himself to a day without his friend when the plump man came scurrying down the corridor and knocked on his door shortly before dinner.

Jack opened it, and invited him in. "Harding, old boy, shall we go down to the cellar for a pint of ale?"

Debtors enjoyed far more freedom in prison than criminals, who lived in positively squalid conditions. Jack generally kept to himself, but confessing both his love and his crimes to Liza made him feel downright gay and thirsty for ale.

"Come on, Harding, just one pint."

"No, sir, we must speak in private." Harding plunked himself down in the only chair in the cell. Then he looked up with a nervous twitch in his eyes, and jumped to his feet. "You sit, Mr. Fairchild, you're going to need the support."

"What is it?" Jack hissed, leaning forward. "Is it Liza? Is she ill? What the hell happened?"

"Do not fret, sir," Harding said placatingly. He patted Jack on the back and nudged him down into the chair. "Take a seat. I'll sit here on the end of your bed. Something very important has happened, Mr. Fairchild. Oh, for God's sake, may I Christian-name you?"

"Of course, Harding." By now Jack's heart was thundering so loudly he could hardly hear, though he hung on his secretary's every word. Harding was his only link to the outside world. "I pray you, tell me what has happened!"

"I am sorry to say, Jack, and yet I am not, for it is an event which entirely changes your circumstances, but for all that, any time something of this nature happens one must reflect on the course of life and—"

"Harding!" Jack shouted, pounding his fist on the table. "Get on it with it!"

The secretary swallowed hard. "Your grandfather, Lord Tutley, has died. He passed on a fortnight ago. Kirby sent word to Middledale, and Giles passed along the news to me here in London."

"I see." Jack sank back in his chair, absorbing the sad news. And it was sad. They had never really reconciled, never been free with the words, "I forgive you." And yet Jack had forgiven him with no expectation of financial reward. At last he felt at peace, and he was grateful that Liza had shown him the power of forgiveness. He only wished his grandfather had learned to forgive before his death. "God rest his soul."

"You know what this means," Harding said.

Jack nodded. "Yes. When I am declared the new baron, they will have to let me out of here."

"You won't have to wait for Parliament to extend the honor, sir. Your grandfather left you his entire fortune. You can buy your way out now. You are no longer in debt. You are, in fact, exceedingly wealthy."

Jack stared a moment in stunned disbelief, then buried his head in his hands and wept. And while the hot tears burned through his fingers, and a ragged pain rent his chest, he kept thinking of Liza. She had been the one to show him just how far one could go for family. She had been willing to give up everything she had to the ones she loved, just as his grandfather had, in the end, given up everything to Jack. With that one gesture, the granting of a fortune, he had given Jack his forgiveness and admitted he was wrong.

The tears stopped as soon as he made that realization. A profound peace such as he had never known descended on him. When he raised his head up, it was as Lord Tutley. He had never been more prepared to accept the gifts and the burdens that title would bring.

He shook his head in hopeful wonder, then looked sardonically at Harding. "Do me a favor, old boy, will you?"

"Of course, sir. Just name it."

"Get me the hell out of here."

"It's already been arranged, Lord Tutley." He shook his head and chuckled in wonder. "I can scarcely believe I finally get to call you that. Thanks to Mr. Cranshaw everything is in order. He certainly knows how to deal with the banks, I'll give him that much—and more. The minute I told him about your grandfather's demise and the terms of his will, Mr. Cranshaw started making arrangements for your release."

"And I am truly grateful." Jack reached for the letter on this table. "I want this missive to reach Liza Cranshaw before I do. Will you see it done?"

"Yes, sir. We won't leave until tomorrow. I'll send it off today."

"And before we leave, I want to visit an old friend of mine on the Strand. He's an art collector. There is one final bit of business I need to resolve before I settle down to become a country squire."

"A lord of the manor, you mean!" Harding said boisterously. "Finally, I'll be secretary to a Peer of Parliament! I always knew I was destined for great things. By the by, sir, Mrs. Brumble has accepted my offer of marriage."

"Congratulations! Shall we make it a double wedding?" Jack said, pumping his hand joyfully.

"Has Miss Cranshaw accepted your offer, too?"

"Not yet. But she will. This time I really won't take no for an answer."

Thirty-one

By the time Jack arrived in Middledale, the leaves were starting to turn. Autumn had begun its golden march, reminding him of all that had happened in such a short time. Jack's life had been utterly transformed. That became poignantly clear when the carriage pulled up in front of the house at Cranshaw Park. It was the most satisfying moment of his life. Liza and Celia ran out of the house to greet them, laughing and weeping, and they were followed soon after by Rosalind Cranshaw and Patricia Brumble. Jack, Harding, and Bartholomew Cranshaw fairly leapt out of the coach in their eagerness to be reunited with their women.

Hugs and kisses were freely given from all quarters, and Jack had the warm, thrilling sense that he was home for the first time in his life. This was his family. And it was a loving family. He was their conquering hero, and the ladies crooned and clucked over him. Jack happily exchanged anecdotes and caught up with the Cranshaws over tea in the parlor, but he couldn't wait for time alone with Liza. He could tell from her looks, which alternated between the smoldering and the sentimental, that she wanted time alone as well.

She surprised him with a picnic at the old churchyard. Aunt Patty and Harding came along as chaperons, though that seemed too little too late, considering her increasing state. Jack hadn't noticed. She was eager to tell him, certain he would be delighted.

They ate and drank and laughed and enjoyed the cool autumn breeze amidst the gravestones. Then Liza invited Jack to stroll with her to her little cottage. Arm in arm they walked through the orchard, savoring their closeness and the brilliant show of russet, orange, and yellow leaves, falling like feathers to the eternal ground.

"Did you receive my letter?" Jack asked.

"No," Liza fibbed. She fully intended to make him pay for his subterfuge with a few moments of extreme discomfort.

"What? You didn't receive my letter from London?"

"No, my dear, I didn't. Was it an important letter?" she asked with false naivete.

"Important? As far as I'm concerned, it had more significance than the Magna Carta."

She laughed, a rich and sultry sound. "Oh my, you do take yourself seriously. What did it say, my dear?"

"I confessed my undying love to you, and I made an offer of marriage."

"I accept both readily, sir."

He tossed back his head and laughed in delight. "Thank God for that. I was afraid I was going to have to kidnap you and drag you off to Gretna Green."

"Now that you mention letters, I received one yesterday from Mrs. Halloway."

There was a long pause. "Oh?"

"Yes." Liza took a deep breath, trying to drag it out as long as possible. "She said she'd received my letters and that she was delighted I had received hers. She has fully recovered from the near fatal illness that forced her to rely on her abigail to pen her last missive."

Liza paused, stifling a smile, waiting for his reaction. All she heard was a sort of strangling sound as he cleared his throat.

"Did you hear me, Jack? Mrs. Halloway also says she has nothing but the highest praise for the reliability of the Royal Mail, and she knows her letters are safe as long as their journey ends at 2 Hanley Street. And she—"

"Liza!" he said, his voice sliding down the scale. He stopped walking and tugged her toward him. "You're teasing me, you wench."

"Am I?" she said, laughing.

"Yes!" Merriment lit his gorgeous eyes. "You did receive my letter, and you did read my confession."

"Yes, but I had figured out your forgery before I received your missive."

"And you still loved me?"

"I loved you even more." She reached up and kissed him. Those firm, sleek lips of his were pure magic. "You're so clever, Jack, so warmhearted and decent. And best of all you're practical. You would never let strict honor prevent you from doing whatever it takes to help those you love."

"We have much in common, then. You'd go to the ends of the earth to spare your loved ones pain as well."

"Jack," she murmured, reaching up and combing his

hair, squinting in the shadowy autumn sunlight. "We have more in common now than you would ever imagine."

He slipped his arms around her waist and nuzzled her neck. A tickling desire crept down her neck and she shivered. "Mutual passion, you mean?"

"Yes." She pressed her hands against his chest, pushing him away so she could look in his eyes. "And so much more than that. Jack, we have a child. A child that resulted from that passion."

Amazement shuttered over his face until he looked stricken with shock. "A child!"

Her heart fluttered a moment with panic. "Do tell me you're pleased."

"Oh, Liza! I'm deliriously happy!" He picked her up in a bear hug and twirled her around. She felt his joy, his complete acceptance of the child in that one embrace. Now everything truly would work out for the best.

He gently lowered her feet to the ground and steadied her. She gazed up at him adoringly as she had so often seen her mother regard her father.

"I love you, Jack. I have since the first moment I met you."

"I love you, too, Liza. I only wish I'd told you that eight years ago. Now let's make up for lost time, shall we?" he said, guiding her to the cottage.

"Be careful, Lord Tutley," she said teasingly as the door closed behind them, "or we might end up having twins."

"With the way I'm feeling today, it might very well be quadruplets."

She smiled as she began to disrobe. "One can only hope."

● ● ● ●

My Dear Mrs. Halloway,

Thank you for your recent letter. It was so good to hear from you after such a very long time. I am sorry to hear that your sister is ill. Please give her my warm regards.

I've already written to you about the extraordinary events leading up to my wedding. Since you could not attend, let me tell you about the wedding itself now that I have a moment to myself.

Lord Tutley and I were married a month after he was released from the Fleet. It was a beautiful autumn day, and everyone was arguing over who made the prettier bride, me or Aunt Patty. She and her new husband, Mr. Harding, are living with us at Tutley Castle. Mr. Harding has been promoted to the post of castle steward, as my husband could not possibly even post a letter without Mr. Harding's help.

After the ceremony and the wedding breakfast at the castle, Jack played the role of the benevolent landlord in his estate room, giving out gifts without any thought to his own pocket. If you knew my husband, you would know that was very in keeping with his character. Fortunately, he can now afford to be so recklessly caring.

To my mother, he gave the portrait of Desiree that Lord Barrington had stolen from Huntly House. Jack had asked an art collector in London to track it down for him. It seems Lord Barrington had abandoned the painting without profit just before he made his escape to India. Lord Osborn has consulted with the Marquess of Perringford to make sure Barrington's visit abroad is permanent.

To his cousin, Arthur Paley, and his wife, Theo,
Jack gave the most impressive gifts. He handed
them thirteen legal documents. The first twelve de-
tailed Jack's endowments for his nieces and neph-
ews. To the boys he generously gave property, and
to the girls he donated dowries so hefty that Arthur
wept before the interview was through. Jack also
gave Arthur and Theo twenty thousand pounds for
their own use, a sum that they assured him they
would never be able to spend if they lived to be a
hundred.

I tell you these personal details, Mrs. Halloway,
not only because we are so intimately acquainted,
but because I want you to fully appreciate what a
generous and dear man I have married. I was especially pleased that he remembered the Davises.
He gave Jacob Davis enough money to rebuild his
chandler shop, and he also endowed Annabelle with
a generous dowry. It is surely significant enough to
help her overcome any scandal that might linger
over her ill-fated carriage ride with Lord Barrington. Mr. Honeycut tells Celia that Annabelle is being courted by a good-hearted farmer from
Waverly, and that his affections are warmly returned.

As for Celia, I believe she will be able to marry
Giles after all. Perhaps in a few years when he is
more established. Jack plans to give him the chambers at 2 Hanley Street as soon as Giles becomes a
solicitor. Jack already has plans to move Giles to
London so he can study at Gray's Inn and eventually go to the bar and become a barrister.

And finally, after all these gifts were given, Jack

and I shared a glass of port with a very special wedding guest—the earl of Osborn. He came from Fielding to see the nuptials. I invited him after giving it serious thought. Papa, that is to say Bartholomew Cranshaw, said he would not mind. And I could tell by the earl's expression that the invitation meant a great deal to him.

He came a day early and visited Cranshaw Park, so he and my mother had a chance to sort through the past and put it all behind them. None of the guests had any idea that Lord Osborn and Mama had known each other before. We purposely had a small wedding so she wouldn't worry about meeting anyone from Society who might remember her days at Sheffield Keep.

I've made it clear to Lord Osborn that I do not want to be named his heir, but I should very much like to be his friend so that my children can understand their true heritage.

In truth, the greatest legacy was given to me by Bartholomew Cranshaw, and my dear sweet mother. They gave me an example of love which I can now share with my beloved husband, Jack Fairchild, former rake, now Lord Tutley. And to think that none of this happiness would ever have come to pass if my first letter to you had been properly delivered. One can never know the importance of a single unopened letter, or predict the significance of the hands into which it falls.

Wish us well, my dear Mrs. Halloway, for you mean more to Jack and me than you will ever know.

Very Truly Yours,
Liza Tutley